City Dreams

Deb & Dale

Family comes from all of the strangest places. Thanks for being part of mine

Kevin R. Campbell

Cover Art by Carlo DeAgazio
It has been a long journey filled with many peaks and some hard falls. I owe most
everything to my parents. What they gave me was an insatiable desire to read at a very
young age and allowed my very active imagination to flourish. (some times to extreme)
I also need to thank Garland for giving the proverbial kick in the ass to finally sit down
and write. He reminded me what was really important at the end of the day.
Finally, Carla, for giving me the time to get all my ducks in a row. Editing out all my
many mistakes and of course for finding some place in her heart to include me.

Prophecy

Some day mankind will evolve beyond this now stagnant existence and move toward a new understanding of the race we were destined to become. The next gargantuan step by mankind since that first step out of Eden is about to be taken in stride. We as a species must salute the conceptual Eve for starting the wheels of evolution in motion.

We now stand alone facing a predestined chance for eternity and finally reaching a spiritual plane of existence. We must learn to break away from our worldly mistakes and join together as we enter the kingdom of God!

Let us embrace the next evolutionary step into heaven, transcending earth and leaving hell to all its minions.

Mankind's Time on Earth is Over!

Fred Drifting Feather
Profit of the Devine Coming
Translated by Dr. Randy Donder
University of the Freedom Faith
3873 A.D.

Trydent

It happened on an evening just like tonight, a storm brewing off to the west. An unnatural storm, a swirling vortex of black with massive arms of electricity lashing down at the earth that howled almost as soon as the lightening struck with its evil force.

When I say it happened on that mystic evening of revolt I am not complete, the tale, no the odyssey that I'm about to unleash only started on that late August evening and ended, (ended, I like that word but even now I'm not sure if it is an appropriate one) what seems like a lifetime away.

Now my life is in constant turmoil, fear, anticipation of what is going to happen next or who will be calling on me to do its bidding. No longer do I control my meager destiny. My life before kept me guessing, wondering from day to day, hour to hour, second to.......OK I won't say it. Let's just say I didn't know where I was always going to sleep or where I might be having my next meal.

Some people would call me a derelict or a bum but these were the kinder names, there were a lot more colorful colloquial expressions hurled in ridicule in my direction as I strolled away with an unpaid for apple or sausage. It was a difficult life but it was mine just the same by my own choosing. The streets were mine, a little niche were I ruled one on one against the elements. Not many beasts (man or otherwise) ever questioned my right to rule, at least not for very long. I have a way of convincing people that the abandoned center of this megopolis belongs to me, its called kicking ass.

These jungles where machines ceased to rule could be mercilessly cruel but I still call it home. Very few dare to roam that vast expanse of abandoned left to be overgrown, given back to Mother Nature to rule with iron law. She only accepted this refuse of man on her own terms, which tended to be harsh. It was a wild and untamed jungle where prides of alley cats hunt an occasional unsuspecting stray human that wandered too close and became the main course for kitty.

Mankind had left these areas centuries ago, moved away to a cleaner, safer, more prestigious part of the City and turned its back on all the forgotten communities too costly to automate. Left to the poor and sickly with a tip of the hat and a flippant remark and of course with an air of don't say we never gave you anything.

Earth is an archaic term now that the entire planet has been given a facial. One complete city, one global city that stretches from pole to pole. The world is divided up and distributed among the various stratospheres of the human race. Suburbs for the proles, a high tech luxury realm for the wealthy (and only the wealthy), and left overs for the dregs of Society. The poor stuck in the mega slums that aren't really fit for the animals that hunt there. Animals that used to purr on your pillow at night, now would claw you to hamburger.

I'm not about to argue that the world has gone to the dogs..... Um I guess I mean cats, but it's my home and I enjoy the seclusion of the Rezidentials. I read a book once about a man living in a place called the Rocky Mountains in an area called Canada. He was almost a total recluse and I stole from his patented style of living. I have a respect for this man that lived in the wilds of his era, a respect unlike two industrial giants view each other.

The knowledge of what happened to this man evades me; he probably met the same fate as the mountains. They too were removed when they were no longer viewed as having any sustainable use anything past aesthetics anyway. Leveled out, flattened to make room for the cumbersome ever-growing population that was soon to engulf the entire planet.

The population explosion came to an abrupt halt, forced to stop because long distant space travel is still not feasible even in the year 2778 AD. Yes I believe that is the date, I'm not sure nor do I really care what the governing populace decides upon.

It was early in the evening and I was deeper into the residential (REZ) than one man should dare to go alone. Cats hunted at night and they liked their prey down to a manageable number. The storm was moving in fast and I decided that it would be better to get out of the open. I took refuge in the lobby of an abandoned old apartment building that had one main entrance that could be easily guarded. I started a fire for all the reasons that one builds a blaze in the REZ; to take the chill out of my bones on a cool evening, to ward off any possible feline attack and to roast up a stray kitty that had the misfortune of wandering too far from the pride. (Better it than me)

Getting up I moved toward and peered out the remnants of a glassless window, long ago given way to the elements. The sky was still spilling those crocodile tears almost as if Mother Nature pitied what we had done to her world, a world beaten down centuries ago.

I was not the first to camp here, to get to the window I had to cross over the charred remnants of what must have been a fire pit. As I lengthened my stride to avoid the burnt out ashen crater in the rotting floor I caught a faint movement out of the corner of my eye. Not quite two buildings down amongst the ever present shadows.

Rationalization was my best defense so I tried to convince myself that it was just the shadows cast by the angry lighting. Rationalizing or not, caution had helped keep me alive over the years so always take the precaution for the probability of cats on the hunt. If I kept a fire going I would be relatively safe {what ever that could mean}, so a quick inventory of the firewood situation was needed. Hellfire there wasn't much wood; I should slap myself sometimes. I kept my eyes riveted on the seemingly lonely streets and saw nothing, but a huge part of me sensed danger.

If my fire went out I could easily become a kitty krunchie; which, in my not always so humble opinion would basically suck the munchkin.

Maybe I was wrong; maybe, just maybe, the wind flipped a branch or a piece of wood from a decrepit building built for another time. I kept reminding myself over and over again to be careful and anything less than this would be extremely dangerous.

Trying to stay calm I began humming an old tune by Sativian Dreams and this seemed to help me keep the feeling of vertigo in check. I had been in a lot worse situations and came out triumphant so I could not understand the lingering feeling of danger that seemed to hang thickly over me.

The feeling in the air was peculiar, something more than just a summer light show; something felt out of place. It was too quiet; the only noise was the whistling of the wind, me humming that old favorite "Die Fighting" and the crying of the earth in an occasional howl of thunder.

The storm was a constant, rearing up to convey its vehemence toward the unsettled REZ. I had a feeling this storm was here for me; somebody or something was out there in the darkening storm searching for my very existence.

A shadow flashed and then again across the decrepit doorway, one hinge long ago forgotten why it was made, no longer a part of the rotting frame. The shadow was blurred but it passed at a speed equal to a man. It was misshapen and small but of human resemblance. I started to relax, call it conceit, call it bravado, but I had yet to meet a man that was my match at staying alive.

Deep in the heart of the Rez, not many would dare venture this far into the realm of the new jungle controlled by once domesticated beasts, played with by young children and the elderly alike. If you were not born to this world you became easy prey to the feral hunters that had become sly and almost sentient killers.

Well I don't believe in anything but a fair fight, so I wasn't going to hang around and let someone sneak up on me, club me from behind and eat my hard earned supper.

The stairs behind me were off to the left about three meters away. To get to them I would have to cross in front of the main door and possibly expose my self to an attack. What the hell I wasn't going to sit around with a sign around my neck saying, "split my skull." Two strides, a dive and a roll, seemed feasible in theory. Now putting theory into an executable maneuver, I must get myself where I needed to go with being no worse for wear.

My retreat up the stairs had no obstacles to bar the way, no doors, broken railings or anything else that might cause complications. I still had to use the utmost cautions falling through the stairs was not high on my list to do tonight. Backing up the stairs and watching below I tried each step before placing my full weight down on those relics of the past.

My body felt like a coiled spring, every muscle tensed for instant action. I was in flight or fight mode but my temperament leans more toward the fight side. I turned, estimating the distance to the top of the stairwell, and my heart skipped a half dozen beats. At the top of the stairs only three meters away stood a man or maybe it was a boy, at the time it was difficult to be totally sure.

At less than half my height and white blonde hair that hung past his shoulders, he didn't come across as intimidating. In fact his slight build and pixie like appearance I almost expected him to utter those immortal words "Avon Calling."

One little thing that seemed out of place and gave the impression that he wasn't here to piss around was resting by his side, a broad sword. It was about chest height and glimmered with faint light. (Well that's how I remember it) The point of the blade was on the floor and with both hands resting on the hilt. Dumbfounded and almost light headed all I could muster was "awe shit" and the silence was deafening as we both stood there for what seemed like an eternity, probably closer to 13 seconds. He was the first to break the silence and just as he spoke lightening flashed to light up his face and I saw his eyes, not young eyes you would expect on this impish face. Not eyes filled with boyish glee but dark sullen eyes with a wise all seeing appearance that clashed against his youthful demeanor.

His first words were not expected and with a very broad grin across his face he said…"Score some weed Dude?"…

Shately Downs

With crushing force the blade sliced the air on the journey down, trying to cleave itself into my skull. Oh please not my face. I moved just in time as the ground behind me sprayed dirt across my face. Rolling quickly to the left I brought up the flat of my blade across my adversary hitting him in the ribcage just beside the sternum. The blow knocked the wind clean from his lungs with a forced gasp. This blow gave me enough time to gain the advantage. I raised my sword high above my head to get maximum swing; I intended to split this Neanderthal in half. I brought it down hard and fast (I love it hard and fast) but he was just able to get his gauntlet up in time to stop from having a split personality.

Holding on to the tip of my blade with his left hand, he grabbed my breast with his right, (don't get me wrong I can like it rough) he made some chauvinistic remark like, "now I will take you butch slut." This comment sent fire to my brain; the stupid bastard should have never called me a slut. In one fast motion my I brought my knee up to his insignificant groin, pushed him away and kicked his left wrist causing him to loose his grip on my blade.

I brought my blade across his exposed throat, searching for that ever-popular jugular. It was a home run, pay dirt, blood sprayed past the glint of my blade with enough force to slap my face as if it was his last act of defiance.

Loosing all his faculties he dropped to his knees and then flopped to his face. A pool was already starting to form under him as I wiped his blood from my face. When I opened my eyes

I could see off in the distance what appeared to be a little man standing and grinning at me.

He was quite shorter than myself and had a full mane of white blonde hair, which, along with a cape, flowed behind him floating in the breeze

By the look of the broadsword he was carrying he gave me the impression of a no-nonsense kind of fella, so I didn't stick around to see what the little guttersnipe wanted.

Turning tail I fled the clearing, I fled the little man and I fled from the already stiffening corpse that lay freshly slain.

I had been fleeing a lot lately and I hoped it was not going to become a habit. I was beginning to really get pissed off.

I believe that at one time the clearing in the Rez had been a park or a community-gathering center. There was a marble slab that lay on a large knoll, on this worn dedication to a past history was a scripture "A gift to the people of New York from the city of New York" Blah blah blah what the hell was New York? I didn't know. The city covered the entire planet; maybe New York was some forgotten subdivision.

I was exhausted and the last thing I needed was to get into another battle with a blade-wielding psycho. At this time the shrimp with the hair matched the description close enough. I decided that back to the Rez were it was relatively safe would be my next destination. I turned and shorty was already becoming a memory....

Actually the Rez wasn't bad once you got used to it, I was raised here. My parents came to this concrete jungle to escape political persecution. After the war of the Colas, Pepsi tried to bring my father to trial for war crimes as a Coca-Cola executive. They claimed he was responsible for the St. Louis Massacre, which I have never been able to believe he could have been responsible for such atrocity.

Fearing for his life and the life of his family, he gathered us up and fled to the one place he felt he would never be found. Deep into the heart of Rez we all found a life and it is the only one I truly remember. My parents died when I was thirteen, killed by a pride of alley cats when they were caught away from the community fire after nightfall. Now I'm twenty-two and still hold a heavy grudge against those feline fuzz balls and I snack on them whenever I get the opportunity.

I've learned to use what I have to survive; I dwell in the company of others for safety when needed. Sometimes I take, sometimes I trade, but always I survive.

The law of the Rez is; survival only happens to those who put a hundred and twenty-five percent into staying alive, everyone else dies. No fanfare, no applause, just anonymously dead.

I headed down an old lane to what had once been an old video theater in happier times. My humble abode was located in the basement of the decrepit movie house that had one time been known as the "Roxy," I tended to call it safe and secure. The building now sagged with the weight of its tired existence, almost as if it was ashamed to be a part of what had once been the domain of civilized man.

Once inside I bolted the door and checked the back exit to make sure it was locked. I had an eerie feeling I was locking myself in with the danger rather than keeping it out. I plopped into my favorite chair and caught two hours of restless sleep not quite loosing the feeling of impending trauma. I felt that I truly was in peril, some form of grave and imminent danger. So my fastest choice (maybe not the best) was to go to a place with a lot more people. Maybe a drink with friends might calm my jitters a bit and maybe, just maybe, help me forget the day's events.

Out the back exit and back into the friendless streets, I decided that my destination would be an out of the way tavern known as "Home."

I frequented this shabby place and thought I might find solace in familiar faces and, of course, getting drunk was always an option.

Getting wasted in the streets by some two-bit slime that thought he was short peoples' fame to Conan was not going to happen tonight. I passed an old school, St. Mary's high; the roof had long ago given up the fight leaving an abandoned shell, begging for the laughter of children, but of course in vain.

Damn it to hell, I saw him again standing alone by a falling building. One wall lay crumbled and scattered along the ground. He just stood there with his passive mockery. His blonde hair and cape fluttering in the breeze and that bloody broadsword gleamed at this distance.

He waved as if he was waving casually to an old friend of many years; oh this guy was an arrogant little shit.

The pace went from brisk to the verge of panic, never before had I felt this kind of uncontrolled fear. I had to get away from him, not really knowing why, but sensing my life would dramatically be altered if he caught me.

Two kilometers, not far when you put it in perspective, compared to Pluto. But at this time I did not have to get to that planet, I had to keep my wits about me and get to the bar called "Home", get off the streets and try and save my pretty little ass.

If I knew what was in store for me I'm not sure what I would have done? I guess I still would have gone to the tavern to find friendly faces.

I arrived feeling significantly winded as I ran the entire way like some scared kid. Bursting through the doors, I startled the local patrons, as they must have thought it was a raid on their unlicensed establishment. "Don't panic It's just me." I assured the crowd, who for the most part recognized me as a regular.

On the far wall across from the entrance there hangs a sign, "How ever humble there is no place like HOME." It hung over the pool table. Now that was a crock of shit, this place gave dive a bad name, but they sold alcohol and I really needed a drink.

A lot of heads turned as I came busting through the doors and most relaxed quickly as they recognized it was me. Trying to hide my obvious emotional disarray I sang out a quick, "Hiya Guys." And walked towards my regular table ignoring the stares of the patrons.

Across the bar I recognized a familiar face, an old friend of mine; we went back to early adolescence. He was one of the few friends I had after my parents died.

Leather Dove was his name; honestly I think that it was the one his parents gave him. They must have had a sense of humor to the whole boy named sue theory. Leather was a trader that usually dealt in, how should I put it, hard to get items if you know what I mean. Nudge nudge wink wink.

Mr. Dove wasn't really a very influential person in these parts but we had saved each other's skin on more than one occasion, so I kept him on my "A" list of company to keep.

I waved him over to join me at the corner table I had just grabbed; it was an invitation that he would never refuse. He walked over to my table, actually it was more of a stagger and by the look of lecherous intent I figured that I had some catching up to do.

The last time Leather and I got blasted together he had green greased back hair and a black leather jumpsuit. This time his hair was bright red and fluffed into an Afro but the jumpsuit remained the same. He claimed it gave him luck because he had never died in it. (Some logic?)

Leather slapped a quarter of a bottle of cheap Tequila into my hand and then he held on to it with his other hand to steady it. "Easy now big fella," I had to remind him he was drunk not me.

He wanted to toast to our friendship and feeling I could use a friend at this moment I kindly obliged him. Killing what remained in the bottle and spilling a little down my front I coughed out a, "To friendship" shuddering at the liquor's strength but pretended it was no big deal.

I slammed the bottle down on the table and saluted Leather with the obligatory comment "How's it hangin?"

Leather sat down and we proceeded to get very drunk, swapping old lies and making up a few new ones, I tried very hard to leave the day's earlier escapade behind me.

I wish that life would have stayed that uncomplicated and dealt me an easier hand to play.

One thing must have lead to another because I awoke the next morning in Leather's bed and his head was nestled to my breast. I hope it was good for me?

I decided that I had nothing better to do that day than visit with an old friend. Sex wasn't a big deal we both new it was a circumstance thing and no expectations or commitments went with it.

It would be good to reminisce and catch up about old times in Sandstone Bluff. Leather looked so very peaceful lying there so I thought I would shut my eyes and try and let sleep over take me again and hopefully dream happy dreams.

My lids were not closed for very long when hope slipped away, the door to our little niche of passion and sin slowly swung open with a long steady squeak of rusted hinges.

I wasn't sure if it was a perverse dream or the start of a day of obscene reality.

Opening my eyes I realized that it was the latter of the two, standing beside my bed was my little blonde man dressed to the hilt in fine orange silk. He bent low to kiss my hand and I couldn't even move.

I wasn't sure exactly what to do, I wasn't even dressed let alone armed enough to defend myself, and I couldn't even pull my hand away.

Straightening up his eyes met mine, a solid gaze that easily held my attention, eyes of both wisdom and sorrow. These eyes didn't seem to belong to this boyish face or match his lighthearted grin. His impish features and youthful physique needed eyes that sparkled and gleamed with juvenile mischief.

These were sad, hardened eyes reaching out with concern, pleading with me to understand. Eyes that had centuries of experience, a complete contrast with the innocence of his face.

He stood there with a broad toothy grin and let out a giggle like a schoolgirl at the prom. What he said next caught me completely off guard even more than the event leading to this encounter. He uttered four words that changed my life forever and even now I'm not sure if it was for the better or the worse.

"Score some weed Babe..."

John L. Morgan

"The puck squirts into the corner, Tyson quickly in after it, holy BEAVERBREATH, Morgan slams him into the boards maybe got the elbow up a bit too. Morgan dipsi doodles around the defensemen, did he ever make the rookie look like a rookie, all alone in the front of the net, Wow! Wow! Wow! HE SCOOOOOORES!!!!!!!!

Inside out and backwards Morgan again turns Wong Pi Tue into a twisted lump in the goal crease, then easily pockets his second goal of the game and his forty second point of these playoffs. I know I say it a lot but John L. Morgan is the best player in this greeaat gaamme, more muscle than Gretzky had unless even when you count Semenko. Maybe as marvelous as Mario even, yes even as good as legendary Brian the BAAAD Boy Hickey.

I love this gaaame! Let's look at it again shall we.... Tyson is going to feel that hit for a few weeks. Does he know his name? Shake it off kid. Now let's slow it down for all you kids out there. Now look, keep looking, there, he pulls the defensemen to the outside, then sidesteps on the inside dragging the puck with him. I wonder if Morgan will send this young defenseman a bill for that lesson. Oh he makes it happen! I give Pi Tue some credit he stood on his head to try and keep that puck out of his net, but watch this left right left and upstairs with gramma, beeaaaauuutiful what...a.... goal. Wrap it up and send it like a present.

We have a tie game at two goals each, fifteen minutes to go before we have to set our hearts for overtime. Oilers up three games to two, in the best of seven, I'm sure this young

Sony team feeeel the pressure building building building, this is all or nothing for the bonsai who look like they may become bridesmaids again this season. All good credits are on the Rexal Oilers and their captain John L. Morgan, who in my humble opinion should be winning the ConSmyth this year. If he doesn't somebody must be bought and paid for.

AAAnd the puck is dropped again at centre and the bonsai win the face-off, Ling boots it back to Randolf and Randolf carries the puck up the left side crossing the blue line into Oiler's territory, he passes across and Ling fans on the shot, he's gonna hate himself tomorrow, the Oilers can't clear the puck out of their zone, Parent keeps it in at the blue line, over to Randolf what a shot, whaaat aaa Saave! Have you ever seen a faster glove hand? I didn't think so....I DID NOT THINK SO. Gumpy holds for a face-off.

The puck is dropped; the Oilers just clear the zone with Lentle dodging Davies along the boards, narrowly missing a crunching hit, looky, looky Morgan is back on the ice and moving fast through the center ice zone. Lentle steals the puck and gets it across to an all alone Morgan a shot BIG rebound HEEE SCOOORESS, Hattrick, Hattrick, Hattrick, Py Tu hardly even saw that one ha ha ha ha....like shooting squid in a barrel, he never misses, what a shot.

This play develops due to a lot of hard work by Lentle she could have given up 2 or 3 times but NOOO; this team knows what it takes to be Stanley Cup champions. Top right corner bing bang booom that's how you play this great game.

Bonsai is calling a time out, cut off the head the nose is bleeding. Two goals in three minutes I guess you call a time out; it's time to pull some magic out of the hat and the carrot out of their asses.

Down at the bench did you see that? Coach Kellor gave Morgan the nod, he gets to use up his last foul, don't go away... action is spelled HOCKEY and Morgan it appears to be given the go ahead to commit his fifth foul...slashing, fighting, slashing, boarding and now the violation of his choice.

Look out the game is starting once again sports fans, now what do you think, can those slippery Bonsai pull themselves out of this one? It's gamma in the circle facing the Oiler's wily veteran Mac.C. his face off ability probably is probably keeping his contract loaded with credits...and Mac.C. easily draws the puck back to his defensemen Solianov who quickly moves up the left side and over to Francis and up to Mactavish, he throws it up the right side along the far boards, Nimlee nimbly picks it up for the Bonsai and carries it out of the zone, the Oilers change on the fly, Morgan Lentle and Fin on the ice for the Oilers, Nimlee beats Fin on the inside, what a gallant effort on the young Bonsai defensemen Heeere Cooomes Trouble... Morgan moving like an astroglide, ouch he almost took his head off, he didn't even bother to hide the elbow. Just went over and tried to decapitate Nimlee, the crowd is going wild....caca on those bleeding hearts that want roughness out of the game, there's no booos coming from this crowd, they love it...THEEY WAAANT MOORE.

Watch out the Bonsai enforcer just jumped over the boards, don't try and tell me he gets a million credits a year to score goals. The officials are trying to control big ol Thumper... what a specimen of a beast. I would be a little nervous if I was Morgan, but of course I'm not so why ramble. Thumper throws aside the linesmen and look at that nobodies going to try and stop him...I GUESS NOT....

Morgan is taunting the big man, he must have coconuts for balls or marshmallows for brains, Thumper grabs Morgan, OH NO, he lands a haymaker...Can Morgan survive this punishment? Somebody stop this, Oh MY GOD Thumper drops Morgan to the ice, we probably need an amblivac, Thumper turns to the crowd as if to challenge them...what's this, WHAT IS THIS, Morgan is back on his feet, Thumper doesn't see him to busy egging the crowd on....somebody tell Morgan to stay down.

Morgan jumps on the Sasquatch's back and it look s like is applying some kind of choke hold. Thumper is trying to shake him loose but can't seem to dislodge him, ride him cowboy, YEEA HAA I love this game!!!! It look s like the big man is weakening OOOh he drops to his knees but Morgan is holding him up, I think the heavy weight champ just lost his crown.

Morgan has him by the helmet and is lining him up, look out heeeere it cooomes. WHUUUMP I could hear it all the way up here, insult on top of injury....

Listen to that crowd! I have never in my entire career as a sportscaster seen anything as GREEEAAATTT as that comeback by JOHN L. MORGAN. I have a tear in my eye, gosh thanks John for that moment......I will treasure it for a lifetime.

The Linesmen is leading Morgan to the dressing room, a chant is starting Johny, Johny, Johny...

What a game, I can't believe I get paid for having so much fun and play a game I love to play as much as I do. I hope Thumper is all right, he is actually a pretty good guy that has a job to do just like myself, which is to sell tickets to that great game called hockey.

The night of the big game everyone was pumped including me, a chance to win back to back Stanley cups, wow what a dream. It feels like a dream now any way. I'm not really sure if we won the game that night. I don't really know much of anything any more. There is no videovision in hell you know.

This is not the hell I envisioned, it is almost like a stasis field with no embodiment, just the mind racing at light speed.

After I go my misconduct and was escorted of the ice, I was still a little groggy from the head shot from compliments of Thumper (actually his real name is Kacey Roberts) and I had to stand in the hallway to the dressing room a bit to stop the world spinning around me. I closed my eyes and tried to shake the widow webs from my brain. When I opened them again there was a very big, mean, ugly beast-like killing machine (for lack of a better name) standing a few meters ahead of me in the hall.

Now this guy looked like he meant business, close to 270cm tall, buck naked, a bright pink skin that looked like it could withstand phazor fire. His massive body was covered with muscles that seemed to bulge everywhere. It had a big set of slimy teeth that could handle brushing, large solid black eyes that were soulless. Each arm ended with claws that extended a three fingered hand (or maybe it was two thumbs and one finger?) Worst of all he appeared to have a very nasty disposition, but I'm guessing he would have made a gracious dinner guest.

I was too stunned to move and my head was just beginning to clear up, he smiled (sort of) in a demonic way (foreshadowing) and pointed a very intimidating clawed digit at me. His speech was slurred and very controlled as if it wasn't his first language. Almost as if he stayed up past his bedtime practicing his little speech.

"I am the lunatic spawn of a million twisted minds, each a crazed schizophrenic maniac, each insane in their own little demented ways. I am the result of a thousand barren souls, raped a thousand times a thousand times. I am what is left of a menagerie of a million putrid demons that push their ideals of perversion on the retched souls of earth. I am your death, I accept you with open arms."

"COME TO ME AND DIE!"

I'm not sure, but I don't think he was interested in going steady nor needed a date to the prom. I decided to act the tough guy and maybe bluff my way through. I figured some quick retorts and a couple of creative threats just might throw mister cheerful off enough that I might just get away.

"Go ahead try and take a piece of me, I just might like it, Sweet cakes. You go a head and take your best shot, you big oversized asshole. I'm just itchen to scrap with some Mama's boy that's nothing but a poor excuse for existence."

I got him there; he should start to cry soon, that Mamas boy comment was good. "You go ahead and come here and I will give you the losing end of the breathing game. I'll be on you like ugly on a nun, you piece of snake dung." Ouch that got him he should be turning and running away soon.

"Your testimonial is brave but......none the less naive, you will die just as I said and you will spend a tormented eternity in hell. Let us end this rhetoric and posturing as it will not change your destiny. I was not sent here to converse with you. I was sent here with orders for your destruction, let us get on with it mortal"

Sometimes you have to say "fuck it" and face the fates of the Cosmic Jesters. "I am ready for anything you can dish out and I have every intention of taking you to hell with me...Let's dance!"

As it turned out the big ugly guy was right, he killed me, he killed me real good. I think I would have had a better chance if I hadn't been so tired and dazed from the battle with Thumper. Now I just kinda hang around in limbo, wondering if I was going to get a Stanley cup ring, (post mortem of course)

Now that I have some time to think, I must admit I've had some good times, even if my life was a brief twenty six years young. I accomplished a lot with the time I had in the City, a sports star, credits coming out my wazoo, adulation of a society that lived and breathed for their sports franchise and I truly believe that I am one hell (no pun intended) of a nice guy.

If the latter of the statements was true what did I do to deserve to be stuck in Beelzebub's playground? Yes, I have had a few moral indiscretions but nothing I feel that would condemn me to eternal damnation. I occasionally get this annoying itch on my nose or at least the sensation that my nose is itchy and there is no way to scratch it, now that's hell. I think I could hate an eternity of that or is this only the start of the process to utter insanity, a few hundred years of itches then it gets worse.

Since I have had so much time to think (really nothing else to do) I wonder if that demon that killed me got any kind of promotion, I hope not. I hope it was a poor execution and he got demoted or got a cut in his demon's salary. I think I got a couple of good shots in before he ripped my body apart and tore my head from my neck. The more I think about it the more I get pissed off!

I DON'T THINK I SHOULD BE IN HELL...

Sir Ogden Timothy Oberhause the 5th

Good Times, fast glides, lots of company, life is good ooh so good
and you know it should be!

Life would not dare to insult Sir Ogden Oberhause, my
family has paid heavily for the distinction of upper-class, and
we have earned the right. Over four centuries my family, the
name Oberhause, has strived to be at the top of the system and
we have paid our dues in blood, sweat and determination. Yes
we can flaunt our power but when shit hits the fan we back up
everything we believe in and recognize our responsibility to
lead and never try and hide from our failures.

We literally turned space travel into a feasible industry and
opened up the universe to commerce.

I was spending a semi-quiet evening at a very posh
establishment known as Le'Ralphe; the evening consisted of
some libation, socializing with a few select friends and the
harmless bantering that comes with inebriation. We had my usual
table against the west windows overlooking the vast expanse of
blinking and flashing lights repeating in a complicated opera of
colors.

The City in all its glory is beautiful in a clustered cluttered
sort of way, showing an ominous strength that reflects
humankind's achievements. Strength is one thing I respect, not
just physical strength but the power to make your enemies bow
down for the fear of being destroyed physically or financially.

When a person can prove their equality to me I can accept
their friendship at face value, but if they cannot they need to
vacate my space before I find them tedious and expose them for
the forgeries they are.

Most people think I am a self-centered, arrogant power monger (jealousy) but I have the power to carry these titles proudly. Why should I show false modesty just so I don't bruise some asshole's ego?

Quite a lot of time passed that evening and the hour was getting late, (disregarding the city never sleeps) the alcohol was beginning to have a lubricating effect on our party of six. A glow was starting to grow across our smiling faces and our yarns took on a more exaggerated flow. I felt the evening, to this point, was extremely entertaining and I had absolutely no inclination that the night would be so controlled with prophecy and destiny.

We had already paired of into sleeping partners so there was no longer the competition of choosing an incubus. The conversation had turned to the topic of sports rather than the petty posturing over sexual supremacy.

After a heated discussion about the upcoming Oiler\ Bonsai game that covered goaltending, rule changes, officiating and every other aspect of the City Hockey League (CHL). Of course this included the dominance of the Oiler's star forward John L. Morgan.

My best friend and Colonel of the Oberhause fleet Bell Anderson stayed quiet already having a little too much to drink while Tobias started a tale of an expedition on a hunting reserve he own on the edge of the Rez. He bragged about hunting a bear that had developed a rare intelligence.

The prey was a cunning opponent and the hunt went over a week with intrigue pouring out of every sentence and B S obviously an active ingredient to the story. The bear died in a rage that would instill fear into a normal man's heart, but my friends were by any stretch of the imagination normal.

Bell drunkenly scoffed at Tobias's tale and the two shadow boxed across the table with the jest of old friends. This tale told by Tobias sparked a memory of a hunt I was the lone participant in, not including the quarry. I was paid handsomely to bring down the most dangerous of all animals, Man...

They all laughed and did the customary doubting, chortling and boasting that they have had shopping trips more dangerous than the story I was about to recall. I took no offence to the teasing and laughed along with my companions.

After we had all quieted down I punched in for a new round of drinks and a couple of serotonin enhancers for later in the privacy and intimacy of my bed chambers. I insisted the retinal scan was on me and nobody even attempted to stop me from paying for the round. I placed the little scarlet pills in my pocket and gave my date a knowing and suggestive wink causing her to smile with a seductress leer.

Taking a long and deliberate slow drink to build some anticipation of my vocal dramatization of danger, I got everyones attention and I proceeded to get engrossed in the narrative that I intended to string one into the evening.

As I was getting into the finer details of the story describing the dark hours of pursuit and struggles in the jungles of Rez, an obviously drunker male from the next table approached. He had apparently been listening to my tale and took insult by it.

He seemed very upset but what was offending him was not a big concern of mine so I asked him kindly to go fuck himself. He said listening to me boast about hunting another human being made his stomach retch. He challenged that he should teach me a lesson, what a dolt TEACH ME A LESSON...

Being the gentleman of virtue that I am I gave the poor lout an opportunity to take his seat again and possibility to survive this night. Unfortunately he did not recognize my Oberhause lineage and persisted in the senseless act of committing suicide by continuing to mock me, not unlike a young boy who should know better than to mock his older brother and eventually needs a cuff to remind him of his place.

Standing I turned to face him, subtlety explaining that this must be the stupidest thing he had done to date as he was still alive. He just laughed and threw a drink in my face.

My physical dominance over this man was slight; he was about six centimeters shorter and maybe fifteen kilos lighter. We circled each other like wild animals (both drunk and swaying) as a crowd was already starting to gather, curiosity bringing them together hoping to see blood. The thrill of the combat was part of our evolutionary calling.

I moved forward quickly and feinted a right cross and came up with a jab to the chin, his eyes already glazing over I dropped down and did a sweeping kick to the back of his legs knocking his feet out from under him. He landed hard like a sack of grain unconscious before hitting the dance floor at Le'Ralphe. I did not feel the slightest bit of remorse for the cad as I did warn him and he got off lucky with just a massive headache in the morning.

I turned and walked away from the very still mass of flesh, OK maybe feeling a little remorse but life goes on and you can't dwell on the folly of others.

Realizing the uncomfortable nature of this specific situation, I thought levity might brighten the mood so I quipped what I thought was a humorous line "at least he could have put up a fight". The words barely left my mouth when a voice behind me snapped, "Well Ogden, maybe I will be more of a challenge for you".

Putting on a smile that a Cheshire cat could envy, I spun around on one foot, a pirouette more for show than anything. I expected to find a large adversary, worthy of such bravado, at the end of my spin. To my surprise the being that uttered the challenge appeared to be nothing but a child.

What sometimes appears is not always so, A lesson my grandfather taught me early in life. A little man with boyish features stood in front of me, the crowd parting like the red sea.

His Orange cape and white blonde hair fluttered behind him although there was no wind in the room. In contrast to his shoulder length blonde hair he carried in one hand a broad sword almost as tall as he was.

He sliced through the quiet air three or four times quite convincingly to get my attention, but even more convincing were his eyes. They were sad eyes that gleamed with knowledge, not youth.

Not breaking his stare he smiled and leaned on the hilt of his blade, then suggested that we converse. All I could mutter was, "Yes of course". At this time I was bewildered at how much control this waif had over me. Not since my father or grandfather had any one ever handled me this way.

Slowly sauntering over to our table with an elegance of kings, he appeared in complete self control. An appearance that I have tried to master all my life and I realized at that moment that I was not worthy.

Before he sat down at our table he cast a backward glance to the crowd, whose mouths were still hanging open like the caves of Jarsenaies, as if to say "carry on the show is over."

The crowd reacted very quickly to his non vocal command. I had never seen so much control from any mortal, a charisma undaunted by any one in the City. Pulling up a chair he sat facing me grinning from ear to ear.

He never said anything for the longest moment; he just sat there and smiled at me.

His first words came as a shock, given a million guesses, I do not believe I would have guessed correctly what he was about to say. I sat there stupefied as he uttered that simple but very succinct phrase!

"Score some weed Dude"...

Jasmine Phillips

Trying to find a mooring space, sometimes, like, I mean really.
The space port is usually busy but the night of our graduation it was pure pandemonium. Two hundred graduates, their families and who knows how many hanger-ons. The crescent moon club was going to be one happening establishment on this mystic night.

My Vette is a small, fast little astroglide, the first year they became single seater. A real collector's item and cherry from bow to stern. My beautiful mode of transportation was a gift from my daddy on my eighteenth birthday last year; I love being spoiled by daddy.

Being cursed with stunningly good looks and an IQ that scares the life out of most males I was unable to get a date for my grad. Unfortunately no guy had the balls to ask me to this night's festivity, so I was stuck going stag. I was graduating second in a class of two hundred, advanced computer literacy doesn't sound very exciting but it appears that I have a knack for that kind of thing. Daddy says, "That's where the credits are," in a gruff baritone.

Having an aggressive temperament and a platinum spoon from birth just compounds the problem with guys felling uncomfortable around me, sometimes it almost feels lonely being me.

Finally I found a space to moor my baby, in the corner beside this bombshell of a glide, made to make sound stand still. A Jaguar XK-36, brand new this year. I figured they could keep each other company.

I only got half way across the dock weaving in and out of all the glides, when I noticed a couple of friends of mine about fifteen to twenty glides down from me. Waving my hands above my head in a crazy motion I finally got their attention.

They must have thought I was drying my armpits because it sure took them a long time to notice me waving like some kind of reject with cerebral decrepitude.

Jar and Choral made a few jokes back and forth concerning my attention getting techniques. Both of their dates were mooring the astroglides so we had some time for that girly chit chat that we're stereotyped for.

Soon their dates, Eldon and Travis, joined us and did their ceremonial bid to get into my pants. They were feeling safe with dates on their arms and no pressure to really chase me. Both of these studs put enough imagination into their teasing to spark a little bit of interest in me, but we had to accept our diplomas and act like a group of good young adults, gag, gag....fat chance.

We promised to behave ourselves at least until we could blow this joint and find a hot private party after this shingding was over and all the pompous ceremony had finished.

The crowd in the hall seemed a bit subdued, but of course the evening was still young. We found our tables and seated ourselves to take a reading of the surroundings. We were seated next to the head table, a good vantage point for watching the evening unfold.

I volunteered to get us the first round of drinks, actually it gave me a chance to see who was here and let the couples do couple things. I had to move around, I cannot sit around for long, I think it's glandular or something.

The trip to the bar was routine, a few casual, "Hi, how are you?" and "Congratulations on your achievement!" etc. Most of the guys kept their eyes averted from mine and some nervously fidgeted in my presence. I really felt sorry for them and kinda for myself as well. A couple of drinks each should get us started with a blast this evening, well keep us going for a while any way.

The return trip back to my table was not as routine as the jaunt there, I passed by this little man in orange silks and long flowing blond hair. As I passed he reached up and goosed my butt.

When I looked back at him he giggled and fluttered his eyes at me. I lost him momentarily in the crowd but kept walking toward my table. When our eyes met again I gave him a look straight out of an Este' Lauder vidiadd that included a smile that said keep pursuing I might be interested.

Not don't get me wrong it's not that I'm a nymphet but this miniature Casanova kinda turned me on. Robbing the cradle really isn't my style but it's not a regular event when a male has enough guts to look me in the eyes let alone make a play for my body.

Not breaking stride I continued back to my table feeling devilishly good, sometimes it's fun to think evil thoughts.

The guest speakers seemed abnormally slow and boring, probably lingering feeling creeping around in the vastly cluttered expanses of my mind that this dude was here to see me.

Curiosity was getting to me (I heard it killed cats which there are totally too many of any way), my mind kept shifting back to that silken clad male who made a pass at me. After what seemed to be an eternity of "thank you and well done," the ceremony was finally winding down. The hall started to change from banquet facility to a synthoteque playing all the latest on the treble charts and the hits from yester year.

My exterior was in my usual calm, cool and confident mode but this was only a charade, a façade to cover my emotions boiling out of control deep inside my body.

I have traveled all over this planet we call City and frequented its spaceports and planetary bases, shopping in the elite of elite shops. I have gotten into bar fights with both women and men but never before felt as unnerved as this moment of existence.

The dancing had started and Travis and Eldon took turns humoring me on the dance floor, both seemed to recognize that my heart and mind were light years away.

Finally my little Sir Lancelot showed his face through the crowded dance floor and started toward me, zigzagging his way through the dancers with the finesse of a hockey player going for the goal.

He came within three meters of me and stopped. He quickly looked to the left; it was the first time I had truly seen his eyes, old sad eyes that didn't seem to belong on that gentle face but still with a twinkle in them non-the-less. They seemed to say more than his youthful body could begin to explain. The depth of so many years radiated from his sadly experienced orbits.

I started to realize that this man was more than he appeared, much, much more. I feared I was beginning the ride of my life; suddenly a crash came out of nowhere a few meters to the left of me breaking the hypnosis that seemed to have enveloped me.

A few startled screams and a mass panic erupted trying to flee from the area of the crash, then I saw him...her...it, one huge mother that looked as if it was designed for murder. A beast that looked like it killed fast and efficient but wouldn't because it would relish the thought of causing slow and excruciating pain before ripping the head from your shoulders.

My idea of savior was not the orange caped wonder that up to this point was just an inappropriate fantasy. But to my surprise he seemed to be the only one brave or stupid enough to oppose this nightmarish demon.

He stood between me and Mr. Ugly and I do mean ugly easily 270cm tall, not a stitch of clothes but complete leather like skin that looked as if it could double as armor. On the end of each mammoth arm was a three fingered hand with very sharp evil looking claws. Its legs hinged in at least four places and three different directions giving it an amazing possibility for dexterity and a broad range of directional movement.

Actually the only thing that did not look intimidating about our unwanted guest was the fact that it was a bright pink, a color more suited for a fairy tale bunny.

The beast was heading straight for me but hesitated when it saw my little elf. Stopping, it growled low and guttural and pointed a long clawed finger at me that put a fear into my bones that I have never felt before.

He spoke to me slowly and menacingly as if he wasn't speaking his own language (or he could have been a bit special).

"I am the lunatic spawn of a million twisted minds, each a crazed schizophrenic maniac, each insane in their own little demented ways. I am the result of a thousand barren souls raped a thousand times a thousand times. I am what is left of a menagerie of a million putrid demons that push their ideals of perversion on the retched souls of earth. I am your death, I accept you with open arms.

"COME TO ME AND DIE!"

Backing down is not a strong trait in my character but at that moment I was ready to turn and run away as quickly as my legs would take me.

The little guy spoke to the demon in what appeared to me as gibberish but Mr. ugly appeared to understand as his attention turned away from me (thank god) and he faced the silken pixie and replied in a similar gibberish and undistinguished jumble of noises.

Out of nowhere the elf produced a very large broad sword (like magic) almost as big as him.

He flashed the blade in plain view and pointed to the exit, it was either one of the greatest bluffs I have ever witnessed or the beast knew something I didn't, because he almost looked intimidated.

Raising both arms above its head it roared with a deafening reverberation that literally hurt my ears. Now this guy was acting like a sore loser, and as if to get back at the little man, he ran straight into the horrified crowd scattering them like bowling pins.

He roared again and ran straight into a plexiwall splitting it as if it wasn't there, the whole time never slowing down. Bodies were strewn everywhere, people in hysterics, they would be talking about this one in the staff lounge for decades to come.

I actually had to consciously shut my mouth as I realized it was gaping open.

I was so grateful for not having been ripped apart limb from limb or any other horrible death imaginable.

I ran up to give my little hero big thanks and a bigillion kisses but seeing how I was much taller than he was I was only able to give him a kiss on the forehead. This seemed to bring him out of the trance like state and he looked up at me as if nothing had happened with a large impish grin on his face.

You're not going to believe what the little imp said, not in a million years.

"Wanna Score Some Weed Babe"...

Trydent II

...Score some weed dude?
The words echoed in Trydent's mind!
Those were not the first words I expected to hear. I couldn't help myself, I actually started laughing and the little imp started giggling right along with me.

I couldn't imagine a day to day drug salesman this deep into the Rez. Hell I don't run into many people at all let alone this little SOB who would probably be out of place every where except a happily ever after fairytale. I like the happy ever after part but I have never been much of a fairytale kinda guy.

He turned and walked to the upper floor and gestured for me to follow with a nod of his head in the direction he wanted me to go.

This is where I should have cut and run but who would have guessed this little elf of a person was going to thrust me into the upcoming torrent of horror and deprivation. A story worse than growing up in an area civilization had abandoned after corporate wars left the land pretty much uninhabitable and left to its misery.

After Sony International defeated the Sanyo Corporation, the use of atomics was prohibited by the City Planetary Unification Department (C-PUD), but that left a significant portion of the Rez contaminated.

Less than a decade later the Cola wars flared up after merger talks broke down between Pepsi and Coke. This time chemical warfare was introduced making Agent Orange look like Kool-Aid. The use of chemical weapons had not been used for over eight hundred years and again a significant portion of Rez was contaminated.

Problems ranged from mutations to rampant death, but the bottom line was that Pepsi was able to secure an increase of forty two percent in the market share of the soft drink industry.

Do I sound bitter? Believe me I just scratched the surface. I would knock the City back to the Stone Age if I could wrestle it away from the corporate giants that controlled it.

Sometimes I can be a complete idiot, I followed him to the room above the stairs for no real good reason, than he had asked me to.

He started to gather wood for a fire and being still somewhat dazed I started to help him; we quickly had a large pile that was easily good enough for the entire evening. Strangely enough I never noticed that much wood when I was looking earlier in the evening. There wasn't a lot of conversation while completing the task at hand and we finished quickly with out a word.

Once finished we sat down and he winked at me from across the fire and said " Well Trydent we should probably get to know each other a little bit better, don't you think?"

I was again caught off balance by the little man, (really not an easy thing to do) how did he know my name? How did he know where to find me? Who was this little man? Questions after questions raced through my mind.

I figured the best way to get answers was the direct approach as this is how I lived life, pretty much straight forward. I sat across the fire and asked a stream of questions such as, who are you? What is your business with me? Etc....

He raised a hand to slow my onslaught of queries and responded with, "All in good time Trydent" Pausing to give me a chance to breath again he continued, "Who I am at this time is not important, although," he paused again with a big smile he continued, "You have probably heard of me."

Not quite getting the joke I continued to listen attentively and not really understanding why, I started to relax and listen to what he had to say.

I had been chosen from thousands of potential candidates that had specific abilities that were needed to help save the City. Who was he kidding I have never been the hero type, yes I'm confident to the point of arrogance, but I usually look out for just myself.

He explained that he could not expand on it any more at this time but the essence of what was happening was that there had been a complete break down of the C-PUD peace initiative and an outside force was feeding fuel to the break down.

This elite group I was supposed to be chosen for apparently had an off chance of preventing the complete destruction of the Cities civilization, but not averting things all together. We had to start to move quickly if we were going to save humanity.

My honest opinion at this time was who really cares; I couldn't give a fiddler's fandangle about another corporate war. And I mean really, how could I impact what was going on at a global level. Society could rot in hell as far as I was concerned; they had done me no favors. I felt I owed this degenerate City nothing and voiced my opinion about it.

He explained that this was very important and I had no choice. To hell I had no choice. I got up and started to walk away. Maybe it was my anger that gave me the strength to break the hold he had over me but I briefly felt I had the power to walk away.

I walked toward the half rotting window sill, glass long ago vanquished, I had every intention to climb out and away from a situation I felt I had little or no control over. I figured it was probably safer outside battling the storm and the cats.

It seemed simple enough to head down the fire escape and into the jungles of forgotten high-rises to take back the control I had somehow relinquished. You have to understand I don't give up control easily, I'm a bit neurotic that way. I moved with a determined desperation and the window held the escape to what I regarded as freedom.

The words sliced through the air like a finely honed blade and hit me hard, "Trydent come back and sit down NOW!" The compelling tone was amazing; I did what I was told for the first time in as long as I could remember. My muscles responded to the voice without my mind agreeing, with the discipline of a private to a drill sergeant.

I found myself sitting once again within a single meter of my new adversary/friend; I wasn't sure at the time. I was sat across the fire and looked straight into those gripping eyes of his, they looked past me and right into my mind, my thoughts, and my soul. A calming feeling again started to come over me, what could I say? What did I understand? Nothing.

He might have been smiling but his eyes were pleading with me to drop the bravado to make things easier for the both of us in the long run.

He must have been able to sense my submission because he slapped my shoulder like a close friend or family member would to ease the tension of an awkward situation and said, "How would you like to go on a wild journey?"

I thought he meant getting high because he handed me some rolling papers and a small bag of what smelled like quality smoke, sheepishly I accepted and proceeded to roll a joint.

He chatted on like we were old friends or would be someday using small talk like a salesmen or carnie. The first drag seemed to engulf my very existence.

The utopic feeling crept up and slowly relaxed my being drifting into a dreamscape that I had never before imagined, brilliant images of dragons and castles flashed psychedelically within my mind.

Looking over at the pixie, he slowly started to disappear, fade out of visual field or was it me that was fading away. I could see him packing up a little bag and I remember wondering if he was going somewhere then the pleasure overtook me and I no longer cared.

How long I was out I couldn't begin to fathom but eventually reality began to seep back into my consciousness and my surroundings began to materialize. I was in a large room with a lot of flashing lights and occasional beeping noises, maybe a computer center or a medical lab. It seemed very sanitary almost smelling clean, a concept foreign to my lifestyle in the Rez.

I was lying in a cylindrical cubicle of clear glass and on the far wall I could see three more spaced evenly across it from floor to ceiling.

Two of the cubicles were empty but one had a body in it, it appeared to be a female and she was dressed in Rez attire.

I assumed there must be two cylinders below me judging from my position on the wall.

A figure was moving just out of my view, then it moved across to a console into my clear range of vision, it was the powerful little pixie. He glanced up and saw me, a large grin spread across his face and he exclaimed "Ah Trydent you're the first to arrive, welcome, welcome."

"Come let us talk, you must be famished after your long journey." Yes I was hungry but until he mentioned it I hadn't noticed.

Sitting up I let the cobwebs slip from my mind, then I followed him to a table of delectables of the finest eateries and proceeded to get my belly filled and my ear talked off.

Ogden II

...Score some weed Dude?
The words echoed in Ogden's mind!

This little man who carried himself like a king was just a lowly street pusher? No I reasoned with my higher powers of logic, this had to be more than a narcotics salesman.

I asked what he truly wanted from me, he replied directly and to the point, "Ogden let's talk a deal, maybe over a small joint perhaps? I need your assistance with a small project and in return I give you adventure, a sense of self worth and of course unlimited wealth.

OK, I love adventure but I all ready have a pretty good self-worth, so it was the unlimited wealth that caught my attention, now he was conversing in a dialect I could comprehend.

He handed me a small pouch of cannabis and some rolling papers, from the delicate yet powerful aroma I was impressed by the quality of the hallucinogen, but of course never letting on that I was.

Nonchalantly I tossed the pouch and its contents onto the table and quipped, "Just who do you want me to kill to receive all that you have so generously offered."

Tobias thought this was extremely jocular and roared with laughter. This must have annoyed my miniature giant as he turned to Tobias and spoke deliberately as if to a child. "If you plan to interrupt I must ask you and the rest of your friends to leave, my business is with sir Oberhause."

Tobias, not used to being spoken to in that manner or treated with such insolence got up to address the remarks that were cast so commonly at him. I let things happen as they would because it was not my place to comment on anything Tobias did under his own free will.

Strangely enough I expected this act of egotistical audacity to be nothing less than an act of suicide on Tobias's part.

Using a very forceful tone of voice, the little Goliath made a request for my friends to leave and to accent his words he placed his broadsword on the table.

Bell put his hands on Tobias's shoulders to calm him and convinced him that this was not the time. Bell was always a very smart man and good friend. My five companions all got up from our table and walked toward the bar, Tobias looking as if he hadn't gotten over the shock of the initial request.

He walked away looking very much dejected at being humiliated and not understanding why he was actually doing what he was told.

My Elfin friend sat down at my table as if nothing had happened, he gave me the impression that he had known me for a long time.

He gave me a brief description of why he was here, another corporate war was looming over the City and this time it looked as if it could be planet wide. Most of the corporate giants were getting involved and an outside influence was manipulating the situation trying to start a war like no others before.

I asked who would want an Armageddon as there couldn't be any profit in it. He explained that this would not be a war for profit but one for power.

He believed that I could be a major player and have a role in preventing the inevitable destruction of the planet that would come with a war of this scale. Since I was in a position of power as the heir to the largest ship building company in known space, he thought I would make a valuable asset to his team.

I posed the question (hypothetically of course) what if I refused to help him? He let those smile muscles work their magic and picked up the pouch of weed and handed it to me and said, "You have never failed me before and you would not fail me this time." Strangely enough I believed him not truly knowing why.

I proceeded to meticulously create the joint he so graciously asked me to roll as he delved deeper into the explanation of the situation at hand. He painted a serious picture of the impending doom.

When I was done he seemed to pick a flame out of mid air to light the tip of my creation.

My first drag lightened my head as if its floating was as natural as flying to a seagull. My frame of consciousness seemed to dwindle at an accelerated pace, faster than THC had ever affected me before.

Flashes of color and visions of flying my ship flowed through my mind and after what seemed to be a life time or maybe a millisecond, the colors and the illusions began to fade. I could hear a faint and nearly inaudible sound of what appeared to be voices.

Opening my eyes I found myself in a glass cylindrical cubical that was located in a large laboratory. It was obviously high tech and sparkled of cleanliness.

The beings that were conversing were out of my range of sight, I couldn't quite make out how many or the genders of the voices I was listening to. Best guess was two males and a female.

I placed my hand against the glass enclosure to see if there was a way of escaping the transparent tomb. As contact was made a buzzing sound started, apparently my enclosure was alarmed.

From around the corner of one of the very antiseptic looking walls came the little giant, smiling as usual. "Well Sir Ogden it was very good of you to finally join the ranks of the living," a simple utterance.

He waved his hand over a console and the glass enclosure slid away, the feeling of being a trapped animal alleviated some what.

He made an offer of food and beverage and a chance to meet my new traveling companions. My curiosity was definitely aroused to find out who else would be considered elite enough to work with me.

Slipping to the floor with the agility of a Rez feline I followed my new employer/captor into the next room, where my gaze fell on two people. One was one of the most stunningly beautiful women I have ever witnessed and the other was a large male who had the appearance of being a bottom feeder from the Rez.

Being the gentleman I was raised to be proud of, I sauntered around the lavishing garnished table of assorted foods and kissed the young lady's hand.

I introduced myself with full title as distinction requires, "Sir Ogden Timothy Oberhause the 5th of the Alanon station at your unlimited and humble service." (OK I've never really been humble)

And almost as if he read my mind the male across the table interrupted with what I believe he thought was humor. "Well Otto you don't seem that humble to me!"

I let the remark pass by me; I could deal with this street vermin later, a task I would quite possibly enjoy. Sitting down I kept my eyes focused on one of the City's master pieces of flesh and did everything in my power to let her know I thought she was interesting.

The young lady turned and giggled to my satin clad friend, "Wow, is he for real?" I wasn't sure if it was laughter of flattery or of ridicule but I was sure I would win her over eventually. Winking at the sweet lass I turned my attention to the lavish meal presented on the table and proceeded to satiate the knowing hunger that clawed at my entrails like a savage beast of the Rez.

Jasmine II

...Score some weed Babe?
The words echoed in Jasmine's mind!

At first I thought he was adding a touch of levity to try and break the obvious tension and panic of the hall. He raised his hand and gestured to me to have a seat at the table ignoring the sense of total devastation coming from the confused crowd.

Although he still had a smile on his boyish face, his gesture seemed more like a command than a request. I'm not the type of girl who easily turns down a man with that much power, besides this little man with simmering silks was a turn on in a rather sad sort of way.

We sat facing each other on opposite sides of a small round table and talked as if nothing had happened, people lieing around bleeding moaning and dieing.

I asked about the pink dude but he evaded the question and explained it was just an old acquaintance. I tried to pursue the topic further and believe me I can be persuasive when I want to be. In a firm tone he said, "We have much more important things to discuss at this time."

What control! I have never had anyone of the male gender hold that much influence over me. It was far more than just sexual attraction; he had an air of power that hovered over him like a halo.

He pulled out a small leather pouch that was concealed under his silken attire, that was straight out a tale of King Arthur. "Can you roll?" he questioned. This was getting weirder by the moment.

I opened the pouch and there was a very high quality of marijuana or derivative of sorts. The THC almost oozed out at me and having nothing better to do I rolled a joint to try and make the best out of a very strange situation.

He told me that I had been chosen as part of an elite team given a mission of utmost importance, a mission to try and stave off a war that would ultimately destroy this planet we call City.

Leaning toward me he produced a flame out of nowhere and lit the hallucinogen I had lightly balanced on my lower lip. The taste and aroma was like nothing I had ever experienced before.

In the year 2778 practically every form of indulgence is legal and I have done my share of indulging in my brief but active time on this planet.

I felt myself drifting off as he rambled on, his words having a hypnotic effect on me, not so much of what he was saying but more of the tone of with which he said it. Colors of exalted brilliance flowed over me and visions of castles and maidens in armor skipped through my consciousness. Then an eternity/millisecond of nothingness took me at last.

How long I was out I'm still not sure, it felt like a year of pleasant dreams and wild colors mixed together to form a very pleasant altered state.

As I came out of it, it became apparent that I was in a large cylindrical glass tube in an outlandishly sterile looking laboratory. I could see two people talking around a table some ways away, one a tall male with the look of Rez all over him; he seemed to carry himself with an air of jungle pride.

The other was my silk clad Goliath looking as if he was entertaining himself by entertaining his guest.

Being still a little bit groggy I wasn't able to get their attention and I was having difficulty remembering how the rest of the evening with my silken wonder went. (I hope I was good!)

The two got up and left to another room, I drifted off for a little while longer into a dreamless haze. When I again came to, the second time, I found I could move, pressing up against my enclosure I set off an alarm hopefully alerting my captor/boss.

I needed to stretch in the worst way as my muscles were beginning to cramp up. I figured even if I was a prisoner my jailor would at least give the opportunity to stretch my tired muscles. After all there is no ransom for damaged goods.

Thank Uncle Elmo, the little dude walked across the room with a large grin etched across his face; he must be connected to the cosmic jesters as he was almost always smiling. In fact, I don't think he went many places without his rizoris muscles active.

He made a sweeping hand gesture and the tube slid back freeing me to sit up and take a better reading of my surroundings.

Hopping to the floor I threw a barrage of questions at him and he laughed at me like I was a child, "All in good time my princess, all in good time." He suggested we go to the other room for a bite to eat. As he said it I realized I was quite hungry, no, more like famished.

He took me into the next room and introduced me to its only other occupant, the man I had seen before. Trydent was his name and yes, he was from the Rez.

A very large finely garnished table was loaded with numerous types of edibles, so what the hell, I gorged myself leaving absolutely no impression of a sophisticated upbringing.

I kept at it as if I hadn't eaten for weeks and realistically I'm not sure if I had, both men watched me and smiled.

Neither said a word, they just sat there grinning as if they were in on a private joke between them and they weren't sharing the punch line.

A buzzer sounded in the back of the lab and the little guy excused himself to go check on it. When he was gone Trydent became quickly serious.

Reaching across the table he grabbed my wrist with an urgency that dictated control and said, "What has this elf told you?"

Seeing a possible ally I began to explain everything I knew, starting with the evening we met at the ball. But it boiled down to both of us being limited in our information. We both knew a war was looming but he was as much in the dark as I appeared to be.

After what seemed to be about fifteen minutes, our silken host returned with a well carried man and equally as well dressed. I wondered how he fit into the whole scheme of things. I really didn't know who my friends were and who my foes were.

When his eyes met mine I could see that (on the make) expression start to light up his face. I was about to meet one of the most interesting men, for lack of a better word, in my life. Sir Ogden Timothy Oberhause the 5th.......

Shately II

...Score some weed Babe?
The words echoed in Shately's mind!

He had to be kidding! This little lunatic pursues me through the jungles of Rez like a pride of alley cats just to sell me some drugs. A surreal moment to be sure.

I pulled my hand out of his grasp with as much determination as I could muster. Leather was roused when my elbow slammed into his ribs from the force of me pulling my hand a way from this mystery midget's puckering lips.

Leather was obviously groggy from being woken up after a night of over indulgence and was slow to react to the situation at hand.

I jumped out of bed stark naked and went for my sword, at this time modesty wasn't even in the back of my mind. There I was nude as a new born, bed head, and hung over, acting tough with a broad sword.

Smiling my silken Conan apologized for the intrusion and said he would wait outside the room until I was properly attired.

Leather must have recovered, because just as I think I'm going to be able to ditch this guy, Leather grabs his cross bow and steps in front of the exit. "Who in the Hell are you?" Leather demanded "And what gives you the right to start barging into a private room uninvited asshole?"

His retort was delivered with the sharpness of a well honed blade.

"For a start I have nothing to do with hell at this time and secondly my business is with Shately and should not by any situation concern you. So turn around and vacate the premises until I have finished having an adult conversation with your female friend."

Now Leather is a trained soldier and fairly disciplined, usually he thinks before he reacts, but in this instance he did not handle the command with his control of character. Leather lost his temper and pulled the trigger of the cross bow.

The arrow whizzed through the air passing the distance between the two men quicker than a heart beat. Straight for his advisories chest the arrow only had about three meters to travel but faster than a blink of an eye, and obviously faster than an arrow the hand of our intruder shot up and plucked the projectile out of mid-air only a few centimeters from his lungs.

The act of defiance was more of an annoyance than a threat to our cheerful advisory and he waved at Leather as if to say "go play". I could see the resistance on Leathers face; he did not want to respond to the request but walked away in his shorts having no control over his actions.

I quickly threw on my clothes and went out to the hall leading to the bar we jokingly call our home. As I entered the door into the main seating area, my orange caped wonder gestured for me to sit with him at one of the tables. The bar was empty as most of the patrons had long ago had some place to stagger away to.

A wind seemed to pick up from nowhere and cause his light hair and cape flutter behind him. He spoke with a kindly, concerned voice, "Shately you're only making it harder on yourself by resisting me, your destiny has called for you and I have come to ask for your help."

He asked if we could start again and try and forget the last few hours. This is were one of the most unlikely partnerships got its start. Although at the time I did not want to commit to anything, but I did listen to his words.

His mood must have lightened as he smiled another large impish grin and his ancient eyes seemed to relax a little. Placing his boots on the table he tossed me a small pouch and asked me to roll one to set the mood. He got right to business by stating he needed help to save the planet and all the souls that resided here.

So what the hell, and I recognized the strong aroma of some very quality pot. Maybe I might be able to learn to like this little guy. Before I even had the joint up to my mouth he produced a light out of thin air.

My first inhale of this wonder weed gave new meaning to the term psychedelic; I began to drift into a land of color and giggles. Castles and queens swirled around in my mind while numbness slowly took me. My last memory was an impish grin spanning from ear to ear.

I gained consciousness in what seemed to be quite a while later, how much later God only knows. I appeared to be in a lab of some sort and wow was this place sanitary.

I was in some sort of clear glass tube that was suspended against one of the walls. I could see three more on the opposite wall only these were empty. I reached up to try and push the glass away and an alarm sounded and to my absolute surprise, the little dude with the super weed came in.

He flicked his hand across a panel that activated my escape and the tube slid away, giving me exactly that, an escape from that tomb and freedom to sit up and stretch.

I followed him into another room that had three people sitting around a table lavishly decorated with various foods. They stopped talking amongst themselves and looked at me. Each one had a look that sized me up trying to figure why I was there.

After about five or ten seconds of awkward silence, the mighty munchkin started laughing and told us to stop being shy as we were all going to be great friends.

He introduced Jasmine, tall, good looking and dressed very posh. She was a computer/electronics whiz from a well-to-do family along the coast.

Second was Ogden, he was sitting next to Jasmine and already making moves. He was a very confident man and dressed in what appeared the finest of attire. It was quickly obvious that his ego matched his attire.

The last man I recognized, by his dress and manner, which he was from the Rez. All people seem to have a certain look in their eyes after spending any long periods of time in the Rez. When I heard his name it all most knocked me over, it was Trydent, a man that was more legend than substance in the Rez. I had met him once when I was little but that seemed like a long time ago this afternoon.

I didn't know exactly why he had brought us all together; he said to avert a war. It was obvious that we were going to make one hell of a team!

Six O'clock News

Welcome to the six o'clock City in review update, I'm Jose Vaschez and this is Fran Temple with sports and your local climactic reports.

Tonight's lead story takes us to the Peace Station "HOPE" as tension is mounting as the peace talks begin to break down again. Wolter Singh walked away from the negotiations stating that Northern City Water Resources was being completely unreasonable with their demands.

The N.C.W.R. responded in turn by shutting down the entire flow of water into the Silicon Valley and threatened to step up their actions with the halting all transport of ice from their mines on Europa.

IBM has warned NCWR that if contracts are not fulfilled countermeasures will be taken at once. Canstar Electrikz has come forward in the support of its sister company which is having a ripple effect throughout the City. Stocks in both companies show radical shifts in a very volatile market.

C-PUD made a statement saying that they are currently at a dead lock and that both sides need to take a step back and leave the posturing off the peace platform, warning that outside interference may result in a possible expulsion from C-PUD.

The general feeling is that war is coming although all companies involved say ship deployment is strictly for defensive purposes only.

Let us hope that there can be some form of silver lining found somewhere on this rapidly darkening storm cloud.

On a lighter side or shall we say the pinker side, tonight a giant pink monster, yes I said a giant pink monster has been reported throughout the City. This beast has been seen in at least six different location causing havoc and destruction.

Nine dead and hundreds more wounded.

Some of the more notable fatalities are hockey superstar John L. Morgan, Dean of religious studies David Fong, Holoscreen star Beth Daniels and councilman and C-PUD executive Mark Coulson.

Here is a Hollovid taken of the alleged beast, now where in God's name did he come from? Outer space? Center of the earth? Different dimension? Already City officials are denying any knowledge of the beast and are assigning a special task force to probe deeper into this bizarre and strange occurrence.

One eye witness claims to have seen the beast at a fast food joint ordering space nuggets and a Pepsi. I'm sure he is sharing a room with Elvis himself! SSHHEESSH what next.

If it wasn't for the dead and the wounded I know this is one reporter that would be writing this off as yet another hoax, but in todays world who really knows?

I just report what you the citizens of the City want, the daily news no matter how strange it gets.

And now a message from our sponsors.

Feeling a bit run down and don't want to stand in those unhealthy lines for a corner Rejuv. Solar radiation wearing you out? How about having the new Home Rejuv installed into your family's life. If you respond now you will also receive free a month's supply of Unsun body lotion with dermal regenerative and anti-depressants for that ever needed boost to get your daily cycle started.

Unsun the smile in the tube that keeps you going. Your friends at Rejuv remind you to use responsibility.

Are you tired of that old astroglide, does it spend more time in the shop than zipping through City traffic?

If you're afraid to take your clunker out of atmosphere it's time to come on up to Satellite motors. Look over our amazing stock of both new and refurbished used astroglides. Don't forget Glides COST LESS IN SPACE...

COMING SOON
Disney Space
August 2779
Prebooking now!

Back to the news:

It was determined that last weeks crash of flight 3612 inbound from Mars was the result of a faulty gravitational stabilizer due to a build up of Martian dust in one of the aft seals. 52 dead and 23 wounded and of course a multi billion credit lawsuit. Max Tupper, an out of worker lunar miner, believed to be one of the survivors, apparently snuck onto the crash sight and pretended to be a victim. It appears that he was trying to collect his share of the settlement that would no doubt be distributed amongst the survivors and the family members of the deceased. Max went to the extremes of actually breaking his own arm, somebody space this idiot.

Space City Flights are currently asking for an investigation into Mr. Tupper's attempted fraud and have filed a counter suit to soften the insurance loss.

OK kids and grown ups alike, Disney announced that their new theme park will be opening ahead of schedule. Disney Space plans to encompass gravity free zones, space walks, mock piloting of jump gate ships, and many more, yet to be mentioned credit drawing attractions. There is a rumor that even Mickey himself may be coming out of retirement for this one.

The final rivet will be in place and atmosphere established in time for a grand opening August 25, of next year. I think Disney has another winner with this space station idea.

In Sports, the Rexal Oilers defeated the Sony Bonsai 5-3 in a *dramatic fashion winning their second cup in a row and their 3rd in 5 years. The game was marred by tragedy as after being ejected from the game with his fifth penalty John L. Morgan was brutally murdered by being ripped limb from limb in the walkway to the Oilers' dressing room. Many conflicting reports have surfaced including tying John to the giant pink beast that has been laying a trail of grief and destruction behind it. Apparently it's a Bonsai fan. Officer Bishop Paxley, the cop assigned to the case will be giving a full statement that we will bring to you at the City shift exchange update.*

City Basketball Association CBA scores:
Micrsoft Jazz 102-General Motors Bulls 99 OT (Jazz has series lead 3-1)
Robotics Nicks 97-Star Reach Attitude 92(Attitude lead series 3-2)
Chrysler Sables 87- Rolls Royce Lords 86 OT (Sables sweep 4-0)
Nutech Energy Dribble 111- MadridOptics Castanet's 86 (Dribble sweep 4-0)

Now here's Fran with the atmosphere update.
Thanks Jose..

Oxygen levels are looking a little low today, getting down to the edge of acceptable tolerances. With City Air withholding the production of clean air but shutting down the Oxygen scrubbers in a show of support for NCWR making it clear to IBM that they mean business. I would recommend that extra O2 be packed if you plan to be walking the surface for any extended period of time.

Radiation levels are at moderate to high levels, so if you are planning a trip outside make sure you cover up. An UV warning has been issued for the northern regions stretching down to the Winnipeg region.

Temperatures ranging from +19 in the northern polar region to +62 along the equator and then dropping again to +13 at the southern polar region of the City. Meteorologists the unseasonable cold weather is due to ash from the current fire that continues to rage out of control in the southern corner of the REZ. The ash is creating a haze thick enough to create a blanket affect throughout the City.

This was a City in Review update and this is Fran and Jose saying

"Live With IT Not Against it."

A chance was being taken, a major chance indeed, placing four egos as large as the ones inhabiting these bodies all in the same room.

Jasmine Phillips

A spoiled, rich, young female that has never been denied anything in her life. A computer whiz that truly doesn't understand the extent of her gift or even cares she that she has one. A filly that may be unbreakable, high strung, spirited with an inner drive strong enough to make her a factor to be considered. This young lady has a destiny with greatness and will go a long way before quitting anything.

Sir Ogden Timothy Oberhause the 5th

The title itself says something about the man, a self centered boor who was born with a platinum spoon in his mouth and could give new meaning to the term arrogant. Ogden was born to power but took what was given to him and created what could be called a small empire. This was a man that had the potential to be as great as he thought he was. Yes, a powerful man but if he gave you his loyalty he would die before he would disappoint you. Can he help rewrite the story of mankind and the journey out of Eden?

Trydent

The X-factor, born to the streets and had no problems making them his own. This was one very angry man and his anger was directed at the human race for the rape and degradation of the planet we call City. This is a man without any formal education but an intellectual wisdom that must be scaled to brilliance. When it comes down to the first step out of Eden this man has the potential to be the Neil Armstrong of Revelations.

Shately Downs

This young lady is as beautiful as a spring flower but as deadly as a cobra to a rodent. Raised in the Rez and parentless at a young age, Shately learned quickly how to survive in an often violent and hostile world. Now this bitter beauty would stand her ground and be as ruthless as the society she has learned to despise outside the confines of the Rez. This girl will join this team and be a force to be reckoned with when a taking a journey into hell.

Four Egos to be reined in and very little time.

Meeting of the minds

The four sat around the table, each gaze unwavering and definitely untrusting. The mood in the room was tense, to say the least. Trydent met Ogden's eyes with equal disdain, both men wary, both men anxious.

"Well, if this doesn't put the pro in Prozac," Jasmine challenged. She started walking around the lab reading labels and handling equipment, looking for some clue to possibly explain why any of this was happening.

"Hey girl, what ya looking for?" Shately pushed a little with a question.

"Anything that will tell me what I need to know to keep my cute little ass from frying" The words me, I, and my where sternly emphasized as Jasmine looked up to retort back to Shately.

Ogden's sneer slowly became a leer, "Now we don't want anything to happen to your ass, now do we?" The mocking emphasis of "your" caused Jasmine to look across at Ogden, almost through him.

"We need answers, we have enough questions to fill an astroport, but right now we need answers. I'm willing to start small and work my way up to complete understanding, but I'm starting now. You guys can do what you want." Jasmine continued to rifle through stuff to look for answers.

"I hear ya sister," Shately agreed with Jasmine "I'll start over here and work my way toward you, shouting if I find anything of interest." Shately was at the far end of the wall before she finished her statement.

Trydent still silent started following Shately's lead and opened a large leather bound book that looked older than time itself. What was written wasn't in English and he couldn't begin to recognize what was scribed there. Trydent slowly leafed through the pages, then shut the volume quickly feeling an icy shiver slip down his spine as the pages slapped shut.

Ogden, talking to no one in particular, queried, "You would think that there would have to be a door out of this place?" Then joined in on the search.

The room was momentarily void of speech just the sound of clinking glass and rustling papers, each sound screaming across the silence.

Everyone occupied, everyone searching, everyone intent on finding answers and somewhat fearful what those answers might reveal.

Jasmine was the first to break the silence and had just a hint of tremor in her voice. "I have found a letter addressed to a Queen Isobel of Praith, High lord empress of the house Brodie, what a mouth full. Something about honor of service and dedication to the raising of the chosen one to the throne of power yada, yada, yada."

It was a very fancy looking document that could have been a thousand years old or made last week. It was hard to tell, although the gold inlaid seal had an official feel to it.

"Has anyone heard of Praith or this queen Isobel woman?" Jasmine asked.

Ogden strolled across the room and took the scroll from her hand, not so grabby, "Ogden, that was your name wasn't it? Sir Ogden blah, blah, blah the 5th." She teased.

"That is Ogden Timothy Oberhause the 5th!" was his abrupt response. He smiled and added you can leave out my official knighthood since we're going to be so close.

"Ya sure, but do you recognize anything about that fancy piece of paper you're holding?" Shately added her two cents into the conversation.

"No, nothing familiar, but it has a fine quality of workmanship for a forgery, the seal is gold and it looks hand scribed not computer simulated."

Shately rolled out another scroll, "shit this is weirdness! Some proclamation of defiance. It appears to forbid access to....now get this." Shately had difficulty believing what she was reading. "The Lord of the Night challenges any who dare transgress the mighty realms of darkness." She had to stop and gain her composure to prevent herself from giggling. "Hell is not to be trespassed and any movement across or through will be considered an act of aggression. A retaliation of extreme prejudice will follow. As decreed by Lucifer; keeper of the dead, Beelzebub, High ruler of the shadows of lost souls and creator of evil."

"What the hell are we getting into?" Jasmine whispered, but loud enough for the others to hear.

Just as the last word slipped from her tongue, a panel in the wall slid away and in strolled the four foot nymph with of course the never ceasing grin.

The foursome was held like they got caught with their fingers in the cookie jar, he approached Shately and neatly plucked the scroll from her grasp, "All in good time child, but not yet, there will be time later for full explanations, Sir Oberhause may I have the document you've hidden behind your back? I still have to send it you know."

Ogden tossed the scroll across the table and was the first of the four to break the silence, "OK little man, you want our cooperation, then you can answer some questions!"

Shately jumped in, "Ya, why would you need us four, where in the blasted City is Praith? Are you a complete lunatic? Why me little man...Why me?" Shately needed to take a long breath after her tirade then she sat down.

A smile exploded on the face of their host/captor, "Slow down child, first you can all start by calling me Drol." He chortled. I've picked you four for very specific purposes, each one of you has gifts, each one has a destiny, please learn to trust me." The last statement was accented with Drol's eyes as he tried to bore into the souls of his audience, eyes that begged trust, eyes that said love, eyes that pulled devotion, sad tired eyes.

As quickly as Drol's expression became serious it just as quickly changed back to levity. "You all must be tired," he gleamed. "Where are my manners, let's all try and relax in more comfortable surroundings."

No sooner than after the last syllable was uttered the entire east wall opened at its middle, exposing a very large room, the opposing wall a window overlooking the City, the City in all its glory. Glass and chrome buildings hundreds of stories high twinkling with a steady stream of astroglides streaking in chaotic patterns across the night sky keeping the City awake.

Lights as far as the human eye could see, dropping off the horizon, a sparkling that blanketed the planet. Drol's apartment must have been one of the tallest buildings, as it easily towered above the symphony of lights that was the City.

The room was lush beyond decadence, thick black carpeting, deep chairs that almost begged to be curled up in and rubbed into their silk.

Rembrandt's, Picasso's, Rockwell's, thirty to forty paintings tastefully adorned the walls. Eight full sets of battle armor decorated the corners and edges of the room, two ancient Oriental, three British, a couple of Aztec and one that could even lack human origins.

The only illumination from inside the room came from a lamp nestled in the corner, the base was a yellow straggly dog with that happily salivating, what can I do for you, smile. On the dog road a white duck with a blue vest, his expression was one of having swallowed a sour pickle and was not at all happy about it.

Perched on each of duck's shoulders were two chipmunks arms outstretched and singing a happy song, brothers in merry bliss. Each chipmunk held the foot of a mouse, a sparkle mischievously glinting from his innocent large eyes, ears that could make a hat and each of his three fingered hands held a bulb that emitted a light that gave an eerie glow to the room.

Jasmine was the first to enter, the silent awe ripped through her "WOW!" whispered from her lips barely making a sound.

Shately was only two steps behind, "Holy fuck my sister," noticing a scowl from Drol she apologized "Oops sorry, I have to learn to watch my shit mouth." Shately half skipped across the carpet and jumped into a velvet lounge chair that sat open to the window's view. A gasp followed by silence, Shately's wide eyed expression said more than any words she could utter.

Ogden slowly entered the room. Very impressive elf, this surpasses even my standards, and you must have some port or sherry on the premises?" Ogden raised his eyebrows as he asked the question and then added, "Just point me in the right direction I can help myself." No sooner had he asked a dark oak shelf lifted out of the floor exposing fifteen to twenty bottles of various shapes and colors but all of finest quality.

Smiling openly Ogden nodded his approval as he poured himself a drink, turning he faced Jasmine, "Salutation, come join me in a drink and a toast to adventure and..." He paused looking for the right words "...and long life." Little did he know the irony that accompanied those words.

"Do you ever quit Sir Ogden?" Jasmine's pronunciation of his title dripped with sarcasm then she added, "Ya pour me a tall one please."

Trydent entered the room taking in every aspect of his surroundings, awe blended with caution. Trydent did not survive as long as he had living in the Rez by letting his guard down completely. Gradually Trydent moved across the room studying each canvas of artistic expression.

He stopped at the third painting that made him smile, It was some kids from a simpler time going for a swim, their clothes hanging on "A no swimming" sign. Each child had a look of innocent joy, an expression lost with the lessons of time.

Trydent's silence was finally broken, "Was there ever such a time? Were did we lose that innocence? Were did we go so horribly wrong?"

Then with a smile that could almost challenge Drol he said. "Hey OTTO the 5th, pour me a double while you're at it." He turned away from the painting, "It looks like were going to get to know each other, well we can start by swapping a few lies!"

Trydent turned to the open expanse of the glass and sighed, expelling the entire contents of his lungs, "I never could get used to the madness that is choking our planet." He took another deep breath. "You better make that a triple, how about you Shately I bet you could use a drink right now."

Shately appeared to be in her own little world half buried in the folds of the chair, she stared at the City in front of her. Beyond the initial stages of trembling, her view never wavered from the multiple layers of lights blinking and streaking through the sky. "I could use a shot, what kind of hooch ya got?"

"We're drinking a 1647 tawny port, you really are clueless." Jasmine's retort had a sense of teasing but definitely an air of superiority poked through.

"What ever has got a kick girl," Shately ignored Jasmine's jibe.

Jasmine took a glass of port and placed it in Shately's hand, absently she grabbed the crystal goblet still mesmerized by the view.

Completely missing any of Jasmine's attempts at a verbal joust, a tear slipped from her eye as the taste of the port hit her tongue. "I had no understanding,' She took another large gulp from her drink. "Absolutely no fucking understanding what it all was around the Rez."

A mute recognition grasped the room as the quartet stared in silence as the power of the City overflowed their senses.

Ogden poured himself another drink.

Drol clapped his hands to draw attention back to him and to try and pull the group back to a functional reality. "Yes it is beautiful, yet I have so much to do. Please forgive my early exit from your evening but I must relieve you of my company. All that I have is yours."

"Except answers," Trydent quipped.

Drol gave Trydent a patronizing look and as quickly as he appeared he exited through a wall that was once again a wall, his last words, "Rest, Indulge yourselves"

But Trydent was right, no questions were asked and none were answered, leaving Shately, Ogden, Jasmine and Trydent looking at each other, not really trusting and more than enough fear of the unknown keeping each on the defensive.

Each person, facing a destiny that was predetermined and far beyond each individual's comprehension of what they were used to in life.

"He is one unpredictable and annoying little guy." Ogden's remark was not meant for anyone in particular.

Back to Hell

Camp time racers sing this song dooda dooda, bet my money on a bold tale ma, ole dude daddy........Yes I believe that is how it goes or was it bet my money on a bob tailed nag.... Day after days creeps into my insanity, boldly going where I have never gone before. He shoots he scores.......RAH RAH Rasputin... flip, my nose is itchy and I can't even scratch it.....Wait, I think I'm insane.....

No...NO....NO...NO......NOOOOOO!

That simple word echoed in John L. Morgan's mind as it slowly yet quite deliberately slipped away. Hell can never be described as relenting; it grasps your consciousness and slams it into your reality over and over and over and over again.

The glass shatters from the inside out, each crack flowing through the mind, causing a tingling sensation that almost feels like emotion. At last count, it was the 3413th sensation that ripped through John's mind, tearing at his memory of existence.

Over the centuries it has been hypothesized that when an unworthy being dies they are plunged into hell, actually it is more like slowly dissolving, an uneasy decomposition of your sanity.

Try and hold your breath for two minutes, go ahead and take a break from the novel and hold your breath for as close as you can to two minutes, did you try?

How close to panic were you? Did you squirm in your seat? Again take the chance and try it or you can just read past this point and lose the experience I offer. Did you make it, probably not; most people can't get past a minute. Now take that feeling of need and multiply it by a thousand. That's the feeling of dread that accompanies going to hell.

It isn't some horned dude with a pitch fork herding you through a maze of fire and brimstone, unless of course that is truly scary for you. Everything you ever feared is boiling up through your senses and screams in your face. Welcome to HELL.

"No let it stop please make it stop, it spins, it floats, you almost have the wheel but you can't seem to drive. Evil has swallowed my mind and foully contaminated any innocence my soul may have possessed. Limbo is not neutral; it very slowly eats away until.....until hope is only a distant memory.

"Hush I smell a rat!"

Dreams

Hours passed since Drol removed himself from the groups' presence. The four protagonists sat together, talking rarely, the flash of the City taking most of their attention.

Shately was the first to drift off, the first time in her life she had been exposed to such luxury. She slept and dreamed, not a deep peaceful sleep more fragmented and tormenting, the incidents of the last hours finally catching up to her.

Trydent watched Shately as she slept, she started to murmur and stir in her sleep. Pushing away things that were only in her dreams the poor girl battled the Rez 375 stories above it.

A barely audible "leave me alone" then again a semblance of peace. A slight smile came over Trydent as he understood the peace Shately appeared to have reached and wished he could remember what it was like to feel that way.

Trydent's gaze left Shately's restless form and slowly crossed the room, stopping at a suit of armor. It was made of light weight metal and shone as the lights of the City twinkled against it. Trydent imagined having armor like that in the heart of Rez, this sent a surge of testosterone through his body bringing exhilaration and guilt.

Trydent smiled to himself, thinking of the damage he could easily inflict wearing the battle armor but then again some bastard with a Laz rifle would melt him in his tracks.

The pale illumination from the mouse lamp fell on a large book in the corner a few meters away. Trydent absently got up and walked towards the collection of words.

The Large hand crafted leather bound book was randomly laying open for display. Trydent approached it with out fear but he did hesitate but caution was in his nature. He could not recognize the text it was written in but suddenly he was hit with its understanding. No better than if a translator whispering in his ear.

Job; chapter 17-"Is there not an appointed time to man on Earth," Trydent flipped through the pages almost with frantic deliberation. *"How doth the city sit solitary, that was full of people."* Lamnations chapter 1.

"And he lay hold of the dragon, that old serpent which is the devil and Satan, and bound him for a thousand years." Trydent stepped back and shook his head to release the shivers that overtook him, not truly understanding what had just happened.

A deep breath synchronized with a full turn to face the liquor cabinet, Trydent downed the last of his drink and lightly whistled. "I think I need a refill," then walked toward the bottles, pouring himself another glass way past social tactfulness.

"Tripod was it? Pass the bottle over here when you're done." Ogden's attempt to get under his skin was momentarily lost on Trydent, but it was filed away for future reference.

Without hesitating Trydent tossed the open bottle towards Ogden, neck over base the bottle rotated evenly one time and Ogden caught it cleanly but stepped aside to avoid the spray and watched it splash against the glass of the window giving a surreal effect to the cityscape as it dripped down.

"Thanks" he smiled, "Sweet libations, nectar of the gods." Ogden continued with out missing a beat "So what's your story, you must be important if you're here, you're Rez Right?"

Trydent stretched hard before replying, "Do you ever wait for an answer before asking another question, my story is, yes I am from Rez, born and conceived there."

"Yes, I thought so; you have that look in your eyes." Ogden's stare never left the lights and glitter of the City. The apartment he kept planet side had a great view but this had to be one of the best in the city. His view from his space station on the other hand was phenomenal.

Ogden brushed his hand through his thick hair absently, never breaking sentence, "I remember I realized that all this was mine for the taking, I was eleven or twelve and visiting my grandfather, who still lived full time on the planet..." Ogden turned to see Trydent looking at him as if to say, "What's your point?"

"I'm sorry I do ramble on sometimes but when I secured my retinal scan on the Teledyne take over it was pleasure beyond ecstasy. My first taste of industrial power compliments of Gramps." Ogden's stroll through memory lane was interrupted as Trydent could not keep quiet.

"You have no clue do you? While you were buying and selling human lives just to feel good about yourself I watched my sister get dragged away as experimental fodder for some drug company, they had to find out if their precious chemicals had any side effects before unleashing it on to society and some worthless female from the Rez was expendable. The elite of this culture must be looked after." The last words were almost spit out of Trydent's mouth.

"That wasn't my company" Ogden appeared hurt by the accusation, but wasn't able to defend himself.

Trydent's vehemence shot up, "You stupid fuck, you are responsible for hate, you are responsible for the death of countless human beings all for the name of profit!" Trydent started to walk toward the startled Ogden. "Do you understand what has happened to this world!"

Never one to back down Ogden began to defend himself. "Yes, Trydent I understand, we are a population of forty six billion and although we have orbiting space stations, colonies on some of the planets, moons in this solar system and.." Ogden's voice started to rise, "have sent numerous ships in a failing search of inhabitable planets. We are stuck on this measly little planet, struggling to keep it from wasting away depleted of everything usable."

Ogden looked as if he was done but then took a step toward Trydent trying to put an exclamation mark to his point. " Population control is not a popular belief let alone understood procedure, but culling this planets population is a very necessary procedure that no one is willing to take on, so I am working to get us out of this system…"Ogden's anger had matched Trydent's, then he added to dare Trydent to challenge him. "If I need a critique of how I run this planet I will ask somebody besides a thug from the Rez who doesn't see past his bitter existence."

The two men were almost nose to nose when Trydent shot back to Ogden's rant, "So why bother, if humanity isn't worth saving? You might as well make a few billion credits off the sweat of it's children since you obviously have such a caring nature."

Jasmine jumped up and slipped in between the two adversaries, "Gentlemen please let us not get upset over misunderstood points of view."

Trydent turned and walked away not waiting to listen to any possible response. Contempt vibrated through his being. "I need another drink; maybe numbness may silence this arrogant prattle."

Ogden opted to stay silent as he put his hands on the large window and watched the City in all its glory and horror.

Shately never stirred from her slumber.

The City never slept, the City flashed, pulsed, continued to live rotating its inhabitants between sleep cycles. The solar cycle long ago had ceased to determine when the populace of earth slept. A million sunsets have come and gone since mankind huddled around a campfire afraid of the night, finally falling asleep and hoping the sun would return.

Now the bustle of civilization was a twenty-four hour neurosis and the daily rat race was a distant memory talked about on educational channels.

Shately slept but not deeply, the events of the previous hours swirled in her dreamscape, a struggle to comprehend, difficult to accept, now surfacing from the deep recesses of her mind.

The cycle of dreams had her walking along a beach, but there were no buildings floating on the water, just water as far as her sight could see dropping off the horizon. That much water scared Shately, growing up in the Rez water wasn't even a common sight three hours after a hard rain.

It was a dream, but to the orphan raised in the Rez, it all seemed all too real. The cry of the gulls the smell of the salt air the wet sand beneath her feet, Shately had never dreamed so real before.

Then a wave on the water started to grow, to lift out of the sea and hover as big as a building. The wave rolled toward shore, Shately tried to run but her feet were leaden, her legs unable to move.

The wave moved closer, picking up speed and increasing in dimension and blocking the sun. Shately found herself trying to crawl up the beach to try and escape the inevitable liquid grave. Lying trapped on the sand, the wave was over her hovering, all Shately could see was water.

The wave spoke to her and she was completely overwhelmed. Each word echoing. "Who do you think you are to stand up to me? You are nothing; your friends are nothing, mere gnats to be squashed under my heel."

The voice increased in volume almost deafening, the scream hurt her ears "YOU ARE MINE Shately Downs, YOU ARE MINE." As the wave came crushing down on her she awoke with a jump, the words still echoing in her mind.

For a brief moment she couldn't remember where she was, and then a flood of memories poured over her, her heart strained under the pressure. The blood of her enemy just two days ago blinded her thoughts.

Ogden, Jasmine, Trydent, these people were basically strangers, a deep breath helped to calm her a little but adrenaline flowed pure in her veins.

Ogden looking in her direction after noticing her stirring, whispered. "The devil tickling your soul?"

"What?" she asked not understanding.

"That is what my grandmother used to call a nightmare." Ogden's voice was soft and sentimental, "Ah Grandmother, she was the substance that held our family together. The only person I ever saw my grandfather bow down to."

Shately still trembling got out of her plush chair and walked toward the window, looking across the great City seeing the lights that were almost as plentiful as stars in the sky. Dawn was approaching and the City continued to pulse, not quite as ominous, but it continued to be very very busy. Shately tried to shake off the still lingering presence but the realness of the REM-scape was indelibly ingrained into her memory. As she stared across the expanse of the City a shiver slowly crawled up her spine carrying with it a looming feeling of dread.

"What ya thinking girl?" Jasmine queried as she stretched off her morning slumber. "Nothing should put that kind of look on anybody's face this early in the morning or do you know more than I do?"

"No, just messed up over a nightmare, just a stupid little fucking nightmare." Her words had anger that was directed inward, almost embarrassed at the fear that gripped her

But Shately's mind continued to whisper the words 'just a stupid fucking nightmare' unsuccessfully trying to convince herself.

Guessing Shately did not want to pursue the topic any further, Jasmine tried to change the subject with as much grace as she could muster. "I could use something to eat, hell I'm kinda famished, and a piece of fruit would do wonders to help eliminate a hangover."

"There must be a food dispenser, how about that lab, there was food in there, how did Drol open this wall?" Jasmine pushed and twisted items looking for a release pin. Trydent spoke for the first time that morning, "I tried that last night while you were sleeping and came up with zilch." The foursome all stood facing one another, eye contact testing, feeling, grappling for more than was being said. But there was no commonality, no understanding, no trust....not yet anyway, not quite yet.

Poor John

Are you brave enough to look into the laughing face of madness, make eye contact with lunacy or even roll the dice to gamble with the game of insanity? Most wouldn't dare.

Can you imagine being a blind man during WWII, hiding away in a shelter during the blitz on London? You would hear the whistle of the rockets long before any one else, more time to get your heart racing. You see with your ears and think with your hearing as you sit gripping what ever or who ever you can find and listening to your would get blown away.

Each explosion a cochlear nightmare, pulse rate beyond acceptable limits, pain beyond understanding and fear beyond belief.

Welcome to John L. Morgan's hell, walk softly and try and deal with the insanity or barge in a find yourself unraveling at the seems.

I give you another chance, two minutes! Am I being repetitive or maybe a tad redundant? John's reality was in steady rotation, each grasp at sanity sliding through his fingers, spinning clockwise for those who remember analog watches.

Distant memories, flashes of familiar faces, why did the chicken cross the road.... That was no chick that was my wife..... Speaking of my wife she is so flat when she sits around the house she actually said quake.....

Poor John nobody ever taught him that hell was so difficult, one minute winning the Stanley cup and then the next stuck in eternal damnation. Life is a bitch and so is the lack there of one.

Emotion blends with sensation crossed referenced with pain. Hell is a trip with out seatbelts and your air bags won't save you so stick your head between your lags and kiss your soul goodbye. Suddenly John found himself gripped by lucidity, almost feeling his body. "Yes this is it, I have to concentrate, I can feel it, so close."

John's frantic attempt to gain back his reality slipped away as suddenly and painfully as it appeared. John wasn't quite ready to walk the caverns of hell.

Upstairs at Drol's

Food supply has always been a dilemma for humankind from the beginning; in fact it was the very first need. Early man foraged for roots, berries and small rodents barely eking out an existence.

The organized hunt brought large quantities of food to the clan long before the concept of tillage and planting grabbed our ancestor's comprehension. The first killing tool to supply the tribe with food was the stone; game was plentiful so only occasionally did one starve to death.

Ways of throwing rocks evolved into slings and we could start being a little particular with our cuisine choices. OK maybe the stick evolved along side of the rock, it's not really known just a lot of speculation opposed to documented proof.

As our species grew, recognition of a necessity to increase food production became apparent and it made early Homo sapiens reevaluate meat eating. The first farmer must have been viewed as a profit or at the very least a genius.

We continued to have a taste for meat so hunting progressed to the domestication of wildlife for ye old taste of roast and potatoes.

Now Biodomes scatter the planet, large half spherical glass skeletons that are both food supply and oxygen factories. These are considered 'zoos for flora' or 'plant life sanctuaries' one of the biggest crazes to catch the public since the hoola hoop. Only advanced reservations assured you a place in line on weekends and holidays. And the credits needed to pass by security were way beyond a simple bribe.

Security was thorough and to the unsuspecting, damn near overwhelming.

Biodomes helped rejuvenate the oxygen supply, the only truly fresh air left on the planet not including bottled air. They were enclosed, controlled, programmed biological environmental spheres.

From parsnip to boreal forest, every ecosystem was given a growing environment and the populace devoured it. One of the City's main food supply had become a tourist attraction. "Food as fresh as the City can produce!" rang across the vid screens inviting Mr. and Mrs. Public to tour the Biodomes.

Every piece of fruit, all the grain for the breads, 90% of the vegetables, (10% window gardens in the cloud layer), acre after acre of cultivated land within a controlled ecosystem. The Biodomes were a marvel of modern ingenuity and necessity of survival.

Farm land was lost with the population explosion of the 23rd century and as a species we needed to feed the masses with more than fabricated proteins with artificial vitamins and color.

Drol entered the room as the wall swished open, "Who wants a bite to eat, 'Food as fresh as the City can produce' you all need to keep your energy up." He giggled, deliberately mocking the Biodomes catch phrase. He pushed a trolley loaded with fruits, juices, vegetables and breads with a myriad of spreads and preserves.

Ogden walked over and picked up a piece of fruit, "OK Drol, you can placate us with good food for a while, but from my point of view if you don't start explaining things with a lot more detail you can kiss my cooperation good bye." Ogden accented the good bye with a bite into his peach.

Not bothering with niceties he turned to Shately, "Mmm good peach." His mouth very full.

Shately still trying to shake of the previous night's nightmare grabbed a slice of multi grained bread and slathered it with a strawberry preserve. "Maybe food will help settle me down some and damn it if I didn't drink a little too much last night, a glass of fresh juice is supposed to help that hairy tongue thing, right?" Shately took a long drink of a fruit punch and smiled, "Wow it's been a long time since I tasted anything that good." She then attacked her bread and jam with aggressive enthusiasm.

"Fill your bellies, satiate your spirits and relax for a little while," Then Drol became serious. "The mission I have asked you to take on is a treacherous one. You must rise to the destiny bestowed unto you."

Shately sighed to herself trying to alleviate her fears and sense of hopelessness. Trydent turned away from the window and gave his attention to Drol anticipating answers. Jasmine helped herself to some breakfast but kept her attention on the silk clad warrior. Mr. Oberhause being the man he was simply stated for all to hear. "It's about time."

Drol continued, "I'm asking for a commitment, one that goes as deep as your soul. Each one of you has a soul that has already reached the greatest of achievements." Making eye contact with each person. "Please look deep into who you are, past your chemical memory, past your mortal existence." Drol literally glowed, his intensity immense. "Look into your souls and remember, we have worked together before, long before, back when you were different people." None could look away the light was bright but did not hurt the eyes.

"Shately you are a proud and noble history, your soul has existed within many honorable people, Mary Magdalene, Mother Theresa, Eve, just to name a few. Join me on a journey into peril and carry a torch of goodness into the battle brewing just off the horizon of humanity."

"Please Trydent, heed my warning and help the cause of righteousness." Trydent tried to look away but was helpless to resist the rapture of Drol's words.

"Walk the path of souls again and remember what it is to be a child of God. Join Gandhi, John Paul, Noah and the many others who have walked the earth with this soul."

Realization unfolded in a flash of his mind, his life, his soul exploded into understanding. At that moment in time Trydent felt all the lives that had existed through out the history of his soul. It was no longer a question for Trydent; he knew he was committed to Drol's purpose without truly understanding what the specific purpose was. At this point he was willing to trespass into the gates of hell if necessary.

Drol turned to Ogden and he, like his companions was gripped by Drol's aura and presence. Ogden was a strong willed individual but at this time he gave his will over to Drol.

"Join me, Sir Ogden Timothy Oberhause the 5th on a quest to save the very existence of your species, like the Apostle Paul, Adam, Armstrong, some great men have shared your soul. And like them all, you have a huge task ahead of you to undertake." At this point there was no question for Ogden, no decision to be made, just devotion to the feeling of doing the right thing at the right time. Lost was Ogden's typical arrogance, his sense of inflated importance, just a pride of a shared soul.

Finally it was Jasmine's turn and again there was minimal resistance, basic acceptance of the predetermined path that was the journey of the soul. Mary, Joan of Arc, Princess Dianna not by any means a complete list.

The truth flowed through Jasmine, everyone that her soul had ever occupied, she felt joy and rapture, she did not possess the ability to refuse Drol no more than she could stop her heart from beating.

As quickly as it started it was over, all four seemed a little confused and each one dedicated to the cause they only understood in their heart.

Jasmine turned to Ogden as she bit into her fruit, "Ya you are right, this is one hell of a peach," smiling at Drol to add to his earlier whimsy, "and Biodome fresh."

Trydent only hesitated a second before digging in. "I guess we all need to eat something to keep our strength up." He surprised himself at how easily he towed the line but he shook it off as he ate a wonderfully delicious breakfast.

Drol smiled one of his great smiles, "Eat, relax a little, get to know each other. In two days hence I need you at Biodome 313.

Your numbers will grow, accept the help, many will be needed to complete your task."

Trydent's voice was slow and with an exacting tone, "Biodome 313 is along the west coast bordering the Rez, if I'm correct. We could be there in less than six hours if we get creative."

Jasmine jumped in, "Why two days? We can leave within the hour and catch an astrocab."

Drol's explanation was as vague as usual, "There are forces at work that will try and prevent you from reaching your destination. You will need to pick up followers, people that will feel a need to join up with you, please accept them."

"How many people are we talking about?" Trydent queried.

"The exact number is irrelevant and I don't want you focused on counting, those who need to join will join. Let's say probably more than a dozen and less than a thousand." Drol was able to smile through anything.

"You will know who to trust, who to accept into your flock," he assured them "but be careful, evil will try and infiltrate your group so learn to trust your instincts."

"So what is it you want us to get from the Biodome?" Asked Ogden, always wanting information and answers.

"When you get there you will be contacted and given directions." Drol replied evasively.

Trydent quipped. "Do you make this up as you go along or do really have a plan?

"Yes there is a grand design Trydent but my plan will be challenged." Drol tossed Trydent a piece of fruit and added "There is always a plan but the path to the outcome is clouded."

Trydent caught the apple with left hand.

"Good catch." Shately teased and in response the apple was tossed again, this time in her direction. In one quick motion she drew her blade and cut it in half.

"Thanks."

Trydent, very impressed with her swordsmanship joked, "Now we know why you were chosen to come along."

"Neat trick but a blade will only be of use for part of your journey." Drol's words slipped back into a serious tone.

Your ability to use a sword is very important, in fact crucial, but let me introduce you to another weapon you might find useful."

Drol pulled a large drawer form under the food cart and displayed its contents to the team. Four compact hand held laser rifles.

"What is so special about blast pistols, I was given a bigger one on my 3rd birthday." Ogden was obviously hoping for something a little more impressive.

Jasmine's agreeing tone seemed almost insulted, "I train with more fire power than this. Come on Drol you can do better? How about some fire power, if you want us to win this war of yours."

Trydent put his hand on the hilt of his sword and said, "Now this is a fine tool and I know how to use it in close quarters, but I will take one of your toys if you think it may come in handy." Trydent hated to be in the situation of not having enough armament going into a fight of any size.

"It's more than you think my children, these are Laz rifles, full pulse, capable of taking out battle skiffs and have the ability to slice through class five shields that are created with a eighty percent pure crystal." It almost appeared as if Drol was bragging.

"Really!" Now he had Mr. Oberhause's attention, "class five, not bad, what's the sonic recoil like?" Not waiting for an answer he added, "Can it be shot accurately with one hand." Ogden picked up the finely crafted weapon.

"It's like pointing a finger, no more jarring than that." Drol explained "but with the fire power to cut a Plexisteal wall in half. So when you play with it, be careful." 'Be careful' was punctuated with slow sincerity.

Jasmine reached down and picked up one of the rifles, "Nice weight." She extended her arm and scanned the room through the sights. "Not bad, if they're really as powerful as you say." She continued to scan the room, stopping at one of the suits of armor, cross hairs resting on the breast plate. She counted to two slowly in her head then whispered "You're dead." Then she continued down the wall and repeated the procedure between Mickey's eyes, then moving across the window to rest on Ogden's back as he was looking out at the City.

Ogden turned around to face Jasmine as she raised the cross hairs from his abdomen up to focusing between his unblinking eyes, "One two, you're dead." She smiled and lowered the weapon, the muzzle pointed to the floor.

Ogden's smile matched Jasmine's and through a chuckle, laughed, "Thank God you're on my side."

"Damn right," was Jasmines simple reply.

"Maybe you should have pulled the trigger." Trydent suggested as he walked across the carpet to pick up a weapon of his own. "Just maybe." His eyes met Jasmine and showed enough mirth to indicate he was joking, just maybe.

Shately was the last to pick up a Laz Rifle and was obviously hesitant, "Point and squeeze the trigger." She took a deep breath, "What is the range of one of these babies."

"There is a fifteen percent decrease in power that is dissipated in the air for every three hundred meters, so at a kilometer away you will definitely start to slow a craft down." Drol seemed to enjoy explaining the weapon to Shately. "Put the weapon on impulse until you're in a real jam then crank it up to full power and watch the fire works."

"Great!! What else do you have little man?" Ogden felt like a little boy at Christmas, "maybe personal body shielding would come in handy."

"Sorry Ogden you know as well as I do that kind of thing is still theory." Drol consoled the disappointed man.

"Until a couple of minutes ago so were those little Laz Rifles we all like so much." Ogden was quick to point out. "My company is working on shield research and was not that far off."

"Yes, yes, Ogden for now, this is enough. Now eat, rest and get some strength because from here on in it is about to get difficult."

Jasmine shook her head. "More difficult than giant pink demons threatening to rip me to pieces...sounds like a party."

Shately, still not recovered from her nightmare whispered under her breath, "Ya sounds like a party."

"Seeing how I don't think I can raise your spirits any more, I will depart and see you all later. Stand proud and believe." With that Drol whirled around and exited his hair and cape flowing, his smile glowing but the most tell tale message was his eye's warning "BEWARE!"

It was hours since Drol's departure and the four rested in silence, Jasmine and Ogden slept surrounded by a City that never did, Shately was afraid to sleep and Trydent rarely succumbed to the REM cycle.

Forces were at work, dark forces that meant to destroy Drol's plan. Death was very close and was reaching to clutch a hold of the four's lapels and drag them to join John Morgan.

It was only a matter of days since Drol had interrupted their lives, but to each one of them it was a life time.

The Demon that tripped the sensors on the penthouse's security system would pay dearly for its mistakes, for it had a master that didn't accept failure well. Its master was by no means benevolent in fact ruthless was a better description.

The alarm system rang loud "Intruder alert" repeating a warning that this morning saved the lives of each individual in the apartment.

Trydent was moving with sword in hand as the first giant pink demon ascended on the sleeping group, his blade making contact on the beast's shoulder drawing what could function as blood.

"You will die a thousand deaths, mortal, for every drop of blood I shed!" The demon spat his words at Trydent. But before the last syllable was uttered Shately's blade came crashing down on the back of the creature's skull. "Remember me you piece of shit?" Her anger over being chased by the beast surfaced quickly.

The demon howled with rage, its scream pierced the dawn but was then cut short as Jasmine fired a Laz Rifle from two meters away, set on full. From chest to skull evaporated as the beam cut the demon down in its stance.

The jerking body fell back and crushed the Disney lamp and knocked over two sets of the ancient amour. A second beast appeared to be completely obliterated by Ogden, "Oh yes I do like this!" almost as if he was enjoying himself.

During the confusion no one had noticed that a wall had opened to reveal a turbo tube. "Wow, can you believe it," Jasmine gulped. "It's one of the pink sons of bitches that attacked my grad the other night, humph he wasn't so tough."

"I'm sure there is more to come; those two may have friends following. We need to come up with a better plan." Trydent yelled to be heard over the alarm.

Ogden moved to were the beasts seemed to be coming from and was not prepared to find what he did. "Holy Shit!" he yelled, "Look what I found!" It was a thermal bomb, big enough to take out a couple City blocks and definitely flatten this building.

Looking at the time Ogden realized that he needed to be heard and now. "We've got thirty five seconds lets move, It's a BOMB!" His intensity caught the others attention and they all pushed hard toward the turbo tube. Trydent grabbed Shately by the arm for support.

As they dove into the shaft Ogden yelled, "get the doors shut." Jasmine was already pounding the direction floor buttons not needing his prompting. The doors slid shut and there was an almost immediate response, the sensation of down ward motion hit each one in the stomach.

"Are we going to make it?" Shately asked.

"Probably not, but we're in for one hell of a ride. Trydent's pessimistic out look on life could surface at any time.

The percussion of the explosion knocked everyone to the floor of the tube. Ogden hit his head above his right eye opening a small gash, not life threatening but if he survived the explosion he would probably have a scar to tell a tale by.

Ogden was right, the bomb was designed for destruction, but he underestimated its power, not only was it capable of destroying the building but a ten block radius surrounding the building and that is exactly what it did.

As the building crumbled around the turbo tube, Shately gripped Jasmine with her hand to her shoulder and her other arm was entwined around the other girl's arm which in turn held on to Shately. The two women held each other as if their very lives depended on each other and realistically very much did.

Over 275 floors of plastisteal, glass and lives came crashing down as that old gravity game pulled at 9.8meters per second into the unforgiving ground. Into 30 sublevels of astroglides waiting in their berths for their owners to return, but none would ever merge again into the traffic of the City.

Each girl held her eyes shut and tight as they embraced each other waiting for an inevitable impact, forgetting to breath, expecting death. Both would have bruising from each other's grip, but that was the least of their worries.

Doug reached in to get a beer from the back of his ultra six refrigeration system, the wall pushed in knocking it completely over Doug. No sooner had it pinned him to the floor, the floor joined the race to become rubble. Doug's apartment was on the 174th floor, 137th, 113th in fifteen seconds and steadily dropping. After forty five seconds Doug was unconscious and his North West view of the City had vanished within shards of rubble and clouds of dust and soot.

Trydent and Ogden crouched down beside each other trying to steady their center of gravity. Both had one hand braced against the wall of the tube and the other arm entwined with each other, drawing strength from the grip. Neither man could remember the argument from the previous evening, at this time it was a petty memory at best.

Ogden opened his eyes to the waiting stare of Trydent's gaze. "This is how we die Otto!" Ogden could not hear the words but knew the words that were spoken; each movement of Trydent's lips enunciated plainly as he gently moved his head from side to side.

Of course it would be silly to kill off everyone now so early in the story so both men would survive to fight another day.

Geoff's world collapsed around him, his fifteenth floor apartment with its meager tapestries and far from elegant décor flattened by the tons of debris. Geoff's survival had to be termed a miracle, 275 floors filled with people, pets and furniture surrounded the five square meters of existence. But Geoff did survive and so did his fish tank, fifty liters of water and a school of seven angel fish. Six orange and black and one scarlet and black (Elvis); which was the only one that Geoff had named, the rest he just called the disciples.

The turbo tube decelerated drastically as it approached the tenth sublevel, the gee-force toppled every one to their sides nobody releasing their grip on the others.

For a brief moment in time all stopped, no one even breathed almost as if God himself needed to catch his breath and recognize that that was cutting it close.

"Wow, can you dig it?" Jasmine exclaimed as time started to flow once more. She finally opened her eyes, "Do you guys think we made it? That was one hell of a ride."

Ogden placed his right hand onto the sensor screen which activated the turbo's doors, opening into a long shaft rising on a thirty five percent grade.

Betty, Frank and the twins never woke; they all died, crushed to a pulp and their remains only recognizable through DNA analysis. But their death was merciful and painless along with thousands that were caught in the blast. They all entered the after life together and would spend eternity as a family.

The four stood in the turbo tube looking out into the rising shaft, "Holy, Wow, we're alive," Shately breathed. Then Jasmine started laughing, more of a release than actually finding anything funny the other three joined Jasmine and they all started with loud boisterous laughter, tears flowed.

"I knew we were going to make it." Trydent choked out his words between giggles, "I never doubted it for a second." The laughter turned to nervous giggles then in unison they all said, "Let's get going."

That set Shately off again as they exited the tube and started their ascent up the tunnel. She might as well laugh at her situation, it was either laugh or start screaming.

"There must be a very powerful shield around the turbo tube and this tunnel." Ogden had always been impressed by power. "I guess we keep going this tunnel has to lead some where." He wasn't talking to any one in particular just voicing his thoughts.

Jasmine had caught her breath by now and agreed. "Yes, it is time to get moving; this would be called fleeing for our lives, now wouldn't it?"

Ogden and Trydent bumped into each other as both men tried to take point. Trydent gave a knowing look and said, "Otto my man why don't you cover the rear."

"Its OK Trypod, I've got point."

"Hey, this is not the time to start flexing egos again, you two had better check that testosterone at the door, Jasmine why don't you take point and I'll cover our asses." Shately's directions were taken with out any overt argument just some grumbling under the two men's breath.

Upward the four fugitives climbed; there wasn't enough room to stand maybe a radius of one and a half meters. The easiest technique was on the hands and feet, similar to scampering. They all got down to the business of crawling up the shaft.

"How's the pace guys?" Jasmine inquired. "I could pick it up a bit if every body wants."

"OK by me."

"Push it girl!"

I'm right behind you, let's go." Shately made it unanimous.

For a half an hour the troop pushed up the tunnel and eventually came to an air lock. "OK we're going out and we should assume that we are still being hunted. Eyes open, keep together we need to move quickly to cover and get a reading on how bad it is."

Trydent didn't even argue he just replied in unison with the other two. "Right."

Jasmine moved to the front, "On the count of three, one, two, three." The doors swished open and a cloud of dust rolled over them as they broke into the street.

The destruction was amazing, piles of rubble ever where stacked with out planning, fires burning lie pyres for the dead, emergency sirens ringing their warning from every direction, pandemonium! Dust and debris still floated in the air choking Shately and her companions.

"To your right," Trydent pointed to a break in the destruction, "let's try and get to that open street!" It was about two blocks away and they would have to climb over the ruins of the fallen buildings but for now it looked as if that was the only option available.

"Let's get going if we're going to do this," Ogden yelled to be heard over the din. With out discussion Jasmine started to move, climbing through the rubble, her companions moved with her scrambling faster than safety warranted.

"This is worse than the Rez, it's got that fresh death sense not that rotting neglected feeling." Shately had spent the better part of her life in the Rez and had to eventually get used to death, but this had a very evil sense to it. A presence that makes the hair on the back of your neck stand up or keep you looking over your shoulder when you're walking alone in the night. Shately felt for sure that it was the same evil presence that invaded her dreams not so many hours ago.

It was dawn but the fires were bright and threw shadows amongst the morning light. It was difficult to see properly as the eyes constantly adjusted to the dancing shadows that played on the rubble.

Jasmine had intensity about her and it showed in the pace she was taking. They came to a fallen wall about four meters high. "Ogden climb on my shoulders and the girls can use us as a ladder." Trydent braced himself against the jagged slab of concrete. Ogden didn't even to bother to argue he just hoisted himself onto Trydent's shoulders.

"Shately, GO!"

The young women climbed quickly up the two men, "Hey watch that scabbard it almost took out my eye!" Trydent complained.

Shately responded almost playfully "You going whine all night or can we get on with this."

"Climb girl climb!"

"If you two can coordinate this, I wish you would hurry, I feel like my ass is hanging out for any fool with a blast pistol can take a pot shot at me." Jasmine's words lacked any of the playfulness that Trydent's and Shately's did.

Shately reached the top and barely got settled as Jasmine started to reach the top of the slab, and was given a helping hand to gain the apex.

"Now you two hold my arms while Trydent climbs up my body." Again no discussion or debate, just action as everyone worked to accomplish the task, the team was growing together!

The wall slowed them down by a dozen minutes but they continued to push, scrambling up and down the buildings that had been reduced to skree, littered with body parts, each one unable to tell their story.

"I'd say we have about another two hundred meters before we get through this," Trydent coughed out the words as his throat was accumulating more dust by the second. He wasn't that far off, he had actually only over estimated by twenty six meters.

The distance took another twenty minutes, twenty minutes through the ruins that had, only two hours ago been towering hundreds of stories into the clouds. This challenge would destroy the average human being, who would be emotionally broken with the horror of the whole ordeal.

Through the dust and debris, they pushed on, "Hey over on the corner, there's an Astrocab call center." Jasmine was the first to view it. The yellow and black checkered post stood out with the flickering of the fires.

The post was a contrast to the church it fronted, already almost obscured by the steady falling dust accumulating in an hundred block radius. Screams and panic could be heard into the morning long past the dust and destruction.

Out of the dusty haze a black craft floated into the clearing that was once a sky scraper now cluttered with debris and rubble, sleek, black as obsidian, the very next technology.

This ship was death and it appeared to be hunting.

"Down," the four hit the rubble and took cover behind a large block of debris; Ogden litterly pulled Jasmine up against the hunk of building. "Not so rough big guy." Jasmine didn't like to be handled period, with out giving permission first.

Shately and Trydent pushed against each other and the concrete almost occupying the same space.

"OK, arm your Laz rifle and on the count of four, every body shoot that ship.

"Armed," Ogden was the first to prepare his weapon.

"Armed," Jasmine was quick to follow; looking at Ogden she nodded her head that meant 'ready', then she glanced questionably at the rest of her team.

Shately and Trydent locked eyes and recognized what they saw in the other, "Armed" Trydent sternly breathed and Shately added, "And Angry"

"One," Jasmine started.

"Two," Ogden joined in.

"Three," All four choroused.

"Four" they all shouted, each one pulling out from under cover and shooting at the craft. Four Laz rifles fired and four hit the target. The ship stopped and hovered, its shields pulsing and fading as the energy weapons did their jobs. The shield held for fifteen seconds, and then in a blast that lit up the City sky it was decimated.

Jasmine very matter of factly said "One two you,re dead!"

"Move, move to the church, now, now, now," and with an urgency that match Ogden's words the four pushed hard toward the church. As they approached another obsidian ship slipped out of the dust cloud obviously searching for its prey.

"Get in before that ship detects us, and even more show up."

"OK, we grab an Astrocab and we try and get to my space station." Sir Oberhause suggested. That is the Alanon station, if we get separated use security code Oberhause Epsilon Three. Ogden found himself yelling much louder than he needed to. As they slipped into the Portico of the sacred ground, two more ships arrived both hunting, both in attack formation. But for now the four were safe. No demons could touch them here, this was sanctuary!

They all took a deep breath!

Cab ride

Credits... What a concept, monetary insanity.

Every citizen with a Personal Identification Code and every PIC had a credit status.

We have come a long way since we carried our coins in a leather pouch hanging from our belt or jerkin. Coppers and Gold but rarely did the common man have gold. Half pence, farthings, terms that went away with the dinosaurs, even a child of the late twentieth century would have looked puzzled over that nomenclature. (Except those on accelerated learning programs of course.)

The demise of the penny was inevitable, when the nickel fell the elderly fondly remembered simpler times as they gathered together in lodges designed for their geriatric needs, if the credits were available.

The dime on the other hand went as expected by every alcoholic philosopher, only surviving its five cent sibling by forty five years.

The quarter, twenty five percent of a buck, (a loonie to canucks), became a talisman. A cry from society to gain control over the mass's demand for more, more, more. Wage and price control was talked about but not seriously. One of the accepted greetings in the early twenty second century was a 'quarter for an open mind', a long cry from 'a penny for your thoughts.' And a world away from, 'credits for submission of your cerebral process.'

The half dollar was the last of the pure coins, ceremoniously made and selectively circulated and never really was part of the monetary game. This doesn't include the yen, deutschmark, peso, lira, rupee, pound or the rest of the world's currencies that were forgotten when the electronic net quickly engulfed the planet.

The dollar started as silver, and then turned to paper as it was supposed to be more manageable. The fiscal restraint of the governing bodies (their words) caused the dollar to go metal again. The evolution of the two dollar coin (Twoonie to Canucks) was supposed to save millions. Then the five dollar coin was born (Finnegan) and met its demise as unimportantly as the ancestral farthing.

The last of the currency system passed on, a very quick death as the world's credit system moved in quickly catching many people off guard.

The elderly weren't used to remembering numbers and the concept of a personal identification code had them screaming warnings about government control and persecution.

Now a world planetary system, where everyone with a laminated card could scan for what ever purchase they desired. Eventually a class system was created world wide with the elite having platinum benefits.

Credit rating means everything; people can be bought and sold if you have good enough credit. An astrocab ride was only as good as your credit would allow, and if it was high enough it would include shields and potential fire power.

The four fugitives huddled in the portico trying to catch their breath. "OK we need to get out of here now! Jasmine do you think you can get to the astrocab caller?" Ogden's words escaped between pants.

"Ya sure, not like I have a date or anything." Jasmine moved to the two massive ornate doors and pushed one open a crack.

One of the ships was moving away from the church about a hundred meters away. "One ship still hovering around but I think I can get to the caller, the trick will be not getting fried before I get a retinal scan."

"How about, Trydent and myself distract the ship while you get us a cab."

"Thanks for volunteering me, Shately." Trydent teased as he was already moving out the door. "You be ready to let us back in if necessary."

Ogden nodded a promise.

"That goes for me too!" Jasmine added.

"Absolutely sister, you get your pretty ass back here as soon as possible." Ogden's sincerity wasn't hidden by his attempt at humor.

Jasmine slid out past the door and crept as quickly as possible, keeping low and against the building. One advantage they had was the pandemonium in the streets, as horrified citizens ran screaming with out any rhyme or reason, drawing fire from the ship of obsidian. But soon enough the church would start to fill as that is what people tended to do in crisis, turn to the church for support.

Trydent and Shately had already started running back to the slab of building that had previously offered them cover. Shately was hit by a feeling of foreboding, a wave that was almost nauseating. She was rarely intimidated by anyone or anything but at this point she felt true terror deep inside her being. Shately needed to dig down and push herself; it was like lifting stone instead of feet.

Heart pounding vertigo growing, Shately pushed on, each step a labor of desperation. "Go, go, go," her thoughts raced as she tried to overcome her fear of the power that controlled her dreams.

Half a block to the corner, it seemed like forever for Jasmine, but finally she reached her destination. She could hear the laser fire from Trydent and Shately but continued to work praying they were safe.

Standing straight she stared into the astrocab sensor letting it complete a retinal scan. The routine flashing indicated the connection was made and now she had to get back to the church. This trip seemed easier than the journey out, tail between her legs she skulked back to the safety of the cathedral. She felt like a mongrel dog trying to evade a beating for taking food off the table.

Trydent and Shately moved again, away from cover and farther from the santuary of the church. When the ship passed out of sight behind a half fallen building they recognized their chance and headed to wait on the other side. The ship glistened in the morning light, the dawn's rays were almost beautiful as they danced on the ship of death.

As the ship emerged on the other side of the building or pile of rubble, it depends on your perspective, they opened fire. This time they did not have the luxury of four new Laz rifles but the ship stopped in it's flight held by the power of the lasers. It got off one shot before it exploded sending rocks and fumes flying at the pair.

"And go fuck your mother!" Trydent stood and yelled at the fireball that was once a ship as it crashed into the mound of rubble that once held Drol's penthouse suite. He sometimes let his emotions get the better of him in battle.

Ogden pushed the door open and caught Jasmine as she rushed to get back to the safety and sanctity of the church. He slowed her fall to the marble floor but let her continue downwards to give her an opportunity to catch her breath and again went back to the door to see if his other two companions had returned.

Neither Shately nor Trydent had ever been involved in a war of sorts. There had been some skirmishes between rival communities within the Rez, it was more like defending the community from raiding parties that were after provisions.

This was different, this was inherently evil that had no other purpose than to cause pain and grief. "The Astrocab post is blinking; it looks like Jasmine was successful."

"Well I guess that's something that went right today," Trydent replied sarcastically. The City continued to spin in turmoil in a fifty block radius and sarcasm was the best he could muster at this time amongst the death and destruction.

Jasmine was already heading back never waiting to hear Trydent's reply, and he had to hurry not to be left behind.

Once they returned to the church, Jasmine had already been back long enough to stop panting, "This is unreal, there is something very powerful after us and I think we are in more trouble than Drol let on." Jasmine locked eyes with each of her three companions trying to convince them of the gravity of the situation.

"But we continue' that's the deal!" Trydent's remark was a question as well as a statement.

"Ya we continue, I believe that is what has to be done, like Drol told us. We have a destiny and as strange as it seems, I guess I believe him." Shately seemed to be trying to convince herself as much as she was encouraging the rest.

Ogden, added "Besides even if we quit we're still being hunted by those blasted black ships, I have been running a ship yard for years and I have never seen that design before and by the looks of them they're of a significant technological advancement.

Trydent extended his hand to help Jasmine up, she was still resting on the floor. "Let's try and make it to your Alanon station, if it has the fire power you claim it does? Then we can figure what we need to do best."

"It has the firepower," almost insulted, "It has more fire power than any other Space station in our universe." Ogden softened letting the remark roll off him as he continued. "Most, importantly we can get Saphrone, now there is a ship! Biodome 313 is about four hours from here even by the fastest Astrocab. We need something faster and my sleuth has the ability to shoot back at these bastards." A hint of boasting slipped into Ogden's statement but he was accurate which helped to tolerate his arrogance.

"There is the cab" Shately was keeping watch between the crack of the two old doors. "We have to move now before someone steals our cab." The word 'now' was emphasized by Shately as she was already pushing through the massive doors of the beautiful cathedral (another time and they all would have been able to appreciate the beauty, but just not this morning).

Trydent, Jasmine and finally Ogden followed her into the rubble strewn street and moved as a group as the Astrocab hovered to a stop to allow access. The cab had already opened its access ports as they approached and they all hurriedly climbed in.

"Welcome to Astrocab." Droned the electronically generated voice of the cab.

Not able to relax Jasmine started yelling orders to the cab's onboard computer. "Code gamma Phillips seventeen, override level eight."

"Hello Ms. Phillips, Destination please."

"Alanon Station, as fast as you can move, put shields on maximum, I mean now not tomorrow."

The synthetic voice lacked the obvious emotion that dominated Jasmine's voice. "Departure started, please buckle up, destination Alanon station, level eight override, which will be a cost of 325,000 credits and will take approximately 22.4 minutes, to break atmosphere Ms. Phillips. Any other requests?"

The Astrocab rose into the air and started along the street; it accelerated and merged smoothly and aggressively into the first level of the global traffic, now being detoured around the disaster. Drol's apartment building reduced to rubble.

Yes an official disaster, (as enough people were killed and significant square footage of destruction to qualify). In the grand scheme of things this ranked low on the top one hundred list in the history of human disasters.

It would be like that time a tornado hit your city and you have a pretty good story of what had happened but when you phone your buddies and one of them was in a building that was leveled after being hit head on, your story just doesn't compare.

Compared to the big quake that hit California in 2062 and again in 2067 when the entire San Andreas finally gave way and let most of California slip into the ocean this was nothing. Hiroshima and Nagasaki completely dwarfed the events of the last hour. The Blitz over London and the bombing of Dresden both killed a lot more people, but this disaster was only starting and before the week was finished nothing would compare. This morning was just the first domino falling.

OK it was a little bigger than the terrorist attack on the twin towers as more lives were lost and a city block radius was at least double. Remember what Joseph Stalin said, "The death of an individual is a tragedy; the death of a thousand is a statistic." But do I need to say more? It was bad none the less.

The cab pulsed into the first level of traffic, this was the transportation lane, three levels of transport ships, merging through was allowed but it was too congested and slow to make any good time.

The cab quickly weaved its way through the lumbering transports and approached the next group of levels. This was the public level, were the average Joe flew his astroglide and ofcourse slower traffic stayed in the lower slower levels. Five levels of steady streams of traffic moving the citizens of the City to were they needed to go.

"Can we go any faster?" Shately asked the cab because she had never been in one before and wasn't sure how the operating procedure went.

"We are traveling at maximum velocity allowed for this level of traffic, for only 13,000 credits I can proceed into emergency mode and increase speed by twenty six percent. Is that a request Ms. Phillips?" the computer was annoying everyone with its slow unemotional expression.

"Yes, that is great, use the credits, what do I need them for?"

"I am not programmed to know how you spend you credits Ms. Phillips." The cab accelerated again and rose through the five levels for public access. "Any other requests?"

Approaching the last group of levels that were designed for high speeds, emergency vehicles, police service, company heads and the rich who could afford the credits that the Astrocabs charged for extra service, the cab increased in speed and feeling of thrust was felt by all occupants.

The glass and concrete of the City was being left behind as the team flew up and away from the dangers that had hounded them. Leaving what once was a lush and amazing penthouse, leaving Doug pinned under his fridge, leaving Geoff, Elvis and the disciples, trying to catch up to their destiny.

"Ms. Phillips we are being scanned," the computer stated its information without subjectivity. "Three ships on an intercept vector, shall I hail them?" "Jam their signal and initiate cloak"

"Cloaking unsuccessful, you do not have enough credits to cover that request." Jamming was unsuccessful their lock is too strong." No change in the monotone voice. "Any other requests?"

Ogden Jumped in, "Credit access Epsilon, Oberhause, override Twenty Five, give us full acceleration and put shields on dignitary level."

"Yes Sir Mr. Oberhause." The computer added a sir for formality (The credits being extremely high) but again did not waver in tone.

The Cab broke through the last level of traffic with the three obsidian ships close behind and on full pursuit. Trydent was the first to see one. "There is one at seven o'clock! And It's moving fast right at us."

"According to my sensors that ship is powering up its weapons array. According to section 132.6 of the flight code, firing on public transportation is illegal." The ships voice was matter of fact and without a care for its potential demise.

"Two minutes and twenty three seconds until we clear atmosphere." The first laser blast hit before the computer was done its statement. The small craft shuddered but its shields held.

"There's another one!" Shately almost shrieked, "Over there on the left."

"One minute and three seconds until we clear atmosphere."

The second blast hit the craft knocking stabilizers off line, putting the craft into a spin upward.

"Shields down to Sixty two percent, I have filed a protest with the space guild." The Astrocab computer continued to spout off information, some had no bearing on the situation but critical facts on shield level kept Jasmine from ripping out the voice synthesizer module from out of its dash.

Too bad it was against space guild policy to allow attack weapons on public transportation, it would give them a better shot at surviving but as far as maximizing shields, they would power up as strong as your credits would make them.

"Shields down to thirty seven percent, thirty two seconds until we clear atmosphere."

Shately could hardly think let alone react to the situation. She just tried to hang on and survive her first trip in an Astrocab. The third laser blast took out the last of the shielding, leaving the craft one shot from destruction.

"Hull integrity down to ninety five percent."

"Shut up already!"

The computer not recognizing the inflection in Jasmine's voice answered her as if there was a basic question addressed to his circuits. "Do you wish the verbal communication mode shut down Ms. Phillips?"

"Yes, yes, I am tired of listening to you tell me the time line of my death."

As quickly as it started, the firing ended as the Astrocab broke atmosphere. Ogden gave the command to the now silent computer, "auxiliary power to stabilizers, stop this spin before I begin to spew."

"Hey where are the warships, why aren't we dead?" Shately's words escaped in a form of a great sigh.

"That is a good question." Ogden replied, then gave a hypothetical answer, "I think they were given orders not to leave orbit."

Lucky for our heroes, shield technology far exceeds laser technology it was also lucky that Drol's Laz Rifle technology wasn't outfitted into the attacking ships. Shields were developed before lasers and were used originally to deflect astral debris. Even in something as basic as an Astrocab's shields were strong enough to withstand an attack from laser cannon fire. (Credit availability of course.)

"You're right." Trydent hated to admit that Ogden could be right. "We're not being followed into space. The ships have broke off the attack."

"Why?" Shately queried. "Since this whole fucking thing started, nothing has been easy, my head hurts with all these unanswered questions."

"Don't knock it sister, we're alive to fight another day and another battle." Jasmine tried to put a positive spin on their situation although she really didn't believe it her self.

"Fight, don't you mean run away from another battle?" Trydent's jibe dripped with sarcasm.

The Astrocab continued to pull away from the earth, colloquially know as the City. The ball glistened with billions of lights and reflected those lights off glass. A glow so strong it gave an aura around the planet, from a distance almost glowing like a star.

"It's beautiful." Shately whispered under her breath. Then more to the others "I've never been in space before, I had no idea." Her naivety showing past her hardened exterior.

"I don't know I always considered it an abomination, we took Eden and destroyed it all in the name of human advancement." Trydent must have heard Shately's whisper and his obvious grudge with humanity surfaced again.

"Yes, the human species is arguably an interesting animal, the hows and whys make a great topic for debate, but let us not get teary eyed until we know it is a little safer. Then we can reminisce and maybe sing a song." Ogden was his usual analytical yet sarcastic self.

"Alanon is about an hour and a half away, and I tell you what I could really use a saniscrub and an hour in the Rejuv to put that spring back in my step."

The Planet slowly distanced itself from the craft which limped its way through space heading on its way to the Alanon space station/ship yard.

With the stabilizers back on line and the auxiliary power transferred to life support, the trip to the Alanon station almost became pleasant; disregarding the numerous cuts, scrapes and bruises to the ego.

"So what now? We have to be at the Biodome in just under two days. I'm assuming you have your own ship that will take us there."

"Why not a little rest while I throw together some support, and you can grab some lunch and recuperate, for shall we say six to seven hours. That would have us arriving at Biodome 313 in about thirteen hours from now."

"Sounds like a plan Otto the 5th but it appears that we are the target of aggression, so I guess that twelve hours would indicate you think were going to live when we get back to earth. Hey, but a plan is a plan and I could definitely use a drink. You do have a bar on that barge don't you?" Trydent wasn't against the plan he just felt a need to give Ogden a hard time.

Alanon station was barely a twinkling light in the sky, but the cab moved relatively quickly and the light started to take shape and grew into substance and eventually gained the majestic beauty that cutting edge technology gave way to, much more advanced than that floating can called Muir.

Alanon was state of the art, the leading technology in space travel, owned and operated by Oberhause Inc.

Again the four survived, again they probably shouldn't have and again they continued on their quest.

"What are you grinning at Otto?" Trydent continued to use the acronym to try and get a rise out of Ogden.

It was simple, Sir Ogden Timothy Oberhause the fifth was going home.

Alanon

I.

Do you think that Gene Rodenberry truly understood those famous words? "Space the final frontier." It was several hundred years since Sputnik orbited a mere three hundred and seventy miles above the earth's surface, which was hundreds of years after the Chinese invented the rocket.

For eight hundred years of space travel, (give or take a decade) human kind was still relatively in its infancy. No easily inhabitable planet had yet been found. Sure there were colonies on the Moon, Mars, Ganymede, Europa and Titan and each colony housed thousands but they were all domed controlled environments.

After all the years of exploring space, sending probes, hundreds of lives lost on long range missions, listening to space for millions of minutes, and still absolutely no proof that there was life outside the planet earth. (Roswell supporters disagree but they are a product of paranoid times.)

Although there was the Saturnian diarrhea, which ravaged through society jut after the first manned landing on the moon Titan, returned. For six months epidemic diarrhea left society with a shitty attitude, but many believe it was a social myth like UFOs, Big Foot, Loch Ness and others that have sprung up along the way.

Space stations were now a fairly common occurrence, in the space that surrounded earth, not anything like Muir or Unity. These two stations in space were twenty five times smaller than space station Discovery, which now houses the museum of space flight, meals and accommodation included. Twelve tours a cycle, but souvenirs cost extra. Now several styles of space stations orbited throughout our solar system, spinning around a central hub, giving a place for the human animal to congregate while away from the safety of the City.

Alanon was originally built to mine asteroids that were salvaged from the belt between Mars and Jupiter, but it never got out of Earth's orbit because it was decided that a larger and less luxurious station would be built orbiting Mars after it became apparent that a lot more credits could be made than originally thought. Making credits in space was only limited to the imagination of the pioneer.

Now Alanon served as elitist housing and several head offices in the space race were located on the floating city. It was sheik to do business off world and often business had a don't ask-don't tell policy.

It wasn't that the Oberhause's conducted a lot of illegal dealings; they typically followed the rules of the space guild but certainly did not police the station by exact rules. The space guild did have a presence on Alanon but rarely were there ever any arrests on the station.

It was an unwritten understanding. Why? It was simply economic muscle and the station was a boon to the economy.

Throughout human history theft has always offered a chance at higher reward than an honest living and as long as Alanon made a lot of credits some leeway would be given to the benefactors that earned them. The benefits of piracy were great but the risk was also great, if caught every asset was confiscated and frequently life was forfeit. The passion for quick huge profit fueled a strong piracy appetite.

Alanon did have to protect the honest as they definitely were the main source of credits and pirates knew what lines not to cross and which companies were offered protection. Big business was business so Oberhause Inc. definitely flexed corporate muscle whenever a regular paying customer needed help with a bully.

The Astrocab, using Ogden's priority codes, moved to the front of the docking queue and carefully limped into the public docking bay.

"OK, we have around six to seven hours, take advantage of it, anything you want just ask; my station is your station."

"I just want to relax, being the target of assassination is tiring," Jasmine's joking nature poked through now that her life had slowed down in the last hour but there still hung a hint of seriousness in her voice.

Exiting the cab was by no means as intense as entering, slowly lead by Ogden each one taking time to bend, stretch, and sooth their aching muscles.

As Jasmine reached down to touch her toes she mused, "I need a saniscrub and a Rejuv and maybe some kind of feathered mattress.

"Are we safe?" asked Trydent. "What happens if an armada shows up at your airlock with lasers arme. My guess is they come in firing and ask question after this space tub becomes solar rubble."

"Don't worry Tripod; this tub can handle any space force made by man that currently exists." Ogden gave a little jibe back to his comrade.

Shately stopped in mid stretch as if she was hit with the sudden realization of a bigger picture. "Sure, that's all wonderbar, but what if," she stepped forward to stand in front of Ogden. "Let us just say 'what if" this force that is pursuing us isn't man made?" she tapped Ogden in the chest to accent her words, "What if that giant pink monster is an alien and this turns out to be an invasion."

Jasmine spoke up, "I know we have no concrete proof but I don't think it is an alien invasion, Drol described the force opposing us as evil not alien," She started to ramble. "But it could be alien evil, human evil is bad enough but alien that's all we need." Her nervous rant had its origin in anxiety but as always her comments were legitimate.

"I honestly believe we are safe, so please trust me as best you can and try and relax, this station has a set of teeth when cornered."

A small entourage of six people arrived to interrupt the conversation. The unscheduled arrival of the heir elite of Oberhause Inc. was already starting a minor commotion.

"Mr. Oberhause, we were not expecting you," the aid was obviously flustered, "and your sister has been trying to contact you for cycles."

The entire entourage waited for a reply from their leader.

"Send a message to my sister that I have arrived. Contact the Alanon council and put the station on alert, I would like to meet the council in half an hour and I will explain things then."

Ogden turned to another aid, "Taylor, I want you to look after my three companions, treat them like you would treat me. Do you understand?"

"Yes, of course Mr. Oberhause. Anything else sir?"

"Prepare Saphrone for departure in six hours, include weapons and shield diagnostics," then turning to his newly acquired friends, "I'll see you all in five and a half hours at hanger one, if you want anything Taylor will look after you."

With his words finished Ogden turned and briskly walked away with five aids hastily recording his whims and fawning over his needs.

The remaining aid directed his attention to Jasmine, Shately and Trydent. "Names would be a good place to start, I'm Taylor." There was a pregnant pause for a couple of seconds and then as if annoyed with the silence, Taylor spoke again, "And who would you be?"

"Jasmine."

"Shately."

"Trydent."

"Now, that wasn't too difficult was it?" Taylor's annoyance turned to insolence quickly.

"Now follow me please, today people, enough with the dilly dallying."

Shately's nerves were already pulled taut from her first cab ride out of the atmosphere, when she was fired upon and almost killed, and she was attacked by a giant pink monster. Yes Shately was a bit on edge!

Grabbing Taylor by the collar just to make sure she had his complete attention. "Listen, Tay-Lor I've had a tough day, hell I've had a pretty piss poor year!" Shately gave the aid a little shake to emphasize her point. "Drop the hissy fit attitude and you and I will get along a lot better."

"Yes mam, I am so sorry, my utmost apologies, it is just my nature miss Shately, forgive my insolence."

"OK enough, where is a saniscrub? I have dust in places I dare not speak about."

"Of course Miss Shately, and Mr. Oberhause doesn't need to know about our little ah...misunderstanding. I humbly ask for your mercy." Taylor knew how to grovel almost as well as he could bitch.

"He won't hear it from me, relax and lead."

"Thank you, right this way." Taylor gestured to the lifts across the concourse. The trip to the room was fairly long, as it was level eight of the inner sector.

The ship yard and the docking bay were part of the outer sector. Ships of all shapes and sizes came to Alanon to do business. Personal Astroglides, Frigates, tourist Hydroglides and always one or two military personnel carriers with soldiers on leave filled the docking bay.

The shipyard was part of the docking bay; this is where repairs, refits and ship building took place. Alanon built several types of ships that were sold to various customers for all kinds of uses. Anything from ore haulers to state of the art war cruisers ready for any corporate takeover. If you had the credits, Alanon would try and make it happen for you with new or refitted spacecraft.

There a number of space stations within human space but none could compete with the commerce that flowed through Alanon.

The main sector held the hub of the station, this is were business and pleasure took place, bars night clubs, restaurants, offices, markets and just about anything the imagination could fathom.

The inner sector had nine levels of living quarters, level one being military births, the essentials but sparse. As the levels went into the station there was an increase in the degree of comfort. If you had the credit rating, life on Alanon could be quite posh and level eight rivaled the accommodations for kings and queens from a forgotten era.

Level nine was for the royal family Oberhause and was decadent beyond most earthly pleasures. Crossing through the bustle of the concourse where life continued as if the three never existed. Cargo was being transferred, people were barking orders, aids were moving to destinations with deliberate singularity, their tasks seeming to be the most important thing in the universe. Oblivious to the pending doom, this was the hub of commerce in the known universe.

Jasmine turned to Taylor, "When you can, could you contact the City," she accented her words by placing her hand on the aids shoulder. "Let Jeremy Phillips, senior vice president of IBM City central, that his daughter is all right and not to worry.

Taylor accepted Jasmines request with out any recording device and then asked if there would be anything else she might need. "How about a bottle of brandy, make it a good year, one of Ogden's finest."

"Yes mam, something from the sixteenth century?" Taylor asked.

"Use your best judgment." Jasmine turned and smiled a mischievous grin and wiggled her eyebrows at her friends revealing that she could get used to this.

The four arrived at the turbo lift and as they entered the enclosure, Shately, almost to herself, spoke, "Last time I was in one of these I almost died."

Trydent showed a rare moment of pathos and softly replied to her, "We're a long way from dead and if you stick with me I promise you death will have to work over time to catch us. Many have tried to kill me over the years, but I'm still pumping blood and intend to continue doing so for at least another hundred years."

"Be careful hero I might just call that bluff."

"I don't bluff." Everyone believed him as the turbo lift accelerated into the world of Ogden.

Level one, inner sector, Down,-Level two. Level...

"Any requests Mr. Trydent?" Taylor asked.

"Ya, brandy sounds like it might hit the spot..." he paused to think, "make it two bottles just to be sure."

Fourth, Fifth, Sixth...

Shately added, "Make that three bottles and I will help drink them, I need to take the edge off a very stressful day and maybe a swig of Ogden's prime hooch just might help me relax."

Seventh and finally "Level Eight, Inner sector." The turbo shafted rang their destination, and then the access doors swished open exposing a vast corridor that traveled the length of the station. The curvature of the corridor was apparent, as it wrapped around the center core of Alanon completing a continuous circle.

Trydent looked out with disdain, over his relatively brief years of existence he had grown to despise human technology. The infestation called humanity was spreading like a virus and threatened to infect the rest of the universe already pushing past the limits of its own solar system.

Trydent's bitterness wasn't due to the fact he felt left behind in the technological jungle, in fact the opposite held true. Over the years he was given the opportunity to join the City's leaders, (there is always a place for someone that commands power) but he could never bring himself to sellout. Trydent's exile was self imposed. As a young man he was the type of person whose opportunity to succeed came easily but he turned down almost every chance at power over his fellow people.

It was the fact that he saw the struggles of the forgotten, the poor who frequently were the victims of crime, war and starvation rampant on the planet that made him resent what the human race had become. Now he was off world and in the very lap of luxury he had grown to hate. For the next few hours he would accept his fate and take advantage of Ogden's wealth and catch up on some much needed rest.

"This way please." The aid pointed down the corridor and proceeded without seeing if the others would follow. The group passed several doors before they arrived at their destination, a set of Oak double doors, very ornate with absolutely no electric access at all that opened to a common room.

Above the doors was a sign made out of similar Oak that said, "Armstrong Suite."

"Do we have access to a communication consol?" Jasmine asked. "I would like to get into the Cyber Net for a while and check my messages."

Taylor looked mildly perturbed, "Yes, of course we have access to the web," then added almost as if he had been insulted, "this isn't the Rez."

Stately spoke up to defend her home but kept a teasing nature. "Watch it Tay-Lor, you're talking about my home."

"Again I tease, Miss Shately, given time I'm sure you will help me pull my foot out of my mouth."

"Actually I was thinking that I would have to help remove my boot from your ass." Shately winked to let him know she was kidding. (kinda, sorta)

Taylor handed Jasmine a small remote, "Here Miss Jasmine, if you want anything and I do mean anything, press this sensor and somebody will be with you."

The three walked into the common room, a huge Holoscreen adorned the west wall and to the north was a large viewer that had an image of the earth rotating its cycles of life.

A large bar faced the travelers with three bottles of brandy waiting as if they anticipated the order before receiving it.

"Yes, I think that will do nicely." Gushed Jasmine as she sunk herself into one of the plush armchairs.

"Each room has a saniscrub, Rejuv and a bed." Taylor almost bragged. "And like I said anything you want, please just ask." The aid then turned and exited quickly and silently.

Trydent walked to the bar while Jasmine walked to Holoscreen. "Activate Cyber Net."

Shately walked to the Viewer port, "Wow that's the City, I'm starting to feel a tad bit insignificant." But the last thing Shately was, was insignificant, the very existence of the human soul depended on her and her three associates (and several key influencers along the way). Together they had a chance to accomplish what previously had been impossible.

By passing the pretence of snifters, Trydent divided up the contents of the first bottle evenly into three tumblers and handed one to each of the girls.

"Forgive the lack of formality," Trying to be as mocking as possible, "but there is no elaborate speech just a simple toast." Trydent raised his glass to, "Survival".

Trydent did not wait for a reply; he lifted his glass and downed the entire contents.

"To survival," came the reply in stereo as Jasmine and Shately both drank their brandy. Trydent had the cork removed from the second bottle as their glasses dropped from their lips.

"Refills Ladys?" Trydent's question was meant to tease, he knew what everyone needed was a chance to feel nothing for a while and to relax putting the last couple of days events behind them for a while the best they possibly could.

Shately extended her left hand forward offering her empty glass. Saying there was a psychic connection between the two may have been an exaggeration but Shately knew he was opening the next bottle as quickly as Trydent thought about the action.

Jasmine broached the question, "What do we know?" as she handed her glass to Trydent, "Besides the fact I want another drink."

Nobody drained this drink in one gulp this time they savored each sip, each one inhaling the fumes to truly enjoy the experience.

"What do we know, yes that is a good question, not a fuck of a lot if you ask me and ah, you just did." Trydent's sarcasm continued to surface exposing his bitter side. "I know it sounds insane but I actually believe Drol when he says that we are important." Trydent tried to be somewhat serious.

"We know we are headed to Praith, I myself have never heard of it," and then Shately added, "but biodome 313 isn't far from were I grew up in Rez and a good days hike if you don't detour for cats."

"Is that Kieper's tribe?" Trydent asked her. "I used to know that man in another life."

"Yes, Sandstone bluff is run by Kieper, he and his wife pretty much raised me after my parents died." Shately's fondness could not be hidden.

Obviously impressed Trydent continued, "Kieper's reputation precedes him, that's why you seem so together."

"So does yours Trydent, probably more than his." Shately's hero worship slipped through, but let us not forget that Trydent is considered a folk hero amongst the people of the Rez.

"OK enough of the fan club, crap, we all agree to accept what Drol is telling us and that tells us we need to work together on a common goal." Jasmine interrupted to change the subject. It was getting a little too nostalgic for her.

"Yes we are" Trydent expressed each monosyllabic word. "But the real question is, are we a dinner date, I could really use something to eat right now!"

"I would kill for some food." Laughed Shately.

"A loaded pizza would be my first choice, with pineapple and ham, I don't care if pineapple is the most expensive fruit out of the biodomes, I'm sure Ogden can afford it." Jasmine agreed with the idea of getting something to eat.

"Ya, I like pineapple, at least I think I do, but a pizza with out cat would be called loosing the battle with the vermin."

Trydent grabbed the remote, and spoke into it. "Yo Taylor, we want a pizza, you got that a large fucking pizza, with ham, pineapple, cat and uhm..." Trydent thought for a few seconds. "Cheese, oh ya, lots of cheese, I can't remember the last time I filled my belly with cheese." With exuberant celebration Trydent took a solid gulp from his brandy looking very proud of their decision to get a pizza.

Jasmine looked at the man and raised her eyebrows. "You don't get out much do you?"

We got a little bit of time before the chow gets here, so I'm going to grab a quick saniscrub and a Rejuv.

The Physiological Rejuvenation process, is the biological science of the human body, hormones, electrolytes, vitamins, stimulants, blood cells, (genetically cloned white and red refreshed and enhanced) Acetylcholine to flush the synaptic gap and increase the firing efficiency of the brain and neuro-muscular system by thirty five percent. Excess toxins are removed from the blood and flushed out of the system making you more alert. This was the generic brand, the run of the slum found on the street corner, bargain brand rejuvs. Line ups were typically twenty-five people deep and almost double that during a shift change.

Ogden's rejuvs on the other hand were top of the line with the addition of pheromones to stimulate the hippocampus and heighten the senses, including perception and memory.

OOH yes the increased testosterone levels in Trydent's body almost had him strutting as he left the Rejuv tube. Feeling like a million credits he walked back into the common room. "Where's the Cheese?" Trydent's attempt at imitating a popular holomercial was lost on Shately, but Jasmine showed a smirk of recognition.

It wasn't long and there was a knock at the door with an aid bearing pizza. Trydent consumed the first piece with the same vigor he displayed with his brandy.

"I feel good!" Trydent gulped down a mouthful of pizza.

Shately's eyes almost glistened with the Rejuv's effect on her system. "Good is exactly how I feel, but kickingly good and the pizza is not bad either." She was new to a lot of what Ogden's life had to offer.

Jasmine smiled at her friend but was quite accustom to the adrenalin rush that accompanied a Rejuv. "I never tire of this feeling, a person could get addicted don't you think"

"To pizza?" Trydent shrugged his shoulders in mock confusion.

Ogden entered the room with a stride of presumptuous stature and boldly stated. "On the way down to your quarters I just came to the realization that I'm having fun." The Rejuv obviously was having the same effect on the Oberhause heir as everyone else.

"You know Otto; I think I'm getting to like you." Trydent replied back. "In a demented, weird kinda way."

"Ah, I see you have gotten something to eat and by the look in your eyes I would hazard a guess that you were able to take advantage of the break in insanity and go for a Rejuv."

Ogden glanced at the meal of pizza, "This better have cat on." and grabbed a piece of Zaa.

For now the four had hope, their spirits were up, but for the most part it was of artificial origin, an after effect of the Rejuv process. The Rejuv was addicting as it lifted the user so high that many people were not able to handle the emotional fall. There wasn't any physical dependency but the fragile ego of humanity constantly needed to be stroked.

The Rejuv was originally invented as a life support unit but a physician with a lust for credits recognized that the marketing potential within the public sector was mammoth and became a very rich man.

To date, there were no physical complications surrounding the Rejuv but in a hundred and fifty years future from Ogden's present, an infection would take hold that would rival the Black Death in the percentage of the population killed. This contamination would spread throughout the city and after a myriad of public warnings; society would not stay away from the Rejuvs. (But this is a story to be told another time.)

For Shately this was a new experience, but it was the boost that she needed to keep her going. She was being taxed way beyond what she was used to in her day to day struggles in the Rez.

"My personal sleuth is being readied as we speak, a diagnostic is being run which includes weapons and shields refit. This time we go in with some help, my fleet is on stand by."

"I think you will like my craft," Ogden continued "she is one very special lady," he almost gushed or as close to it as he was capable of.

"We still have a few hours before we disembark, why doesn't somebody pour me a drink?"

"Sure, why not, after all it's your brandy." Jasmine handed Ogden the bottle.

"Good boy Taylor, this is good brandy but not my best stuff. Someone remind me to give him a raise. How is everyone's drink?" Topping all the tumblers Ogden then poured himself a liberal amount into an empty snifter.

"Queen Isobel seems to be an ally," continued the conversation as if Ogden hadn't walked into the middle of the previous discussion. "And Biodome 313, is that where we find out how we get to Praith?"

Jasmine continued on the web, like most youth who grew up in the City, surfing the Web was second nature to her. "Well nothing comes up for Praith although I have a hit on Prath, which is a small colony on one of Uranus's moons, Oberon. But it is a research station funded to look at the viability if mining the rings of Uranus. Nothing about being run by a monarch."

"We really don't have anything else, how about giant pink monster or better yet four scared silly humans with their heads up their asses." Shately must have been a little relaxed as she was able to make a joke and her mirth brought a chuckle from everyone else.

"We can stay in stealth mode before we're through the atmosphere and even send out phony tracer signatures on other ships or drones." Ogden changed the conversation to focus on his ship. "Once in the City's atmosphere we will have to rely on shields and maneuverability. I want to sneak in and not be seen, but worst case scenario Saphrone has teeth. Jasmine can you handle targ and scan?"

"Count on it."

"Trydent, you've got navigation, do you know were we are going?

"Funny boy, Otto thinks he is funny, ya I choose to reside in the Rez but I have piloted a couple of shuttles in my day."

Again the two men started to push each other's testosterone buttons and Trydent's shuttle comment got his partner's dander up but he recognized the jibe as a deliberate attempt to get him going and was able to keep at a joking level.

"I will have you know that Saphrone is not a shuttle and much more than an astroglide, she is an Excalibur class vessel and literally is a one of a kind. She has deep space capability but hasn't been past Jupiter." The ship magnate tried to control his enthusiasm but felt a need to keep adding. "She can't take on a battle cruiser head on but is designed to be more than capable in a fire fight. I will introduce you all to Saphrone soon enough and I know you will be impressed."

"Excalibur class, put it back in your pants." Jasmine smiled "Very nice, I have not as yet had the privilege of traveling in such a vessel. Does Saphrone, it is Saphrone isn't it? Have a positronic matrix as her core; I've heard rumors that the technology gap was finally bridged."

Ogden clearly liked the topic of his ship. "Rumor is verified young lady and she surpassed all projected capabilities."

"Isn't a ship a ship?" asked Shately.

Trydent walked up and put his hands on Shately's shoulders adding security to his words, "In theory, this means that the ship has the ability to think for itself and some would argue that it actually is sentient."

Ogden; obviously proud of his greatest technological achievement, jumped in, "You can include me in that argument, just trust me when I say you will have to meet her." He was willing to go on but at this point rest was more important.

Jasmine stretched hard and walked toward one of the sleeping quarters. "I'm going to try and get a couple hours of sleep, so nobody bug me while I catnap. If we are attacked by monsters, alien ships or any other insanity, can one of you guys handle it? I need to rest these eyelids." There was a joking tone but in all seriousness Jasmine did look tired.

"Hell of a good idea young lady." Agreed Ogden. "I think I will catch fifty winks myself."

Trydent also got up and headed to one of the sleeping quarters. "Two hours is a luxury I'm willing to indulge in right now."

With their decisions made they all turned to se if Shately was going to take advantage of the same opportunity. Shately looked back and felt compelled to explain what she was doing but really she was thinking 'leave me alone; mind your own business and fucking go to sleep.' But her actual reply differed from her thoughts, "If you don't mind, I will just sit up for a while, maybe I will get tired if I just relax for a bit." Shately did not sound very convincing, not even to herself.

Sleep came quickly to Ogden, Trydent and Jasmine, but Shately battled the overwhelming desire to sleep. Fear of what was waiting for her in her dreams gnawed at her psyche. For her, dreams were the unconscious connection to the enemy. That foreboding presence was able to manifest itself and come out of hiding from her subconscious always waiting, waiting, waiting....

But sleep did claim her and terror waited for her as she crossed into a dreamscape. Shately found herself trapped on a five foot island in the middle of a torrent of water. A massive river of dirty viscous liquid that overflowed its banks bore down on her. The water was littered with bobbing debris as the rushing flood waters indiscriminately destroyed all that opposed it.

Chunks o f earth crumbled into the water as the flow tried to erode Shately's tiny island. "You and your friends are doomed!" a voice boomed out of the sky echoing all around her. The island continued to wear away, erosion from the rising flood waters slowly eating away at her island of hope.

"Give up foolish little girl, you are no match for me, you are nothing." Each word seemed to take a bite out of the island bit by bit. "I have existed since the beginning of time; I will crush you like the insignificant bug you are."

A large wave crested the horizon and started down the swollen river towards Shately, only three meters high but with enough power to sweep the island into the raging torrent, Shately saw a floating church pew going by and recognized her chance. Mustering all her courage she jumped out into the water hoping that the bench would float her away and eventually to safety. Everything was in slow motion and Shately hit the icy waters shy of her target and could feel the under currents of hell drag her down, just a little bit farther........

CAT: The Other White Meat

Earlier that day...

Ogden's mind shifted into action, things to do and only six hours to complete eight hours work. He quickly moved into the turbo lift and headed into Alanon, deep to level nine the Oberhause home and the heart of Alanon station pulsed with the bustle of people rushing to get ready for the unscheduled return of their heir.

There was ass to be kissed and it belonged to Sir Ogden Timothy Oberhause the Fifth.

Priority one refit was the orders to be passed along the station, Saphrone would be upgraded, recharged, armed and fueled. This would include shields, torps, lasers, life support and normally a complete refit would take up to ten hours with out a big push and eight in a priority, but Ogden would push his people to rise up and complete the task within the six hours available.

He walked onto the bridge giving orders, "Thompson I want three crews on Saphrone, she needs to be fully refitted and ready for flight in six hours."

"Six hours boss, your kidding, right." All eyes were looking at Ogden with bewilderment.

"I know, I'm asking a lot." Ogden raised his arms in an encompassing gesture and with a reassuring smile he tried to appease their fears. "And if you pull it off, you all know everyone will be gratefully compensated for their effort."

Ogden turned to his long time friend and colonel of his fleet. "Anderson, I want land gear for four, no make that five I will bring Taylor with me." More to himself than to anyone else

"Taylor is always useful. You might as well make sure dragon fly is ready to fly also ready to get in a fight."

Bell Anderson remembering the night in the club when they first met Drol and recognizing the urgency in Ogden's orders immediately pressed the communication actuator and gave his old friend an "aye aye sir!", and carried out the expectations with out delay.

The bridge command crew were used to unusual requests, the Oberhause's were unusual....ly busy people. The family Oberhause was fair and elicited respect from their people and the bridge crew was passionately dedicated to their leaders. They had lead them from the beginning of planetary exploration, past mars and into mining the belt. They had defended against hostile takeovers, survived meteor showers and a myriad of major and minor incidents.

"How are we with the new shield technology, when I talked with engineering two weeks ago I was told that we were on the cusp of a serious break through." Ogden raised his eyebrows in an expression of hope.

"We have the new sodium crystal defense grid, but by no means has it been tested outside the laboratory." Thompson replied.

"But, it is a sound theory, right?"

"Very sound sir, but to take a chance with direct laser canon fire, I'm not making any promises" Thompson's concern was so obvious that his voice almost slipped to a whisper.

"Do you believe in your theories Mr. Thompson?"

"Yes," was the one word response.

"Then I believe in you, I want the new sodium crystals installed before I depart."

Ogden paused to look at his crew, these were men and women that he trusted, people that would go to war for him.

Peter Simpler, on communications, was a second generation Alanon bridge crew. Peter's father was the helms first with Ogden's father, and Rosa Balachez was security/weapons and her mother before her was part of the officer's quarters cleaning staff.

Duty officer first was a huge man, not quite as tall as Ogden but his girth was one and a half that of his leader. Greg Hanson was an earther but unless you knew you would never guess he had nor grown up in low gravity.

Sally Molzahn, a third generation spacer, she had only been to the City four times in her life and actually preferred it that way, was helm/targeting first.

Finally Anderson, second in command and the one everyone turned to when Ogden wasn't on the station. Bell was one of Ogden's childhood friends and as loyal as friends typically were, even when your best friend was also your boss. Anderson wanted desperately to grab his friend and have him explain that night at Le'Ralphe as he had been going crazy trying to sort out what really happened. But a telling look from his boss let him know that there wasn't time and they would try and catch up later.

It was time to move thought into action, "I believe humanity's soul is at risk so we need to succeed no matter what the cost."

"Sally I want Saphrone's signature loaded into an Excalibur class ship and I want it fully operational by remote. The ship needs to be unmanned; we need to get the forces on the City to think Saphrone will be leading the charge, they can't realize that ship isn't for real. You will need to add my genetic signature into the new ship and the signature of all my companions, they're staying in the Armstrong suite right now and include Taylor's genetic scan in there as well." (Five was now six)

Hardly taking a breath Ogden's plan materialized as he spoke. "I want a cloaking system put on Saphrone to mask all life signs; I want to be able to reach the surface of the City UNDETECTED!" Ogden stressed undetected to make sure that everyone understood his needs were paramount.

Col. Anderson turned to the bridge crew, "Everyone to their stations you heard the man, I want to start to see sweat."

Before Bell's words were finished, Ogden had bent at the hip as a gesture of gratitude, turned and exited the bridge. Now he was formulating thoughts to address the Alanon counsel.

Ogden walked out of the war room with an uneasy feeling, it wasn't that he did not believe in his people, in fact he was sure they would lay down their lives if he asked them. He hoped collectively there was enough strength left in humanity that we had the outside chance of surviving what was waiting for him back on the City. Keep your chin up was something that his grand-father used to tell him, but at this time it seem just a bit too casual.

Ogden intended to face this head on, proving again that the Oberhause line had a destiny that was written in the stars, but he felt more like he was heading to hell. With an air of foreboding doom riding on his back, Ogden kept a brave face for his people. A battle was coming and he knew his crew was up to it, now he had to face the Alanon council and convince them to go to war......

Asmodeus

A very very long time ago, when humanity still foraged and hunted with sticks...

The tribe was hungry as the hunt of late had not been going well. Nothing more than a couple of squawkers and their eggs, barely enough to feed the hunting party let alone remove the tension that went with a gnawing belly. Apprehension ran high among the tribe, tempers flared and pockets of violence erupted over the smallest of conflicts.

Trerl was trying to keep her spirits up, but she was only twelve seasons old and not yet a woman. She ate almost last and her subsistence of grubs and beetles were keeping her alive but not healthy. She longed for meat, a chance to feel satiated with the juicy meat of a tusker or even a squealer.

But this hadn't happened in many darkenings and if the tribe didn't have a successful hunt soon, she would probably become the brunt of the tribe's ire as she was the youngest female, not even able to be a hunter. In the world of Homo habilis a female's worth wasn't great, yes they were a pleasure to be grunted with, but often they just got in the way or lagged behind during travel to better hunting grounds.

If food wasn't found soon a move would take place and frequently the weak of the tribe did not survive a move.

Trerl was wandering away from tribe, looking for beetles amongst the rocks at the edge of the jungle, far below the community shelters nestled on the mountain side away from predators. Before she realized it, Trerl found herself out of earshot or smelling distance of her tribe.

Trerl was an inquisitive girl who always had difficulty staying put and the longer the tribe went with out meat the more she felt a need to distance herself from the growing tension and potential violence that was inevitably heading her way. She already nursed a swollen cheek after an unsuccessful hunter took out his inadequacies on her with a forced grunting.

A squawker startled her as it flew up from under a bush and noisily headed through the jungle; Trerl checked the bush for a nest and was rewarded with a single egg. She knew she should return this prize back to the tribe for the leader but selfishly sucked the proteins from the shell, greedily licking each fragment until all sustenance was removed.

She had almost forgotten that a squawker was in her grasp, she cooed happily as she headed in the direction of the semi-flightless bird. Trerl got her name by the way she rolled her tongue when she was very happy or trying to sooth a potential aggressor, hoping to avoid a beating or a forced grunting.

But at this period of her brief life she was happy and if she caught a squawker, it might go a long way to help her avoid any beatings in her near future.

It took Trerl awhile but she eventually lost track of the bird and recognized that she had no idea where she was and the darkening was approaching. The jungle at night was no place for a little girl, actually it was no place for a lone hunter, because even the top of the food chain can get eaten by a toother, whose feline claws make very short work of the frail flesh of even the mightiest of hunters.

Trerl turned her attention to returning to the tribe, and she knew that when going home you always go up hill. So uphill it was and as luck would have it she wasn't heading in the right direction, she was heading up the mountain but easterly instead of westerly.

By time she got into the protection of the rocks the darkening was upon her and she was able to crawl under an outcropping of rock and shiver with fear and cold. The sky above her was bright as the orange orb was almost full and the landscape was cast with long blackened shadows. Trerl whispered her name at the light in the sky hoping it would not come down and feast on her, because that was the way of her people, the way to keep the moon at bay.

But like every darkening it was followed by light and the morning sun started to warm the rocks around the young prehistoric girl. Trerl arose out of her restless slumber thrilled to have survived the darkening. The light brought hope again and Trerl climbed onto a large boulder to look for a familiar sight, and what she saw filled her with elation, a tusker.

This was a young beast that must have been separated from its herd, it was limping and obviously in distress. Trerl's first impulse was to move toward the young beast that had now started trumpeting and with a change in direction she found herself heading in the direction of home. She dared not approach the tusker, who was not yet a tusker as its age was not that of maturity to warrant the growth, but she got close enough to see that the beast's back leg was broken. Broken legs meant death, which was the way of the world a million plus years ago.

Trerl started to recognize some of the landmarks of home in the distance and hurried amongst the rocks and boulders to share her news of many meals to come. As she approached the crude gathering of shelters it was obvious that the mood of the tribe had not improved as everyone stayed away from communal contact and when two strayed too close they would posture and bark and hit if the hierarchy was distinct enough.

Trerl approached jabbering and yelling, she was quite excited and had difficulty finding the words to explain that she had just found a young mammoth with a broken hind leg and everyone needed to hurry before something else stole their meal.

She approached one of the older males and tried to explain that they needed to follow her, but language wasn't a strong point of Homo habilis and Trerl's excitable nature did not help her cause. Tronk slapped her with a back hand knocking Trerl completely off her feet.

This caught the immediate attention of Cheld a younger male that hadn't earned much status but was proving he had the strength and power to someday be a leader. Cheld had an eye for Trerl and had grunted with her when the opportunity arose.

The slap did not help the young girl gain her composure in fact it had the opposite effect and Trerl started to scream. She was trying to explain the importance of the situation but it came across as emotional gibberish.

Cheld approached and rolled his tongue, holding out his hand, knuckles forward in a none-threatening stance. Trerl accepted the approach and was able to explain with a few gestures and pantomimed trunk movements that she had seen a tusker.

Cheld recognizing that there could be some importance in the girl's ramblings approached the chieftain to explain there could be a possible hunt developing. Tronk decided he wasn't done with the girl and started to hit her with a slender branch he had pulled from a tree, whipping her across the back and legs.

The Chieftain barked at Tronk to stop and when his subservient did not shoved him to his back. Tronk quickly took the passive position curled on his knees head down with his hand extended out. The Chieftain ignored the gesture and went to Trerl, grabbing her by the hair he expressed his desire to know were the tusker was. She was able to point to the west and was shoved into the lead so the hunters could follow.

The tribe was in a commotion as the word of a hunt spilled through gestures and broken sentences. Spears were gathered and off the tribe went. A lot of pushing and jostling of position took place and the green eyes of jealousy stared at Trerl and Cheld as both seemed to have gained status and Tronk would have to work to retrieve what he had lost.

It took a concerted effort on the Chieftain's part to keep the hunting party quiet as the anticipation vibrated through them, many openly drooling with the potential of meat with in their grasp. The kill was easy as the poor beast could not maneuver amongst the rocks and it was quickly stoned to death with large rocks as the party was able to get on a ledge above it and make quick work of the kill.

Using a piece of sharp rock the Chieftain cut the first slice of their meal as the tribe impatiently waited for their opportunity to feast. Everyone praised him on his prowess with cheers and cries of his name. "Topla"

Topla gave the ok for the tribe to eat and they rushed in a maddened frenzy to fill their bellies with the spoils of the day. Trerl was quickly forgotten and she again waited to eat after several attempts were thwarted by larger females who in turn had to wait for the males.

Bellies full and the concerns of yesterday forgotten, the tribe cut up the remains and returned to their shelters with enough meat to last them through several darkenings. They no longer squabbled or barked, now gentle touch and community returned, the tribe had prevailed.

As the darkening approached the orange orb was in full cycle and looked down on the happy society, and they looked up and yelled and pointed. Boastful and proud they started to yell their names at the powerful entity.

Topla was the first to feel brave enough to shake his fist at the full moon and bark his name; a chorus of "Topla, Topla." came from the adorning tribe. Each took their turns and when Tronk sang his praises to the light in the night sky many snubbed his reply, causing his anger to fester.

Trerl enjoyed this full moon, she felt good, good enough to willingly let Cheld grunt with her and when she felt brave enough to yell her name the tribe all laughed at the attempt but all repeated her name as she had become one of them.

But this night's start of her acceptance wasn't her only change, as a young girl becoming a woman she carried her first egg and this would be fertilized. Tonight she would conceive a son. She watched Cheld from across the enclosure hoping to catch his eye and his attentions.

After a couple of furtive glances were exchanged, Trerl slipped away from the shelters hoping to draw a mate, and mated she was, for as she entered the shadows Tronk lay waiting to enact his revenge on the poor girl.

Trerl did not see it coming; she was hit in the side of the head with a rock bigger than her fist, dazed and terrified she could not defend the advances of the older male as he forced himself on her with a vicious grunting, his evil moving inside of her, to eventually swim to her egg and at that point the conception of Vermin unalterably took place. This was his first existence of many evil filled lives.

The child was born prematurely and if it wasn't for the strong physical genetics' of the father (I use the term loosely, he was nothing but a sperm donor) Trerl's child would have probably died in hours. But unfortunately the birth weakened Trerl due to loss of blood and she struggled to stay alive. In her weakened state she slipped and fractured her tibia just below the knee.

Again the tribe felt the need to move, to try and find better hunting grounds. The chieftain made the decision to move not caring if Trerl could keep up. He had hard choices to make and he couldn't worry about an injured female and her scrawny infant.

The tribe moved and at first a few hovered back to encourage Trerl but none would be left behind for her. Eventually Trerl had to drag her infant son by the foot as she did not have the strength to carry him. Her maternal instinct would not allow her to abandon him, even after the baby was dead for two days Trerl continued to crawl after the tribe and drag her child. Eventually she succumbed to the difficulties of Homo Habilis, broken legs meant death, which was the way of the world a million plus years ago.

The child ended up in hell through trickery and deceit on the Devil's part, a fallen soul to be molded for a greater purpose, to again walk among humanity and to inflict evil where ever he went. Asmodeus, demon of lust was born.

The Plan unfolds

War has been a common part of humanity's history, even before it started to be recorded. Keeping in mind that victory was one of the most important factors in human evolution and history is only the reality of those who survived. Reality is a complex negotiation between the observer and the observed and it usually is the point of view of the victor not the vanquished. Much of history died in the last breath of the subjugated.

The question is: Are we evolving on earth to ultimately face an aggressive universe, preparing to defend our existence from others who rose to the top of their food chain on their lonely little planet ready to take what is ours if we don't know how to defend it, or are we going to be viewed as the hedonistic aggressive animals that we are?

As early as man learned to pick up a club, Neanderthals were willing to beat other tribes senseless out off fear and misunderstanding.

The English invented the long bow and defeated the French's far superior army. Bow practice was compulsory as early as age eight and a seventeen year old boy would march off to battle for his king or queen. For over three hundred years the bow and arrow was the most dominant weapon of war. (Then the bullet came along.)

Gun powder actuated projectiles changed the face of war. Yes there was an attempt to keep it civilized by making up rules and etiquette, but from the evolution past the single shot musket all the way to Mr. Gatling's rapid fire gun and beyond, the bullet was an effective killing device.

Smart bullets, heat seeking missiles, grenade launchers, nuclear warheads and many more atrocities have been designed to effectively and efficiently kill our fellow human being.

There have been many reasons for war; our species have fought over square footage of land, oil, water, race, religion and lately corporations fighting for potential sales.

After the world economy broke down the barriers that the petty borders tried to uphold, the corporate wars started. At first espionage was brought in to help outsell the competition, bombing of supply lines, computer viruses, but eventually full fledged war broke out between rival companies. When all avenues of corporate bullying failed, many turned to incapacitate the enemy on the battle field before the enemy did it to them, which brings us back to evolution and the survival of the fittest.

The government tried to chastise and warn, but unfortunately the one human certainty is war.

The corporate wars followed man into space and will probably continue to follow humanity all the way to first contact, possibly uniting everyone with the common hatred of the alien race.

Oberhause inc. has been to war, in fact the Alanon station was involved in three battles for control of specific areas of space. Each battle, a hostile attempt to take over the shipping lanes that Ogden's family had developed over generations.

Ogden was a young boy the last time Alanon station was involved. Ogden grew up abhorring war but understood the necessity of standing up to a bully even if it meant spilling a little blood. Ogden did not know who the bully was this time but he really didn't like being pushed around. Now Ogden had to make sure that the Alanon council was going to back his play.

When Sir Ogden Timothy Oberhause the Fifth spoke, typically people listened. As far back since he was a child, he had humans do his bidding. It was more than the fact that he was heir to the Oberhause throne, he had a presence even as a young boy.

As Ogden strode through the corridors of level nine of the Alanon station his people turned to watch him pass and he made an effort to make eye contact with each and every one of them. This was his team and they needed to know they were valued.

Ogden hesitated as the access portals slid back allowing him entry into the central core. The hesitation held Ogden to a single breath to help ready himself for what was ahead; it slowed him somewhat as he stepped into the arena of Alanon station.

This was an agenda of vital importance and it needed the trust of the ruling body of the space station. He was about to try and explain how he wanted to defend against the latest enemy but could not explain truly why, just that it was very important. It would take more than guile and perseverance to convince his command and family to follow his lead with partial blinders on.

The council sat around a large triangle table with a look of anticipation, with a mix of concern and trepidation blended in.

Slowly the last of the conversations trailed off into whispers as Ogden approached the command table.

"Let me get to the point because we really don't have a lot of time for discussions. We need to get past talking and move quickly to action."

Getting the full attention of the council the young heir jumped into the fray with out hesitation. "I need a full battalion of ships to move against the City."

The idea of an attack force entering the atmosphere of the home planet again caused a commotion of whispers and gasps.

"Please, please!" Ogden encouraged as he gestured with his palms up toward the council. "We are not attacking the planet, as everyone has obviously heard by now; it appears that another corporate war is brewing with attacks already starting. These attacks are not by forces I recognize and it appears that their goal is to start a war and I mean a big war. The ships that attacked me earlier are not of any design that I am familiar with and they are powerful."

Ogden had the full attention of the room. "I have no intention of actually attacking the City as there will be a large force waiting for us as we enter the atmosphere that is our target. My plan is to use the attack force as a diversion to help me take a single ship and make it to the planet. I don't want the first ship manned,as I want the enemy to think that it was able to destroy me and my friends. I already have the bridge crew making the proper procedures."

Ogden could tell that some of the older council was starting to think that he was doing a lot with out council approval. "I'm sorry for getting things started without your rubber stamp but priority and time dictated that the wheels of motion get started right away. The first ship will go in unmanned and engage the enemy over the South Pole with lasers and torpedoes blazing, the enemy can't find out that the first ship is unmanned until it is too late." Ogden slapped his fist into his hand to emphasize his point.

"Who is this enemy?" interrupted Kelsey Montague, the interruption was acceptable and expected. Kelsey was Ogden's father's childhood friend and rose to power as a trusted advisor. Kelsey was a man that controlled a significant amount of power and influence within the council and was highly respected by the other people at this table.

Once again Ogden's vagueness had to be enough. "Kelsey, do you trust me?"

"Of course I do but you have to admit that your request comes at a very high cost and is out of the ordinary even for you."

This got a lot of nods from some of the other council members.

"You trust me as you trusted my father before me and for now that has to be enough," explained the Oberhause heir. ": All I can tell you, and that is only because I don't truly know everything, is that the future of humanity is dependant on our efforts here today."

There was a significant moment of silence as the council thought about what Ogden asked of them then Kelsey stood up and said, "Bottom line Ogden I do trust you, I trust you with my life so you have my blessing and please come back to us quickly."

The rest of the council stood and expressed their well wishes and with that Ogden thanked every one and left the central core through the swish of the access portal. Leaving behind a commotion of communication as each one of Alanon's elite actively prepared for Ogden's return to the City.

Ogden's team was more than dependable; they were some of the best and the brightest of humanity's space fairing pioneers. It has been said that Ogden Oberhause had cobra venom flowing through his veins and the Alanon crew thrived on his confidence. It was difficult to find anybody on the space station that wouldn't go to the edge of space and beyond for this man.

Ogden started his trek back through the space station but on his return to his new friends he had one more stop to make along the way and that was communications.

Alanon spun in space, a beacon of hope for commerce amongst the stars; the satellite was built for personal gain because the accumulation of stuff is the human way. Being at the top of the food chain meant more than satiating hunger, it meant completely dominating every living creature they came in contact with.

The Oberhauses were 'good people' as far as humanity was concerned and Ogden had no problem keeping his chin up as he walked with controlled deliberation to the communications center.

There was a big hope that all communication channels were being monitored by whomever or what ever controlled these obsidian ships. It would be great if those ships would be waiting for Ogden, because he would shove the Alanon fleet down the throats of those pink skinned demon wannabees.

Communications was actually a small room compared to the vastness of Alanon, only twenty by twenty meters, and the lady at the power switch of these electronics was Ogden's big sister Sarah, his senior by three years. The two of them were close and Ogden frequently came to her with his hopes and dreams and occasionally with his concerns and fears.

As children the two spent plenty of nights staying up hours into the sleep cycle, mentally exploring the known universe, dispelling myths and sharing dreams. Sarah would shut everything else out and listen to her brother's stories, ramblings and ideas of the future. She learned early that her younger brother was different from everybody else.

Passing along the central level of Alanon, Ogden reminisced over the joys of childhood and anticipated seeing his sibling again.

Alanon pulsed, as it reminded everyone of its alert status. Ogden hardly recognized the flashing amber lights as he approached communications. Even on alert the people who frequented Alanon's central core, its other eight levels revolving quietly around the hub, had a look of determination on their faces as they scuttled through the halls. Everyone recognized their leader and felt a mix of anxiety and relief that their strength had returned.

Each room was an individually sealed unit and as the portals swished open the heat from the electronics flowed past Ogden as he entered communications.

Sarah's gaze slowly left the screen she had been intently monitoring; she broke out into a vivid smile when she realized her baby brother had returned. The two moved to greet each other in a warm and loving embrace.

"Hi big brother."

"Hey little sister."

"How have you been?" they spoke as if in stereo, then laughed and hugged again.

Sarah stepped back and raised her eye brows in a tell tale fashion as if to say 'what are you up to now?'

"OK Oggie doggie." Sarah teased him with a nick name from their youth. "What the hell did you bring down on Alanon now? Nana always said you would bring destruction to the Oberhauses."

Ogden quickly replied "Well Nana tried to beat the devil out of me on a couple of occasions" and through laughter giggled, "and the 15ml fiber optic cable stings like a damn." He could almost feel the welts from being caught buying black market X-rated hologames.

"So really now brother, what is going on?" Sarah again inquired. Making sure that he wouldn't try and change the subject.

"Let us sit, little sister Do I have a story to tell you and I'm not sure that you will believe me." The two sat across Sarah's com station and Ogden started his tale.

"You remember Tobias?" Ogden started.

"What does that bonehead have to do with this?"

"That bonehead happens to be my friend and to answer your question, we where just having some fun and he has nothing to do with this."

Sarah's brows rose with doubt. "Ya right."

"Whatever, Tobias, Bell and I were at Le'Ralphe with a few young ladies....."

Sarah interrupted, "Bell should know better, I will kick his ass personally."

"......having a few drinks when we were approached by this weird little man, who basically drafted me into his cause." Ogden paused to look for a reaction from his sister but got nothing so he carried on. "Later on we were attacked by giant pink monsters."

Sarah's interest increased. "There were several sightings of these monsters on the Prime City News."

"So you are going to believe me, are you? But believe me, my story is going to get even stranger." Ogden continued on with the previous days events and even he couldn't fathom that only a short time ago he had no idea that Trydent, Shately and Jasmine even existed and now he felt a connection with them like no other before.

Ogden explained Drol and the mysterious pot that transformed him to Drol's penthouse and their eventual escape back to Alanon being pursued by the obsidian ships.

"I've been instructed to return to earth" he said.

"And do you intend on following these instructions? Are you completely off your rocker?" Sarah's concern for her brother's choices at this point in his life could not be hidden.

Once again Ogden found himself asking the people around him to trust him, but his analytical side screamed in his mind that the trust was misplaced. His emotional side believed everything that Drol had said so far and he had every intention of completing Drol's quest even if it meant dying for the cause.

"I know this all seems very overwhelming but I need your support, I have already convinced the council to back me. I really need you to believe in me right now."

"OK, you can count on me." Assured Sarah as she placed a caring hand on his arm for support.

"Great, here is what I need you to do." His need to save time showed clearly through. "I need you to send a message stating that our forces are returning to fight. It doesn't have to be to any-one in particular as I am sure all Alanon channels are being monitored. I want you to encrypt it with every trick you know, dazzle me with your magic."

At first Ogden was going to withhold the fact that this whole attack on the City was a distraction, a feint to draw away from the real plan. Again Ogden paused as the events of the last hours spun past; this was enough to remind him that family should know everything.

"Listen Sarah, I'm sure that the encryption will be broken and I'm not trying to burst your ego bubble but Drol assures me that this is just fact, but I need you to be very convincing." The last two words were punctuated with a clenched hand stressing the importance of what he spoke.

The entire Alanon fleet was to enter the City's atmosphere above the South Pole, as Saphrone and its crew tries to sneak in through an area that was once known as Sangudo along a reclaimed river called the Pembina. Rivers were natural channel ways to help move the flow of water to the city's populace after it was mined off Europa. They are going to attempt to slip in undetected and fly down to biodome 313 hopefully under the radar. This is where they would learn destiny's plan.

Ogden gave himself fifteen minutes of quality time (A self indulgence) before returning to the Armstrong suite, before returning to his new friends, before returning to his destiny.

Farewell to Alanon

Rejuved and ready to rock and roll, the four ordered breakfast. Of course it was a Kellogg's breakfast of champions. (Just kidding) Actually it was proteins blended with carbohydrates with enhanced vitamins and minerals. Most importantly it had flavor to resemble bacon, eggs and hotcakes.

The coffee was real as Shately had made sure that she had ordered a fine blend of the City's finest, enough for her to take some back with her for a personal indulgence if she ever survived.

Jasmine awoke to a personal excitement, she wanted to meet this Saphrone and make her own opinion of the craft.

Space travel was not a new concept for Jasmine, she had traveled to the edge of the solar system, the base colony on Pluto, but that was aboard a deep space freighter which was converted into a luxury cruiser. If you had the credits you could take this voyage and experience the edge of known space. The sun was just a large star from this vantage point.

Her parents thought it would be a great present for her fifteenth birthday. Jasmine actually finished her high school on Ganymede, a moon of Jupiter. It is mostly an ice ball on the surface and a fluid ocean that would rival our oceans of the past.

Jasmine's Astroglide was an amazing piece of technology, but it wasn't a craft that could handle more than a quick trip to Mars or the moon. The asteroid belt would quickly make a mess of her Vette, not having the shield technology or strength that it takes to take the battering from asteroids at high speeds.

But for now Jasmine finished her breakfast and mentally prepared her self to ride Saphrone back into the maw of evil.

"You know this is a pretty good meal for someone like Otto to serve." She teased.

Trydent was quick to jump on the band wagon. "Hey Otto I know it tastes like bacon and eggs but really now, what is it?"

"OK, enough with the yuk yuks, lets just say it is good for you and will give you the strength and energy to face the day ahead of us." Ogden's words were more than accurate because they all understood that getting through the day was a long shot at best.

Shately was still trying to shake off last night's terror and she was worried that they were going to become a regular occurrence.

Jasmine turned to her female companion, "Hey girl, you're still looking rather pale and puckish, didn't you catch any sleep. I haven't slept so well in a month and I didn't even get laid."

Trydent looked over at Jasmine and asked, "Don't you ever take a breath between sentences?" and then did his best to try and imitate her, "I mean really"

Everyone laughed openly including Shately and some of the tension of the previous couple of days slipped away.

"So Ogden, when do we get to meet Saphrone?"

"Right now all we have to do is to walk to the space dock and climb aboard." Ogden simplified his answer. "Here is what I've set up. I have assembled Alanon's fleet, 30 ships in total; including eighteen battle wagons, twelve light atmosphere cruisers and ten Excalibur class invaders which include Saphrone."

Saphrone was an Excalibur class invader by name and blue print only; she was refitted with the cutting edge technology, including a very experimental computer core, an artificial brain that was designed from a plasma base and a positronic neural net. Not many would dare to say sentient but Saphrone her-self may argue.

The shields were developed from sodium chloride crystals that are grown in zero gravity to increase symmetry, then a harmonic resonance of specific pitch is directed through the crystal creating an artificial force field that can repel everything from asteroids to man made projectiles and even energy weapons.

Lasers would be quickly absorbed, dissipating the energy across the surface of the shields. It was highly difficult to penetrate a shield that was created with a crystal that was rated at eighty percent structurally pure. Saphrone's were rated at a salty ninety percent true. How, you ask your-self, did Drol's Laz rifles take out the enemy ships so effectively? There is no scientific explanation at this point to fully understand the technology at Drol's disposal and unfortunately that is the best that can be said.

Pulse cannons are bursts of energy based on a chemical reaction, three chemicals, all relatively harmless on their own but when mixed together creates an energy discharge. This release, when fired can reduce the effectiveness of a top of the line shield by fifteen percent per blast. The percentage drops according to efficiency of the crystal powering the shields. So if a ship is hit enough, shields will stop to function and be vulnerable even to low caliber projectile weapons.

Ogden continued to explain his plan of including the Alanon fleet. "The fleet will move in mass with Excalibur class invader leading the charge. This is a sister ship to Saphrone with-out all the bells and whistles. Our genetic signatures will be down loaded into the ship."

"Does this ship have a name?" Jasmine inquired.

"It will probably be a newer ship that hasn't been christened yet, something expendable." Ogden continued, "But it wont be a ship like Saphrone as she is literally a one of a kind and her primary neural matrix is a prototype. So far no other ship deserves a name like Saphrone. This ship for all intensive purposes will appear to be us and when scanned it will show an Excalibur class invader registered as Saphrone with five crew aboard."

Shately feeling some-what better asked, "Who is the fifth? Ogden I know I'm not the smartest," feigning a simpleton like presence, "but I only count four in the room."

"Yes Shately," Ogden replied in a mock condescending tone, "I have asked my personal valet to come along. You have all met Taylor. Trust me when I tell you he is very dependable and has always proven to be useful."

All four of Drol's champions were obviously pumped and full of adrenalin. Each one considered his/her fate and was a semi-willing participant in the battle ahead of them and all hoped Ogden's plan would work as they were tired of being shot at.

"I hope the demon ships will think that we are returning with a vengeance and will meet the fleet head on. If they fall for the attack, I believe that we can slip into the City undetected and make it to the biodome before the last shot is fired."

Trydent being the eternal pessimist brought up the idea of weaponry, "What kind of fire power will we be packing?" Through out his entire life, Trydent had made it a habit to never get into a fight that he would lose due to the lack of offensive toys.

"Of course Saphrone is armed with both Lasers and pulse cannons but nothing as powerful as what Drol gave us, I am leaving one behind to be taken apart and examined by my engineers down to the bolts, but they could never harness the technology this quick. I am hoping that Saphrone's shields will be solid enough to get us to our destination unscathed." He then added, "We will still have three of Drol's fancy dancy Laz rifles and I will have a collection of hand weapons added into Saphrone's stores."

Jasmine asked the next question, "How about rations? I may get hungry on the way." She smiled a smile she learned when she was young as a way to always get what she wanted.

"Of course......and we will even have a built in Rejuv on board if we need one."

"Great," Jasmine jumped in, "let's get going and meet this ship of yours.

"Ya I'm as ready to get started as I ever will be." Shately needed to have something to do. She was slowly having a break down and sitting around and waiting wasn't helping her disposition.

At that point every-ones eyes met with an understanding, a wordless acceptance that it was time to move on, time to grab the demon by the horns and ride, time to get the show on the road.

They travelled through the levels of Alanon station on their way to the space dock. With the station on alert, and news of the prodigal son of the Oberhause Empire having returned, word was spreading fast through-out the station which was a murmur of rumors and conjecture.

A crowd had gathered outside the ship yard and was steadily growing; it had started when a complete communications ban was imposed station wide.

Ogden lead the way out of the Armstrong suite and into the turbo lift and out to the last level, it opened to a throng of people trying to get a glimpse of.....let us just say the rumors varied from, a demon killing commando unit, VIP's from the surface and even a counter strike team assembled after the Oberhause interests were attacked.

Of course everyone had watched the Prime City news as Fran Temple was the highest rated newscaster. The Vidnews had been reporting the insanity that had hit the City and the escalation of retaliation since the earlier attack. Corporations were blaming each other and threatening counter attacks.

The crowd was split as Taylor pushed his way through. "OK, Ok, enough already LET ME THROUGH!"

Taylor grabbed the pony tail of a tall male journalist and pulled him out of his way, "I said make some room dipshit."

Ogden turned to his new team and with a large smile said, "I told you that Taylor is always a handy man to have around."

"Hey Boss," Taylor made salutations. "I got your message and Saphrone is ready as per your request."

Taylor again turned on the crowd, "I told you to get out of the way or I will have you thrown out of an airlock." He pointed at the tall journalist who immediately moved out of their path. His reputation parted the crowd and due to the rising volume of the growing gawkers, (rubber neckers as they were called in the twentieth century). Shouting seemed to be the only way to be heard, "Follow me."

The troupe obeyed and pushed through the curious crowd. The din was loud and steady and it took a concerted effort to weave their way toward the launch bay, closer to Saphrone, closer with their destiny with hell.

The launch bay seemed like an eternity away and the station turned to slow motion. Taylor pushed his small frame as the lead and continued to chastise anyone that lingered in his way. The bay was a-bustle with commotion but it was a controlled deliberate mayhem as the Alanon fleet rushed to get to battle ready.

Anderson met the gang as they entered the bay, ships were lined up and ready. Each ship's crew moving as extension of the vessel. A battle wagon had a crew of sixty eight and that included a chef. Twenty forward lasers, four unidirectional pulse cannons and five aft lasers (the thought was- why run from a fight) and of course shields. (As earlier stated, shield technology far out weighed fire power)

"Ogden we're ready." Anderson explained with confidence "The fleet is on alert and ready to depart on your orders. The only problem I can see is we will need to man the ship with your phantom signatures. The life sign emitter is not running at an efficient capacity so we will need actual bodies."

Ogden responded, "I trust that you tried everything you could, have you asked for volunteers?"

"I already have four volunteers and I plan to pilot the ship and it will be the dragonfly."

The words were simple enough but to Ogden they meant so much, he didn't even attempt to talk his childhood friend out of this decision as he wouldn't accept it if the roles were reversed.

Ogden leaned over and hugged Bell, "OK you give them hell." It was kept short and sweet sensing that death could very well interfere with their ever meeting again.

Anderson was flying the Dragonfly into the jaws of hell and the chance of survival was slim to nil.

"I'll be with you in spirit."

"And I with you." Ogden replied. The two men shook hands and moved on, Anderson to the Dragonfly and Ogden to Saphrone, both to an unknown future.

Saphrone pulsed as she floated in her slip; antimagnetic anchors kept her floating in the busy launch bay, waiting anxiously for a chance to fly again. The ship had no idea that she was considered so important or how truly special she really was.

She boasted the first positronic neural net that allowed her think for herself, feel emotions pure and raw and even dream (a subconscious tool to deal with life.) Nobody, not even the Oberhauses' her complete and so unique ability.

Ogden had grown very fond of his ship and never referred to her in anything but the first person.

Saphrone had yet to be in a fire fight; Ogden was hoping she had a chance to mature emotionally before unleashing her aggressive capabilities. Being of the cutting edge technology, she was equipped with a laser cannon that would slice through a shield operating at sixty five percent like it was butter. Her shields were third generation Gryphon sodium crystals and even her own lasers would only make a dent.

It was a giant leap since Sputnik took the world by storm, the small satellite that started it all. Saphrone would not accept an ancestry to Sputnik no more than the puritans of the early eighteenth century accepted their lineage to early primates.

Crews had been working nonestop since Ogden and his company arrived on Alanon. Refitting, upgrading, making Saphrone the elite of the elite that she was. Not nearly as large as an ore hauler, small and sleek, her bridge could accommodate eleven but it was still significantly larger than the astrocab that brought them to the space station.

The team arrived on the flight deck during the heat of preparation; Alanon's extensive workforce hurriedly got the squadron ready for battle. At T minus half an hour it was no longer about repairs it was more about tweaking the fine adjustments and coming to terms with your existence.

Waiting to send them off, Sarah stood below Saphrone encouraging and inspiring the young ship. As the group approached she addressed them, "So what has my brother gotten you all involved in?"

"What makes you think that your brother is in charge?" Trydent asked. "He's just the guy that has an armada of ships."

"Ya, we're just letting Otto hang around for his liquor." Shately teased.

Sarah couldn't help but smile, admiring the optimism that was exhibited through the humor. "I wish you the best of luck." She then turned to Taylor and added, "I don't have to remind you to look after my brother."

Taylor scrunched up his brows in a mock scowl, "Now why would you say something like that? Are you trying to be hurtful? Don't I always look after our little Oggy?"

"Oggy?" All three of Ogden's new companions spoke the nickname with questioning mirth.

Sarah quickly continued the conversation saving his brother a little dignity from having to explain the childhood moniker. "Like always Ogden my brother, you're heading out with your heart on your sleeve to grab the proverbial demon by the horns, I ask you, please..." Sarah accented her words with love and sincerity that only a big sister's advice can carry. "...be careful, slow down and look before you leap.

Ogden gave his sibling one last hug. "We don't have that luxury right now, both feet are plunging toward the City and I can't even afford to blink."

Jasmine walked straight for Saphrone with a twinkle in her eye and a longing in heart, she was eager to meet the ship and strap herself into one of the helm's chairs. Her astroglide was a nice piece of engineering but her Vette was not comparable to Saphrone.

Of course Jasmine had been aboard an Excalibur class ship before but nothing as new and renowned as this ship. Jasmine's family was wealthy but not to the extent of the Oberhauses, Ogden ruled a world, albeit an artificial one, made of steal, plastic and the sweat of a dreamer named Ogden Timothy Oberhause the second.

Ships were already amassing into battle order; the Dragonfly was preparing to take its position to lead the fleet into battle against the dark forces that already occupied the City. The phantom image of Jasmine and her companions was imprinted into the ship, hopefully giving them a little more time.

Saphrone was sleek and elegant, at least twenty times the size of Jasmine's Vette, long smooth and hardly an angle on her hull.

Jasmine slid her hand across the hull as she crossed under the nose. With contact she whispered, "Hi beautiful."

Saphrone's outer lights pulsed with an appreciative greeting.

With a click and a whir she opened her access port in anticipation of her passengers.

Jasmine, Shately Trydent, Taylor and Ogden gathered at the stairs leading up to the catwalk that led to Saphrone's entrance.

Jasmine led up the ladder with an obvious excitement about meeting the wonder-ship, she literally had a skip in her step.

Trydent followed, he had a look of cold determination, each step up precise, ten steps closer to the City and retuning to his destiny.

Shately was quick to follow her fellow Rez inhabitant; she was still swirling after the events of the last days. Her haunting dreams continued to swim along her sub conscience threatening to surface when she let her guard down.

At this point in her life Shately believed that being close to Trydent was probably going to extend her life past the next week. She wasn't sure about the next five minutes as she found her life suddenly beyond the security of the Rez and exploding into the twenty eighth century.

Taylor kissed both cheeks of the heir to the Oberhause fortune that spilled out into the Solarian universe, turning to go up the ladder he started shouting directions to the group. "Jasmine, move a little faster this isn't a sight seeing tour." Taylor's attempt at humor was lost as Jasmine had already entered the sleek craft.

Ogden turned to face his sister and say his goodbyes, but it was Sarah that spoke first, "Just come home safe."

Ogden gave his sister a wink and a hug, "Don't worry, jumping in with both feet has always worked so far."

Sarah returning the hug, "MOM and Dad would be proud."

"Thanks."

Getting professional Sarah moved the conversation to logistics. "I just came from communications and the City sky is swarming with unknown crafts, an estimate of over thirty. I'm going to hit the air waves with as much chatter as I can, hopefully this will confuse the enemy long enough for you to make it to the City."

With a knowing nod Ogden turned and climbed the metal stairs to join his team. At the top of the stairs he noticed that the sound level had dropped to a steady whir of the machines, all eyes were on him and as he scanned his met Bell's.

Both men nodded for luck realizing that in a couple of hours from that point everyone involved could very well be dead.

Taylor stuck his head out of the port looking for his boss, "We have to go sir, address your troops and get this show on the road."

Ogden, with a raised voice, addressed the audience that was still in the launch bay finishing up any loose ends.

"Today we go into battle, we fight not for ourselves but so our children may see a tomorrow.....Live long and die with honor."

The crowd repeated the last six words in unison. "Live long and die with honor." While they raised their right fist above their heads in salute.

With that Ogden Oberhause turned and climbed into the command chair of the most advanced space craft in the history of humanity.

"Hello Ogden," chimed Saphrone's very feminine voice, "I have missed you!"

"Lock up and prepare for departure." Ogden told his ship in his very professional voice, Then in a gentler tone added "I've missed you too Saphrone." Ogden's sincerity almost seemed out of character for the hardened corporate giant he was known as.

"We're going to war my shining beauty and I need you at your best or all our work will be for nothing," Ogden spoke to his ship.

"Ask and you have my complete support, I will fly into any battle you wish me to. My shields are feeling wonderful since the Alanon crew completed my refit. Thank you for that."

"Wonderful Saphrone, Now let's get going."

Jasmine piped in "Is it possible to have some music to help me relax, maybe something that is emotionally moving."

Saphrone responded to Jasmine like they were old friends, "How about something from Orf, Is Carmena Burana moving enough for you?"

"Yes that would be perfect."

"Not to loud, I will need to concentrate." Ogden advised

'Fortuna Imperix Mundi' slowly touched each person with its haunting melody.

Ogden addressed the force over the flight com, "Everyone knows the plan, lots of chatter, talk about vacation plans or birthday presents but I want the City inundated with radio noise, call your mothers, sons or cousins. I want confusion so Saphrone can blend in."

The ship disengaged the docking magnets and moved toward the bay doors with the assistance of a tractor beam. Saphrone slipped out of the space station and slowly moved, jockeying for position amongst the ships heading to the blue planet.

The fleet aligned into battle order with the Dragonfly in the lead, as Saphrone tried to blend in by moving toward the middle, keeping to the edge allowing an easy opportunity to slip away unnoticed.

'Happy birthday' was heard by all the ships involved; that was the command to move the fleet toward the planet. A move toward a battle of destiny and hopefully toward victory, freeing the City from the evil force that occupied it and allowing Saphrone passage.

The mass of ships surged forward.

"Planet atmosphere in sixteen minutes Ogden, and my shields will be at full capacity in three minutes."

Each one of the troupe sat comfortably in what would be considered plush by any standards. "Do you even fly this ship?" asked Trydent noticing there were no controls.

"Actually voice activated controls respond to my commands and she is capable of reacting for her-self if she needs to, but she takes orders from me."

"It's ok Saphrone," Trident joked. "Otto isn't the worst boss you could have."

With an obvious admiration for her commander that showed in her electronic voice she bantered with Trydent, "It is better than being a long distance ore hauler or tanker."

She continued, "We are emitting a carrier frequency of a transport barge and let me tell you that is as close as I want to come. The flow of civilian traffic has us taking a flight path that will move us along the Delton space way." (Designated industrial for transport traffic)

"I see an opportunity to merge behind an ice transport from Europa."

"Works for me." Ogden replied, then addressed the com system, "This is Transport LX315 on access to Ardco Smelter 55, City side, arriving in forty-five minutes, atmosphere in eleven minutes."

A reply came back. "This is Ardco 55, LX315 we have you locked, please dump load at bay G-3, access code G-3 LX315-2A."

"Message received Ardco. Transport out." The rouse was starting to come together; it was time to start crossing fingers.

The Alanon fleet moved forward to address the enemy with Dragonfly leading the way, shields on full, lasers on line and torpedoes armed and ready.

As the Armada approached the City the obsidian ships broke off their search pattern and aligned themselves to create a wall to repel the Alanon force and finally destroy the humans, Jasmine Phillips, Shately Downs, Ogden Oberhause, and of course Trydent but the four had their own ideas and none of them intended to die without a fight.

Saphrone had left the fleet behind and under the mask of deception moved with the barges, transports, tourists and the rest of the steady stream of traffic that was headed toward the City from the many places that man had colonized in this solar system.

Biodome 313 was a simple enough of destinations, but a possible life time away for the company of five seemingly forsaken people, but Saphrone bore them with pride and determination on to the next step of their unknown path into oblivion.

Flight to the City

I.

Space travel, the basic concept is easy, the problem as Einstein explained is how fast and how far. Putting it into perspective, The Planet that is now referred to as the City is 149 million kilometers away from the sun. Not everyone remembers that Earth is really the name given to our home planet, but the City has evolved, 93 million miles, approximately 8 light minutes away.

Now back to perspective, Sedna, one of the last planetoids in our solar system is over four billion miles from our sun, which takes approximately three years to travel if we go at the speed of light. (Something we have not been able to accomplish with any modicum of safety.)

Following the planets is the Ort cloud which is a massive accumulation of ice and rocks surrounding our solar system and very difficult to navigate at any high speed, so again another obstacle to humanity exploring space.

Continuing out into space, we look at the next solar system to ours, Alpha Century. This is four and a half light years away from the edge of our known space. It has no gas giants to draw in meteors and comets, with a massive gravitational pull. So any planet with the potential for life was pounded into oblivion by massive space debris. Jupiter has protected our planet for billions of years from thousands of life ending meteors, like the one that destroyed the dinosaurs. Without Jupiter's gravity, humanity probably would never have evolved past early Rodentian.

Needless to say we have spread across our solar system with bases on planets and moons. We've tried to seed the moons that have a supply of water, with cold tolerant algae and microbes, and then fish were introduced to flourish as a food supply.

Long range multi generational ships have been launched in the hope that over the centuries we may eventually find another planet that when can inhabit. Unfortunately all contact has been lost from these ships leaving the outcome unknown.

As far as we know we are alone in the vast chasm of space, (until a few days ago) when the first ships not made by man flew through the City's skies causing devastation at will.

Saphrone stayed in the queue behind a barge loaded with alien fish, destined to help feed the billions of inhabitants of the planet. The steady stream of ships that kept the commerce of space moving.

Merging through traffic Ogden coaxed Saphrone along the long line of ships passing through the City's atmosphere. Shately, Taylor, Trydent, Jasmine and Ogden floated toward their goal in the belly of a very special ship. For now everyone was comfortable, Saphrone enjoyed keeping her passengers comfortable.

Not much was being said, everyone content with watching screens and portals for signs of the obsidian enemy. The choral sounds of Carmena Burana continued to flow through the ship, each crescendo building quietly in the background.

As each ship merged into the planetary traffic, Saphrone made no effort to stand out; blending in to the bustle of flying vehicles was the plan of the hour.

Jasmine was the first to break the silence, "Dragonfly should be getting close to breaking atmosphere pretty soon."

No sooner than the words were uttered Trydent jumped in. "Enemy ship at five o'clock and moving fast."

"Saphrone don't scan the ship directly," Ogden advised. "We don't want to draw attention to ourselves."

"There is another at seven o'clock," Jasmine chirped in.

"Two more behind that one sir," Taylor added. "But they're not slowing down to take a look at us they're going somewhere fast.

Shately whispered, "Live long and die with honor Dragonfly."

2.

Dragonfly passed into the City's atmosphere on full burn, with the Alanon fleet close behind. Lasers on full, torps to the ready and shields fully charged.

The plan was to punch a hole through the enemy's defense and pull them away from biodome 313.

As Dragonfly broke through the stratosphere, Anderson started barking orders. "Target the lead ship!" his voice swam throughout the entire fleet. "On my mark...FIRE!"

Dragonfly roared straight into the center of the waiting obsidian squadron. The lead ship was hit hard; it started to glow as its shields absorbed the laser fire of most of the thirty ships. The explosion was intense sending a wave of confusion and debris rippling through the enemy.

"Live long and die with honor," the battle cry filled the airways as the "fire at will' order was given and the sky lit up with laser fire and explosions.

Fran Temple was being given enough news to win an award, which of course depends on our heroes success and that she isn't a collateral statistic.

The Alanon fleet gave Dragonfly enough room to move farther into the frenzy and it was engulfed by the evil mass of ships.

Ships from both sides were being lost; explosion after explosion inundated the city's sky line. Ultimate sacrifices helped push the Dragonfly deeper into the heart of the enemy.

"Shields at forty percent, we can't take any more hits before we will be open to the elements with our ass hanging out."

Anderson responded. "Stay with the coordinates given and transfer power from aft lasers to shields," a deep sigh. "Continue firing."

"We are being scanned, Sir." A cheer from the Dragonfly crew went up, as the enemy scanned what they thought was Saphrone, the ruse was set.

All the Obsidian ships turned their attention to the Dragonfly. "Take her into traffic helmsman." Colonel Anderson expected to die but he was going to lead them on one hell of a chase before he let those bastards snuff out the fire his existence.

3.

Saphrone continued down on the other side of the City away from the Dragonfly, at this time oblivious to the forces searching for the group of six as they hurled toward the biodome. Saphrone kept her scan to close traffic proximity as was protocol for all industrial ships.

The four obsidian ships took off at full burn, eager to join in on the hunt and eventual battle. It was a close call but Saphrone was not detected and was disregarded as the transport LX315 on the routine oar haul to the City.

"OK Saphrone let's get going." Ogden urged, and then added to his crew. "By the books contact the smelter facility."

"Ardco, this is LX315, T-minus five minutes." Jasmine tried to keep her voice from shaking.

The reply was routine. "LX315 you are clear to dump at G-3, 3rd on queue."

Trydent turned to Taylor. "Let's get the gear ready."

"I'm on it." Taylor pointed to the storage compartment and asked for help. "Can you get out he packs; I have one for each of us?"

Taylor moved toward the armory, "Hey sweetheart can you get your fanny over here and give me a hand and help me with these power cells for our hand lasers."

Jasmine always ready to enjoy some spirited banter as a way to relieve some of the building pressures, "You're looking to get my boot up your fanny if you think I'm responding to sweetheart, little man." She was moving before she even finished her response and Taylor recognized the playful nature of her tone.

"Put four in each pack," then to Ogden he meekly added, "Hey boss I went down to research and development last night."

"And?" Ogden's single word was an obvious question.

"Well let me tell ya," Taylor quipped. "Remember the body shields that they were working on? Well I was able to appropriate the prototype."

"Appropriate?" Ogden asked, "Sally is going to eat your balls for lunch!"

"She could be so lucky."

Ogden raised his eyebrows and with a smile addressed his ship. "Did you get that recorded Saphrone? You will have to let Sally hear a play back of that statement, I think she might enjoy it. Taylor you might be the one needing to wear that body shield."

"I would love to listen to you two all day, but I would like to hear more about this body shielding, I thought that this technology wasn't developed yet."

"Actually it hasn't been invented yet." Ogden gave Taylor a look of 'what have you done now' but answered the original question. "It functions under the same concept of ship's shields, only it attaches to a shoulder harness. We are trying to develop a small yet consistent crystal that will generate the power needed to absorb light laser pistol fire. Not enough to save your ass if a ship locks on to you but a lot more than a toy also."

"So what you are saying is 'don't wear it to a knife fight'." Trydent teased.

"You're an impetuous son of a bitch Monodent." Ogden shot back more cutting than teasing.

"Boys, lets get along please." Shately had been relatively silent up to this point. "I need to know that we are all on the same team." Her anxiety was surfacing again. "I need to get my feet back on the ground." Spoken more to herself than to the rest of the ships passengers.

Shately did not seem to be as strong as her new friends, but a lot had to be due to the fact that she was completely out of her element, when she walked the Rez she walked with confidence.

Ogden congratulated his aid for acquiring the body shield but added "But who gets to wear it? I could do enie meanie mienie moe."

"You do have conceptual rights with ownership of Oberhause Inc. That would give you every reason to wear the shield sir."

"Give it to Jasmine, I promised to save her pretty butt." Ogden expected to get a rise from his female partner but she didn't bite.

"Thanks Otto." Jasmine took the harness without addressing the chauvinistic remark. "How do you put this on Taylor?"

Taylor helped Jasmine adjust the shield harness, "Just press this button and it should activate the crystal and you will be safer than I am."

Indeed she was and the shields hummed as she felt the power envelope her.

When the building fell Doug was knocked unconscious and did not slip back into reality for two days. He was disoriented and it took him hours to truly understand the gravity of his situation. Actually gravity was the problem, when the building was attacked Doug's world came tumbling down on to the streets.

4.

Feeling around in the dark Doug was able to take stock of what he had. Food for over a week or until it started to go bad, vacupacks of wine and beer, but unfortunately the water container had spilled leaving very little to sustain him beyond ice cubes.

What the hell, he took one of the packs of beer and tore it open, needing a drink he downed the first one quite quickly, the first led to a second and a third........until he was very drunk. He passed out and stayed unconscious again for several hours.

Doug woke up with a hangover, he started vomiting and his head ache rang clear the lesson of how stupid his previous actions truly were. Now he had the smell of puke to deal with until he was rescued. Doug had always been a survivor and was determined to get through this. He just hoped it didn't cost him his sanity.

His decision to buy the Ultra-six had been a good one, twenty five cubic feet with loads of shelf space. He could remember the vid-display ads and thought, 'I don't need anything that elaborate; seventeen cubic feet would been more than adequate.'

He now wanted to give the sales girl a big hug for convincing him that he actually needed the extra eight cubic feet. Lets be realistic Doug wanted to give the girl more than a hug the moment she came up to offer her assistance. Once again girls perpetuate the myth of 'bigger is better'.

Doug opened one pack of beer hoping the hair of the dog would help alleviate his throbbing headache, but his stomach wasn't quite ready for any food at this time.

5.

Dragonfly was battered and wounded, each shot taking its toll on the ship and its beleaguered crew.

The ship broke through the last of the enemy forces and dove deep into the lower levels of traffic. Carnage and wreckage followed them as innocent astroglides and transports became casualties and were blasted out of the way as the enemy pursued. Three obsidian ships broke away from the battle to follow the lone ship into the traffic.

"We have lost shielding power by ninety percent. We can not afford to take another hit." The crewman was obviously emotional and his voice could not hide the fact.

"OK lets fly this baby like there is no tomorrow!" Anderson's words had more meaning than he had intended.

Down through the many levels of traffic, swerving and dodging astroglides, at this point Colonel Anderson couldn't worry if he was causing any accidents. He would be saddened if he knew the people that died but for now he was flying for a bigger cause.

The ships closed in on Dragonfly, even though the crew used every evasive move in the handbook, and a few that would be considered too high a risk.

"They have a lock on us." Cried Corporal Maxwell, Everyone braced themselves to die.

As quickly as it began the hunt was over, all the pursuing ships broke off their pursuit and changed course, turning and heading back into the City.

"The phantom probe has been knocked off line," The crewman half yelled. "They know we are not Saphrone!"

"Live long and die with honor Ogden." Anderson whispered, and then he spoke aloud to his crew, "Set a pursuit course, we aren't out of this battle just yet."

"Aye, aye Colonel."

Dragonfly banked and followed the enemy ships, the chase was on.

6.

Shately kept telling her self that it would be all over soon. This adventure that seemed to have kidnapped her was moving out of control. As a young girl, a refugee growing up in the Rez, she had never flown before let alone left the planet's atmosphere. She was hoping that they arrived at biodome 313 with out further incident, actually at this point in her life she would settle for getting both her feet planted on good old terra firma.

"We are being scanned!" Jasmine announced, "Wide band, a general search pattern."

"OK, Saphrone be prepared to run." Ogden advised his ship; he hoped that she would be able to perform her duties without letting the fear of the situation get the better of her.

"Packs loaded and ready." Taylor laid a pack beside each passenger of the ship. "Everyone strapped in?"

"Here we go again, two ships moving hard, at one o'clock." Trydent showed little emotion, he had learned a long time ago that emotions could interfere with survival when big decisions needed to be made. There was time for emotions later.

"Would you like me to try and lose these ships?" Saphrone's sexy young metallic voice chimed to her commander.

"Let's try and hide first." Ogden wasn't quite ready to give up his position.

Saphrone was basically a child; she had been taken out on some basic missions but nothing that would prepare her for war and the difficulties that would lie ahead of her, a flight to Mars and back on her maiden voyage, nothing taxing at all. In the twenty-eighth century this was a trip made by college students on their spring break. Saphrone had imprinted on Ogden on this trip, she was completely dedicated to the heir of the Oberhause fortune.

"Drop down a couple levels, slowly, try not to draw attention to us."

"There is an ice hauler just below us, I will attempt to merge in behind." Saphrone tried to please her owner.

"Let's stay alert everyone, when we make the break for the biodome, we have to be fully committed and ready for just about anything." Ogden reminded his crew but he really did not have to as they all recognized what was at stake.

Jasmine responded to Ogden with a minimal amount of mirth. "OK, but lets try and get there with out being shot at any more. I hate being killed before I have lunch."

Saphrone continued to weave her way through the constant traffic that circled the City. The obsidian foe continued to scan, searching for the ship and its crew. The enemy armada withdrew quickly from the battle against the Alanon fleet no longer fooled by the rouse. Hopefully Dragonfly had bought Saphrone the time she needed to reach their destination. But once again hope was snatched away as one of the ships changed their broadband search to directly scan into the very soul of Saphrone's workings.

"I'm being scanned directly!" Saphrone was sounding scared. "I can feel them inside my mind; they know who we are Ogden!"

"Calm down Saphrone." Ogden tried to sooth the young ship.

"Two ships on us hot." Jasmine could feel her heart racing, this wasn't unfamiliar, she felt this adrenalin rush whenever she went into battle. Hand to hand in the holovids was the usual but today it was for keeps.

Shields on full, lets get low Saphrone, drop down below traffic and try and put some distance and a couple of obstacles between us and those ships."

"Transfer all laser power to aft lasers; chances are we are going to be chased."

Saphrone detected a significant gap in the traffic and dropped into a full dive, past the industrial traffic and into the no fly zone.

"Transport LX 315 you have entered the no fly zone, do you need assistance?" The local traffic ordinance hailed Saphrone.

"This is Transport LX 315; we have two aggressive ships firing on us, permission to pass through." Ogden continued with the rouse.

"OK what are you trying to pull, we have you on visual and you're obviously not a transport, you look more like an atmosphere class invader to me."

"OK you got me, but I really don't have time to explain right now." Ogdin continued "Saphrone full burn."

The police moved to pursue and were charging lasers when the first black ship broke through the last line of traffic. The law enforcement ship was scanned, targeted and destroyed as the first ship fired a full barrage of torpedoes into the unsuspecting cops. They had forty-five minutes left in their shift and sergeant St.Lois only had sixty-four shifts left until his retirement and only one hundred and fifty dark hours to work the night shift. Amanda St.Lois was left with an excellent widower's pension and the family mortgage was cleared of all debt. Both men qualified to eventually be decorated (posthumously) with the highest honors the City had to offer (the Columbia Cluster) in honor of the gallant astronauts that gave their lives in the pursuit of space travel. Long live the space race.

Saphrone dove low and tried to hold the pavement, she sped down the street that had once had the local bar at the intersected of main street. This was another world that existed centuries before. She flew low under the wheat pool house and banked a hard right at the Doug McKean Park right across the street from the Sangudo Hotel. (That would be the H-1 square on the game of Sangudo)

The crew was pinned in their seats as Saphrone lost sixty percent of her main stabilizers as she accelerated down Main Street between Big M Foods (B-2) and the machinery sales yard. Past the pop shop and in a blink sailed past Woody's Lumber (F-3) and bumped the hill under the legion hall.

"Hang on!" Ogden yelled but it was unnecessary as everyone was holding to what ever they could find as Saphrone went into a side spin over the Maybelle Scheidl Park.

"Power to stabilizers!" Saphrone explained that she had got things under control as she pulled out of the spin in time to skip off the protective energy barrier covering the Pembina River.

The grid (aquabarrier) that covered all waterways was based on the same science as shield technology. It was a very broad band of energy that kept basic contaminants out of the water system of the planet.

A steady stream of cosmic ice was transported regularly to specific water purification factories that battled to satiate the ever thirsting planet.

The grid was set to go to maximum when a proximity sensor was crossed, which set off an emergency override that charged the specific section of the barrier to full capacity. This was a very expensive system, so anyone that activated an emergency pulse was charged for the cost of the energy it took to activate it.

As Transport LX 315 skipped across the Pembina the automated system announced, "Transport LX 315 you have been charged seventy five thousand credits for activation of sections 125 and 126 of the Pembina waterway. Charging Oberhause Inc. verification Ogden 3341 epsilon."

The closest ship boar down on Saphrone but was unable to pull up in time and slammed full force into the aquabarrier. The automated charge system buzzed and whirred but could not trace the ship back to any corporate account.

"Great flying!" Jasmine encouraged Saphrone, but Shately's ashen face told a different story, she needed to dig down deep into that hardened discipline that comes from being raised in the Rez. She needed to find the girl that would kick more than your ass if you ever pissed her off in some alley of the Rezidentials.

It was everything that Shately could do not to bring up her breakfast, spew, puke, vomit the morning meal compliments of Alanon station, but she resisted the urge and concentrated on Trydent because she felt as long as he was with her she would be there to see the end...and she couldn't help but be impressed with a man that screams 'YEEEAA Haaaaa' as Saphrone skipped past Ma Campbell's acreage on the bow of the Pembina river and accelerated hard toward the Hagarty building.

"Hold on every body!"

"Will you stop saying that!" Shately exclaimed, "It's not helping at all."

Saphrone warned, "We are going to take some hard Gees."

"Closer, Closer....Now." Ogden gave the order for his ship to climb straight up the Hagarty building. The second enemy ship tried to follow but like its counterpart culminated its existence in a fiery end as it crashed into the building and pieces broke through on the other side.

The human body is not designed to handle that kind of Gee force and these five bodies were no exception as each on of the occupants of Saphrone faded to black.

Saphrone, recognizing the immediate threat was gone, decelerated so attention would not be drawn to her, but to the steady stream of death and carnage that had hit the city over the last hour. She pulled away from the burning high rise and slid back into the ever present traffic. Astroglides whizzed by, trying to get were they were headed, with out becoming a statistic.

Jasmine was the first to get a grasp of her facilities. Groggily and somewhat surprised she mentioned. "Hey we're still alive."

"Welcome back Jasmine, now what should I do?" chimed the ship.

"Just continue doing what you're doing, just keep us alive, try to blend in and head toward biodome 313 just like before." Then Jasmine added, "And thanks Saphrone that was one amazing bit of flying."

If the ship was capable of blushing Saphrone would have, unaccustomed to praise from someone besides Ogden, Jasmine's words made her feel proud.

Trydent started to fade back in, "What the....." then with a smile and a shake of his head he said, "Can we do that again."

"Please God can we just get back to the earth." Shately looked a little green. "Before I spew."

"Hang in there sister, we are almost there," It wasn't really a lie because Jasmine really did not know how much longer it would take to reach their destination.

Before Ogden was able to regain consciousness another ship passed through their vicinity. Saphrone announced that she was being targeted again and dropped into a line of traffic that was traveling the fastest and accelerated hard to catch up to the flow.

Five levels above a second obsidian ship joined the chase, at this point stealth wasn't required and the ships blasted their way through the traffic in pursuit of Saphrone and her crew.

Saphrone broke through the south bound flow of traffic and caught a west lane heading toward the biodome, which was just located on the other side of the Rez.

Ogden regained his senses as Saphrone nervously explained that there were now two ships on a pursuit course after them.

"OK, Saphrone there is the Iona building approximately five kilometers ahead, as you pass by it hit your retros and wait for the ships. Full power to the lasers, take one ship out and then dive." Ogden explained his plan to the ship.

Buildings flashed by, "There's the Iona." Jasmine pointed to the largest that looming ahead of them on the horizon.

It was a good thing everyone was strapped in because when Saphrone cut behind the Iona building and slammed on her brakes, Taylor's unconscious body would have slammed through the windshield and skidded across the highway. (OK maybe in 1977)

Saphrone fired both retro boosters at full capacity and waited for the sleek black enemy to fly by, lasers were fired quickly, each shot reducing the enemies shield by thirty-five percent. "Enemy shields at sixty-five, thirty, shields down, targeting pulse drive, fuel ignited.....haha," she giggled, "ship is destroyed." Saphrone's obvious excitement could not be hidden by the young ship as the enemy exploded into a ball of fire and light.

"Good girl, really good girl." Ogden's ship quivered with excitement, this truly was an adrenalin rush for the young ship, if of course Saphrone was controlled by neurotransmitters. Maybe more of a synthetic Dopamine or something that resembled Serotonin but emotion pulsed through her matrix.

Saphrone was pumped. "Now I dive. Lasers recharging Ogden."

Again Shately had to work to prevent from loosing her lunch.

Ogden let his ship taste the pleasure before he reminded her to control her emotions and focus. "Focus little girl, focus, focus."

Saphrone flowed with the pulse of the planet; she felt the traffic flow by the exploding ship, a lot more than a drive time nuisance. Rarely was there ever more than a thirty astro pile up, but occasionally like today, ships scattered on the horizon creating a confusion that helped hide young Saphrone, she followed her orders and she dived looking for the next enemy.

Traffic continued to flow past as Saphrone dropped towards the ground, still concentrating on getting to biodome 313.

"Let's not get careless Saphrone." Ogden reminded "We're almost there."

"Rez is just ahead and on the other side of that, is the biodome, I think we are going to make it." No sooner had Jasmine spoke when the ship was caught by a direct hit.

"Laser fire, I've been hit, let me fight back they're trying to kill me!" Saphrone was beginning to sound frantic.

"Sorry little girl, we have to make a run for it."

"Put me on the ground and place a blade in my hand and give me an enemy with substance." Shately was used to hand to hand combat, not hurling through the sky. She would get her wish soon enough but she should have learned long ago to be careful for what you wish for. Right now her head spun, her stomach churned and a continual sense of foreboding desperation hung over her like a gallows.

Again lasers hit Saphrone as she raced to their destination, shields were down to eighty-six percent. "There is another one! It has me targeted." This time Saphrone was hit with a full barrage of laser fire.

"My shields are down!" She proclaimed in a passionate plea.

"Lose them!" Jasmine yelled. "I will accept the hard Gees."

"I would rather die." Shately groaned.

Saphrone headed straight toward the last building between the group and the Rez. Trydent felt an unexpected draw to the Rez, but then again he was born and raised there. He gave out another yell. "Yeeeaa Haaa."

"Shields back on line." Saphrone sighed, if a space ship has the ability to sigh.

Both enemy ships locked on Saphrone's trajectory and charged ahead on a collision course with the sky scraper. Saphrone was again hit; this volley of energy knocked her stabilizers off line again.

"Transfer all power to shields, including life support." As quickly as Ogden gave the order her shields glowed full, this was the last order that Ogden's ship would be able to fulfill, Saphrone slammed into the building...

Crash landing

Corporal Maxwell was the helmsman on the Dragonfly. "I have Saphrone on sensors Colonel Anderson and she has three ships on her and is taking hits."

Anderson directed the remains of the Alanon fleet to converge on Saphrone's coordinates and then gave the command to engage Dragonfly into battle. The crew of the Dragonfly responded like an elite trained force, mostly because they were.

"Saphrone is in trouble sir."

"Push engines beyond regulation, they have to survive." Anderson's orders showed a little emotion but his training was able to keep it check.

The Wake of destruction was easy enough to follow as they passed an astrocab that had its upper half sheered off from misdirected laser fire of the earlier battle. The bottom harnesses still held the legs and lower torsos of Mia and Frankie, a blind date that ended badly.

The electro cabbie could be heard simultaneously quoting the lords prayer in three hundred and fifty two languages. Drives still functioning, the cab would take days to come back to earth; in fact it would take society centuries to overcome what will transpire over the last few days of modern humanity. The astrocab continued to float through traffic that is the City....as on earth as it is in heaven.....

Religions would be written and some might even get it right, but unfortunately wars would be fought over interpretation of these very events. God doesn't always speak the same language.

The Dragonfly moved to support the flag ship, lasers on full and prepared to fire. The race was on to catch up and make sure that Saphrone made it to her destination.

......Saphrone impacted the building at high speed shattering through the seventeenth floor; fortunately it was an electronic maintenance floor that was minimally staffed.

She didn't bother reporting shield strength as it was quickly depleted. She shut down her sensors in a panic that gripped her hard. Simultaneously, Shately shut her eyes, and both rode out the crash anticipating death.

With shields down to five percent the ship and its crew broke through the other side of the building and plummeted towards the edge of the Rez at the hands of the merciless gravity.

Two of the attacking ships ended their chase lodged three quarters through the building; their shields not nearly as effective as Saphrone's.

A pride of cats scattered, their hunt interrupted. The leader, mostly of Manx descent arched and hissed as her pride scattered and abandoned the prey. (An eleven year old girl)

Saphrone saved the girl's life without realizing that the hunt was even on, but this was a day of coincidences. She hit the ground hard and parted the Rez like the red sea. Dust, sparks and debris sprayed as she furrowed through the refuse that had once been a thriving part of the human civilization.

Silence was the most dramatic sense that dominated the ship and it was a full thirty seconds after grinding to a halt before anyone remembered to breath.

Trydent was the first to move and he blew the hatch on Saphrone and exited the craft with Laz rifle in hand. "We have to move, NOW!" he encouraged the rest of his companions by emphasizing the importance of continuing to push forward.

He dropped down in front of the battered ship and scanned the sky for any possible enemy attack. Raising his hand up in the air he flipped the bird in the general direction of any possible pursuing ships. "Fuck you, it will take a lot more than that to kill me you sons of a bitches!" he screamed.

Jasmine had to help Taylor out of his restraints; he was still struggling to get his thoughts back on track.

"I'm alive!" Shately murmured, as the sudden realization that she was alive hit her, she scrambled out of her harness and started throwing supplies and back packs out of the hatch. She had an urgency about her but she was able to pause to help Jasmine help Taylor out of the ship. "Come on sweet cakes this is no time to be slacking off."

Taylor must have been hit by flying debris and was very groggy, he tried to make a snappy comeback but the best he could muster was "I'll show you sweet cakes."

Tomorrow he would find that he was going to have one hell of a head ache and a shiner that would rival a prize fighter. Of course only if he survived until tomorrow, because it seemed death was stalking the troupe.

Ogden sat at the helm trying to sooth his ship, "It's ok little one, we will get you back to the station and before you know it you will be as good as new ." Although he wasn't really sure if he believed it himself.

"Just hold on."

Saphrone did not feel pain but she felt emotion and she was very scared.

"Use your distress beacon." Ogden soothed. "Someone from Alanon will come."

Anderson gave the order, "Open a channel to Saphrone; I want to talk with Commander Oberhause, Now!" He accented the word now with an urgency that everyone on board knew was intentional.

As Ogden was reluctantly preparing to leave his ship, the voice of his boyhood friend and commander of the Dragonfly piped through the communication system of Saphrone.

"Saphrone this is Dragonfly, are you reading me? I figure under the circumstances radio silence has been lifted."

"Bell where the fuck are you? Saphrone is hurt badly and she needs a pickup."

"We are approaching the Iona building, holy shit Ogden did you do that? Three floors are at a steady burn. How bad is she sir?" Bell used the term Sir purely due to the horror of the moment and reverted back to military protocol.

"I'm almost there Saphrone." Bell tried to assure his friend's ship.

"You save her now, make sure she gets back to Alanon, we have to keep going and head out on foot."

"Incoming enemy ship." Announced Corporal Maxwell.

The black hunter moved around the burning building and Trydent spotted it right away. "We've got to go now, and I mean NOW!"

Jasmine had Taylor out of the ship and was moving toward Trydent.

Shately was gathering up all the gear that she had thrown out onto the ground. "Here guys grab a Laz rifle."

The ship banked toward the crash site and scanned the area for life signs, using a heat sensor. Heat signs were everywhere as the pride started to regroup, so it delayed its fire until it could identify the specific target it hunted.

"Relax, you will be OK, you will be at Alanon soon." Ogden's final words to his ship were meant to assure her as he climbed out.

The Dragonfly did not see the second enemy ship as it fell behind the sky scraper. "Corporal Maxwell be ready with targeting, I need a lock as soon as you can.

"Aye aye sir."

"OK on the count of three," Shately Trydent and Jasmine all aimed and fired their Las rifles at the incoming ship.

"One, two, three." Each laser hit the charging enemy ship.

Ogden saw the second ship hiding beside the edge of the building and yelled out a warning. "Look out there's another one, it will see where you are."

The second ship attempted to lock on the three as it sensed the energy pulse from their weapons. They misjudged as they destroyed the ship that was barreling down on them, it would take too long to recharge as the second ship prepared to destroy them where they stood.

Dragonfly pulled up behind the advancing ship, "All armaments locked sir."

"Fire everything we got."

The enemy ship was hit; enough to knock off its targeting as it missed the group on the ground the stray laser fire strafed an empty section of the Rez.

"We won't recharge in time for another shot." Corporal Maxwell continued to keep his leader informed.

Recognizing he had no other choice, Bell gave his next order without hesitation. "What the fuck...Ramming speed..."

In the late twenty-seventh century the electronic media became very convoluted with the evolution of truth laws. Basically all information had to be verified before could it be used in a holocast. This all but eliminated the anonymous source.

This new expectation within the truth laws caused the corporate City to hit a proverbial wall that significantly impeded business and inturn sales dropped, bankruptcies occurred in record numbers. Around the same time security with in big organizations was starting to get extremely beefed up.

What started as paranoid security enhancements to counter espionage turned into small armies that raided and destroyed supply routes. Assassinations and blackmail followed.

A domino effect happened throughout the corporate world and eventually an arms race followed. Corporations gave hostile takeover a new meaning as they quickly grew impatient waiting for legal declaration and so espionage lead to raids which lead to wars.

The wars started small but alliances were made and eventually the top one hundred corporations were dragged into the conflict.

The Oberhauses built space craft so they quickly moved into a position of power, somewhat due to wealth, somewhat due to connections and alliances, but mostly because they always had the cutting edge technology in spacecraft design.

Consortiums fought consortiums and for thirty-five years the planet was ravaged, leaving barely inhabitable areas that came to be known as the Rez.

Some areas still ached from the radiation and the result of the biological weapons used; leaving behind more than death, mutations at all the levels life followed.

As all this came to pass the City continued to grow, ultra skyscrapers started in an area called Japan and quickly spread as income from space technologies soared. Iron was expensive to mine, but the belt between Mars and Jupiter offered an almost unlimited amount of raw ores.

The Oberhause Empire was responsible for the first space mining operation to supply the state of the science shipyard.

The City grew relatively quickly compared to other eras of human history, but that seems to be the nature of the beast. The human animal tends to breed exponentially when given the opportunity. Part of the privilege of being at the top of the food chain.

Hoofin It

I.

Full planetary war was eventually quashed but corporate battles continued and skirmishes to control sales turf were rare but not completely unheard of. For example, When a failed merger between two leading soft drink suppliers turned ugly, chemical warfare solved the problem.

The Oberhauses and five other great family businesses signed a unification pact and C-PUD (City Planetary Unification Department) was formed. This helped establish a planet wide military presence that helped to police the City.

The Cola wars forced Shately's parents to flee for their lives into the heart of the Rez. Fortunately Mrs. Downs got pregnant. It was unplanned and really a dangerous thing to do while hiding even if it was ten years later.

Shately was raised by a tribe in the Rez after her parents were killed when she was around five. In the Rez the human animal had learned to band together in a tribal community. The governing body of the City tried on a couple of occasions, to control and disband the tribes of the Rezidentials but was not successful.

Social engineering, although in reality is probably the only way of controlling societal norms, has never worked. Diverse thinking and dissidence has always gotten in the way of any attempt to control the human population even if the theory behind the social engineering was sound.

The Obsidian ship, sleek and deadly, bore down on their position. As Ogden hit the ground Shately tossed him a Laz rifle.

"We have to move" She urged.

Jasmine half carried Taylor as they hurried to distance themselves from Saphrone and find cover in the ruins of the Rez.

"This doesn't mean we are going steady," She used levity to try and take the focus off Taylor's injuries.

It must have worked because it sparked Taylor's playful side. "Listen sweetheart if you ever had me you would be spoiled for other men."

"If I ever let you have me so would you." Jasmine's banter helped Taylor forget about his pain and move quicker to cover.

Ogden joined Trydent and Shately behind a crumbling concrete wall. "The Dragonfly is coming." The enemy was almost upon them. Trydent set his rifle to overload and tossed it back toward the City, Ogden looked at him like he had lost his mind. "Oh great now we have one less rifle."

The alien craft fired on the rifle giving them a ten second recharge time on its lasers to head deeper into cover. They all pushed hard and scrambled behind another long forgotten wall.

Trydent replied to Ogden's earlier dig through pants of breath. "Any...other....questions?"

"Ok, you get that one."

Shately watched the Dragonfly come racing past the last building between the City and the pocket of Rez and she pointed at the sky. "Here comes the Calvary"

The Dragonfly hit the ship with its lasers which obviously had some effect. The group of three took the opportunity to catch up to Jasmine and Taylor.

"Taylor, can you make it?" Ogden asked his aide.

"Yes, I have probably scrambled my brain and I expect to have an amazing headache but I won't hold you back."

Taylor was able to stand on his own, the cobwebs slowly clearing. "A stim shot will have to do. A Med lab or a Rejuv would be great, but sez-la-vie, point the way."

Jasmine administered a stimulant into Taylor's left shoulder. "Be brave this will only hurt a little." Taylor just smiled and let her do her work.

Shately pointed to the south west. "As the crow flies biodome 313 is that a way, but we should go through Sandstone bluff community. Otherwise we could encounter some unfriendly types from Billingsley point."

"Billingsley is full of a bunch of unfocused bullies; we should be able to push right past them with minimal opposition. But you're from Sandstone aren't you? Sandstone is not really out of the way and we could probably get a warm drink on the way." Looking up at the sky Trydent added "it looks like we may get rained on before this night is over."

"Then let's get at it, how is the stim working Taylor?" Ogden asked.

"I could run a Martian marathon," Taylor tried to stay positive

So that was enough, the five headed into the Rez, right into a deep pocket of the refuse of human kind. It was difficult for Ogden to leave Saphrone so vulnerable but he knew that the Alanon crew would continue to fight to make sure his ship would be returned to the space station.

Dragonfly flew hard and directly at the enemy ship. Anderson had full intension of destroying his ship and himself to protect Saphrone, recognizing the true uniqueness of the ship.

The Dragonfly flew past the remains milliseconds after it finally exploded, it was protected from the heat as it easily dissipated into the shields.

"I want a one minute landing; drop a retrieval net, Corporal Maxwell you're with me. Pack some weapons and move double time.

Dragonfly swooped in low and took a hard landing, Bell Anderson and Corporal Maxwell moved fast as the ship performed a bounce landing and dumped supplies. Both men rolled and ran for cover with lasers on full.

Dragonfly pulled away and banked over the Rez circling to organize a pick up.

"Corporal secure the perimeter." Maxwell's well trained senses scanned the horizon then the main accesses by land.

"All clear sir."

Anderson moved fast to unpack the retrieval gear, which included a net strong enough to hold the weight of a ship. Two more ships arrived and pulled into a defensive position.

The next enemy ship to breach the area would be met with a destructive force and be blown out of the Cityscape.

Anderson and Maxwell moved quickly to attach the retrieval net around the remains of Saphrone, her sleek hull crumpled and twisted. She was now a pile of debris with a very advanced brain.

With the nets secure Anderson climbed inside Saphrone's hull to explain what was happening. "The fleet is here to take you back to Alanon, you're going home."

"How is Ogden?" was the ships reply.

"Fine, don't worry."

"Go after him commander, make sure he is alright, and make him safe."

"Just as soon as I get you on your way, I promise." Bell assured Saphrone.

Corporal Maxwell attached the cables that connected the retrieval net to the capture ring. The whole assembly is attached to a balloon that when filled with hydrogen raises the capture ring to a level so that it can be easily grappled and whatever is in the net is retrieved.

"Ready to inflate sir."

"Gotta go Saphrone, I have to go catch up to Jasmine."

"Thank you Bell, go help my friends, tell them I'm going to be fine." Saphrone was hoping she would be fine but wasn't really sure herself.

The two men watched the capture ring float up to a waiting transport, then turned to pursue their superior officer and his comrades in this whirlwind adventure....

The sun started to set onto the troubled land called the Rez and storm clouds were rolling in. Shately and her small force moved cautiously yet deliberately. Shately took the point and Trydent followed up protecting the rear. Shadows were very long as they danced off the broken dreams and fallen walls.

Heading into the Rez the shadows that were hanging over Shately's heart were beginning to lift, she was going home.

"We have about an hour before we arrive at Sandstone Bluff communal and about three hours from there to the biodome. I'm sure we can get food and rest a bit at the bluff."

Ogden looked over at Shately and commented, "It is good to have you back, young lady."

"It is good to be back, Otto."

Past the fallen buildings, brick and mortar crumbling, lanes of debris that were once roads to a world long forgotten they continued.

Trydent gave the first warning, "I have seen a couple of cats moving with us, if there is one there will quickly be a hundred. Keep your eyes on the Rez as well as the sky.

Jasmine queried, "Are cats as bad as the urban legend makes them out to be?"

"They're even worse. Do you want to stick around and test the theory?"

"Five o'clock," Jasmine yelled, as another ship entered her line of sight against the evening sky.

The five took cover in a building that looked like a rave gone wild, rotting walls covered with graffiti and the windows long ago had lost their transparency.

2.

As quickly as the ship was seen, an explosion followed. The Alanon fleet was looking after them. Destroying the enemy before they could catch up to the fleeing five-some.

Saphrone was being raised up into the sky and Anderson and Maxwell took one last look before heading west in pursuit of there commanding officer and his friends. It was a good thing that the tracks were obvious because neither man was an adept tracker.

"Corporal, take the point, we need to move quickly."

The young man responded with the standard military reply for yes. "Aye aye, sir."

The first half an hour went smoothly but then they lost the trail, "Sorry sir, but I have lost them, what are your orders?"

"We will need to back track."

"HELP!" The cry came from off in the distance.

"Sir did you hear that?"

Anderson stopped with an ear to the wind. "HELP ME!" This time he heard the cry.

Maxwell pointed to the south. "Over there."

Both men were running in the direction of the yelling, as they approached a clearing it became obvious who was calling for assistance.

Anderson's heart sank when he saw a young girl high on an abandon monument of some local dignitary centuries dead and buried.

The young girl was obviously relieved. "How about a little help."

Corporate Maxwell dropped to one knee and aimed his Laz rifle, locking in on the potential enemy.

Anderson addressed the young girl. "Have you seen a group of five people pass by in the last little while?"

Coming off as a bit sarcastic she replied, "Actually no, I have been a bit preoccupied. If you haven't noticed I'm surrounded by cats."

"Give the girl some relief." With this command the young corporal began firing, fur singed, kitties scattered. Several of the beta felines arched and hissed before scurrying of into the shadows and of course hunger would dictate that they would regroup and begin the hunt again...

3.

The troupe continued at a steady pace staying on a westerly path, taking turns on point and helping Taylor. Trydent fell back protecting the flank. Over an hour passed with out any break from the movement. No ships, no demons, no significant cat presence.

"We should be arriving at Sandstone Bluff soon," Shately assured Taylor. It was her turn to assist the aide; he was tiring and needed to rest against a large pile of crumbling brick.

"I'm ok, just need a little breather."

"Yes, maybe we all could, who is up for a water break." Ogden offered.

"Go ahead I will take first watch." Jasmine offered, she didn't trust the Rez, unlike Shately she never had a very high opinion of the scum and reprobate that tended to frequent the streets of the abandon city.

"Wow, what a fucking day!" Trydent laughed, and then took a long swig from the water flask. "What next, a herd of elefates?" He paused and thought about what he had just said. "No I think they were called elephants."

Everyone knew that Trydent was just being Trydent, and he really thought he was funny, but right now nobody felt like laughing.

"Ouch, tough crowd." He tossed Shately the water and asked for her opinion. "I think we are being watched, what do you think?"

With a toss of his head over his right shoulder he directed her attention. "I believe a couple of spotters."

"I have seen at least three signs of spotters so far." Shately accented the 'at least'. "Pretty standard greeting party wouldn't you say?"

Ogden looked at Shately and Trydent, "What are you not telling us?"

"We are entering the Sandstone Bluff community perimeter; the locals will do what they need to protect themselves. Don't worry sometimes that means doing nothing."

"And," Ogden paused, "what does that mean?"

"It means we let them know, that we know they are watching us and that we would like to talk They need to know we are no threat."

Shately walked toward what was once a side street and raised her hands above her head palms forward.

"My name is Shately Downs, I am from the community of Coffey Ridge but I lived with you and yours as a youth. I wish that we be allowed to pass with your blessing."

There were a couple of moments of silence as the spotters deliberated on what to do next. Then a voice came from beyond sight. "All your weapons on the ground, NO exceptions!"

"You heard them, everything down." She slowed the last word down to emphasize the point "Now"

Ogden hated this, he was out of his element and now he was supposed to give up his weapons and leave his ass exposed. But he trusted Shately, so he slowly lowered his Laz Rifle and his side arm to the ground. He removed several small blades that were built into his gear made a mental note and nodded to Shately. "I think that's everything."

Trydent stepped back into the shadows of the darkening evening, not willing to give anybody the upper hand.

One man walked out of the Rez to address the group, he had a bit of a swagger and didn't appear at all apprehensive about approaching the area. He was either very confident of his ability or he knew something that the others did not.

"Shately Downs, in the flesh." He had a lilt of humor in his voice that wasn't quite arrogance. "I have heard of you!"

"I hope it has all been good." Shately engaged the approaching spotter feeling out intention and potential aggression.

"Actually, some of it has been great." He continued to play the game.

Shately suddenly recognized the voice and with a big smile she said. "Holy fuck, Leather, long time no see."

Trydent moved through the shadows circling to get behind of the unsuspecting spotter.

"Shately baby, Are you responsible for this? The holovids have been going insane. What war are you fighting; you have never been much of a joiner."

"Nothing more than the battle for humanity's souls!"

Not taking his friends response seriously, Leather started to laugh. "Shate, you kill me some times."

"Ah Leather, you do me some times."

Leather, trying to get a little information continued to pry. "So, really, the vids talk about fifteen percent of the City burning and in turmoil. Was that you?" Leather was sincere about his inquiry and never saw Trydent slip stealthily behind him.

"Trydent, I have it handled!" Shately half spoke to Trydent and half to let Leather know that Trydent was behind him.

"Trydent?" Leather half cocked his head in the direction of the approaching man. "Really, thee Trydent." Slowly he turned to face his adversary.

"You have me at a disadvantage, I don't know you. Leather was it?" Trydent's mocking tone was a little more obvious than the blade he had palmed and ready.

Leather started to back down, giving Trydent a chance to relax. "Ok, I respect the rep. But you guys have got to understand, this little war of yours has everyone on edge."

"Boys, boys, enough already, let's play nice." Shately stepped between the two men and threw her arms around both.

"Ok, problem solved." Ogden said as he picked up his weapons. He smiled under his breath when he picked up the Laz Rifle. He was happy to have his new toy back in his grasp....

"Ok kid, where do you live?" Anderson asked the young girl as she climbed down from the monument.

"Thanks man, you wouldn't have a spare Laz pistol, would you?" The young girl was not at all shaken over her previous ordeal.

"Slow down kid, let's try and make thirteen before you ask to handle a weapon."

"Yes I admit that I am only twelve years old but can you give a break on the 'Gun permit' who are you my mom?" The lass used her fingers to parenthesize her sarcasm.

"Ok corporal move out, try and back track and pick up their trail again." He turned to the young girl and addressed her.

"If you want to tag along until you feel safe you're welcome, but you will need to be quiet."

"I understand, a little less lip, sooorry siiir." This kid could teach flippant at the university level. She shook her shoulders as in a la-de-da mockery.

"Enough with the banter kid or we will leave you behind." Anderson turned to follow his corporal and as he turned his back on the girl she stuck out her tongue in defiance.

She sighed and let out a, "Yes Sir." And scrambled to keep up and stayed at a good pace not to be left behind.

"My dad is kinda important and if your friends were in this area, let me tell ya, my dad would know." She seemed very proud but had to add the caveat, "Well he isn't my real dad but he raised me mostly."

"Take a breath kid." Maxwell encouraged.

"Did he give permission to speak corporal?" She countered.

"Listen you snotty little…" Anderson cut in recognizing they needed to take a different approach with this child. "Take us to your leader."

"Ya, sure, you guys got any food?"

Corporal Maxwell looked at his leader for permission and after receiving a nod offered the girl an energy ration. "Here Kid, it's not bad, healthier than actual food."

"Thanks"

"You got a name kid?"

"I'm sorry, I thought it was kid," then decided to give it a rest.

"Call me Jewel." She beamed. "And what do I call you guys?"

"I'm Corporal Maxwell and that is Commander Anderson of the Alanon station."

This information seemed to please Jewel. "Alanon station? Wow, what do you fly? Are you guys involved in the war that is going on? I saw these huge black ships! Are they yours?"

"One thing at a time kid." Anderson cut off the girl's rambling. "Can you get us to our friends in a very short time?"

"Ya sure, but remember you said you would call me by my name, well actually just a nickname, my real name is Julie." Jewel stopped long enough to eat part of her energy ration.

"This isn't half bad." She added to herself as she wolfed down the remains of the troop ration.

Both men looked at the young girl impatiently waiting for her to start to focus and lead them in the right direction. Recognizing that they were waiting on her, Jewel huffed as if the weight of the world was resting on her shoulders and pointed into the Rez.

"My community is that away about a two hour hike."

"Let's go Jewel, you lead we will follow." Bell half bowed and swept his hand in a westerly direction that Jewel had earlier pointed out.

The girl took the lead and as proud as a peacock showed the two military men the way to Sandstone Bluff...

"Now let's get a quick drink." Shately tried to change the subject to something that she knew would interest both men.

"How about introductions, Shately darling." Jasmine asked with a smile and a wink. She let Taylor borrow a shoulder for balance.

"No problem, Leather, this is Jasmine and Taylor, the guy packing all the armory is Ogden and of course you have already met Trydent. Guys this is Leather Dove, hair and all."

"Hi, any friend of Shately's.....well has already earned my respect just for that accomplishment alone." Leather explained.

Five became Six.

It was a quick twenty minutes to get to the community hub, even with Taylor still struggling to keep from slowing the group down.

News of the newcomers rippled through the community, whispers of "Trydent with Shately" or "Trydent's Army" even "Shately's return with her thousand warriors to liberate the Rez." The rumors ran rampant through the Sandstone Bluff populace.

People awoke to, "Wake up you're not going to believe this." And after shaking off the cobwebs that come with being woken up before you're ready, the town turned out to get a first hand view of the army that marched through their streets.

Shately had come home.

4.

There was a very large welcoming committee as the six approached the communal fire, all jockeying for position to get a better look at the truth. Nobody knew exactly what was happening but they knew the truth of the matter was something important was going down.

One man who was evidently important met the group as they approached. "Welcome Shately, it has been too long."

His open arms were an invitation for a hug to which Shately honored with a heart felt embrace. "Kieper, it is good to see you again, how is Roxy?"

"Why don't you ask her yourself, she will be here soon."

"We wont be staying long, we need to keep moving and be at biodome 313. It is imperative that we get there before sunrise."

Trydent approached the two as they ended the embrace. "Trydent this is...."

"Kieper you old dawg." Trydent extended his hand to greet the man.

Kieper grasped the outstretched hand with both of his. "Welcome Trydent, what kind of trouble have you gotten our little Shately into?"

"Nothing more than the usual." Trydent replied then introduced the other three. "Kieper, this is Jasmine and the one sporting the beautiful shiner is Taylor, he is the attaché to," he turned to introduce Otto, "Sir Ogden Timothy Oberhause the 5th, but we just call him Otto."

"Quite the place you have here." Ogden shook the community leader's hand.

"Every man has his castle.'

"Yes, I guess we do." Ogden agreed. "I guess we do."

"Join me by the fire and partake in a drink, what shall we drink to? How about friendships, new and old." Kieper offered the flask to Ogden then added. "It is probably not as smooth as what you're used to but it will help warm your soul."

"I hope it is better than the last rot gut you and I polished off." Trydent kidded his old friend. They hadn't crossed paths for nearly ten years but in their younger years they had been known to get into some predicaments. Mostly it was having fun but a few bullies had to be put in their place along the way. Kieper took the power offered to them and Trydent walked away, not wanting the responsibility.

Ogden drew long from the flask then handed it to Jasmine. With an exaggerated shiver, Ogden coughed out. "This isn't bad, I've had worse." Smacking his lips he smiled at Jasmine, who was still hesitant about taking a drink.

"Are you going to take a drink or just stare at it? Because if you're not interested I know I could use a swig of that." Taylor asked Jasmine

Jasmine broke under the peer pressure and swallowed from the flask; she looked happily surprised and took another drink then tossed it to Taylor. "But be careful it may knock you on your delicate little ass."

"You do realize that one of these days, your shots will get my boot up your delicate...little...ass.

Jasmine smiled. "Ah, you're feeling better."

Thanks for the Disciples

How wasn't important, why didn't seem to concern him, but what happened absolutely intrigued him. Geoff regained consciousness. He found himself in a pocket within the collapsed building. At this point he was just happy to be alive. He would worry about his sanity later.

Feeling around in the dark, Geoff found his fish tank; it was intact, upright and full. He wasn't a betting man but he was sure the odds were astronomical. He moved to the left to see if the bureau was still there, as he was sure there was a glow torch in one of the drawers. Again eureka, let there be light and then there was.

Elvis was alive and all six of her disciples and the tank held seventy-five liters of water. Geoff wasn't sure what happened, but he was fairly confident that there would be a rescue attempt, at least within a week and he had enough water to last way beyond then and if he had to the disciples could be replaced. Especially the one with the odd tail fin, he renamed it sushi and giggled for no reason beyond being overwhelmed.

A week, ten days at the outside, it would be easy, Geoff was already rationalizing. He tapped the glass to get Elvis's attention "Hey, boy we will be ok."

In his frantic mind he was starting to believe he could live for ten days trapped in here but he didn't know that he would be there for much longer than ten days, much much longer...

Greeting Party

"Commander, I've spotted two men following us."

Jewel said, "Actually the standard is four but you would never see the fourth, they are there in case of trouble and run for reinforcements. I want to be a spotter after my thirteenth birthday, but mom says not a chance. I am pretty sure I can convince dad though, he usually is a push over and if I have to I can always cry that almost always works."

Anderson gave the young girl a glare that said 'shut up already' and Jewel turned up her nose with a scowl and stopped talking. Well for a little while.

"Can you get their attention, Jewel?" The corporal asked the girl.

"Sure, why didn't you just ask?" She was just a little indignant from being asked to be quiet. "I even know all their names," Then she tested just a smidgen. "I bet if I started screaming they might even shoot you."

"Because that would make you the victim instead of the hero and I think you're hero material." Anderson played on the young girl's vanity. "So lets get this thing happening and introduce us."

Jewel started to yell and wave. "Hey Dudley, these guys are ok, you can come out now. They're headed to Sandstone and hired me as their guide." She turned and smiled at the Alanon soldiers expecting a hero cookie.

The man Jewel referred to as Dudley, cautiously walked out of the shadows of dusk. He knew that his back was covered but it was always dangerous to make contact in the Rez.

"If you are headed to Sandstone Bluff you had better pick up the pace, cats hunt mostly at night and there is a pretty big storm heading this way. What do a couple of military types want with Sandstone Bluff any way?"

Jewel jumped in to explain her version of the latest goings on. "This is General Anderson and Captain Maxwell, so maybe you should just stop being so pushy and take them to my father."

Dudley turned to the young whelp, "you're in enough trouble missy, what in god's name are you doing this far from the Bluff this late at night? Just think what your father is going to do when he hears where we found you. So you just keep your little yap shut." Dudley had dealings with the young girl and was frustrated that he was given the task of baby sitting. (Again)

Bell stepped in to defend the girl. "We need to get to Sandstone. We are looking for our companions, and two of them are from this area, Trydent and Shately. Jewel was kind enough to offer her assistance. This is very important."

The name Trydent caught Dudley's attention; he turned his attention away from Jewel and back to the matter at hand. "Trydent's involved in all this hoopla, I should have known. That rapscallion is going to be the death of us all."

Jewel still miffed over her perceived poor treatment at the hands of the spotter hhmphed and took a shot at him. "Say that to his face, I dare ya."

Dudley ignored her and spoke to Bell. "We can be there in just over an hour at a medium pace."

"Let's go." Anderson nodded and followed the young man. "A faster pace would not hurt my feelings." He urged the spotter.

The pace quickened but no more words were spoken between the two men, no words were necessary, from here on in action was needed.

Jewel on the other hand felt she needed to continue to prattle on and on and on. "It look likes its going to rain pretty hard, those clouds are awfully black and rolling, my dad says their devil clouds, a sign that something bad is coming, I like the rain, I know it doesn't happen very often but I remember the last storm. It was so cool, lightening and water, it smells nice too..."

Jewel wasn't at all ready for what happened next, she would have never thought that the commander would reach across and cuff her lightly across the head. But that is what happened.

Jewel glared at Bell with a stare of daggers and malice, daring him to try it again. She put some distance between herself and the commander and sulked all the way back to Sandstone bluff and never really stopped talking...

Sandstone

I.

It was nice to warm themselves by the fire.

"Who ordered the rain?" Shately bitched after swigging from Kieper's flask. "Haven't we gone through enough without spending the last few hours trudging through the rain?"

The rain started light and the wind was picking up, it was a storm for sure. Lightening started to crash down into the Rez and move toward the group.

Ogden turned to warm his back by the fire, his grin was wide as he saw his old friend and a young corporal approaching. "Anderson who gave you the order to abandon your post and follow us here?" He yelled across the community square.

"That would have been Saphrone sir, just before the retrieval team transported her back to Alanon. She is away and safe."

Ogden gave his friend a hug and whispered into his ear. "Thanks can't be put into words Bell."

Six was now eight.

"Dad, I found these guys and brought them in, I told you I could be a spotter." She was beaming and even let Anderson ruffle up her hair.

"She did very well."

The earlier cuff forgotten, Jewel stood very proud. Hoping that her father would take notice.

"You and I will talk later, you know what I'm alluding too." He addressed his daughter sternly. He then added, "Were you well behaved Julie?" using her given name to stress expectations.

But before she could say a thing Corporal Maxwell remarked. "Like a well trained soldier sir."

Dudley's snicker was contained to his spotting group.

Jewel's smile rivaled any child who though her parent was proud of her.

"We are packed sir, energy rations and extra power cells for the Laz Rifles, just waiting on your orders."

"Why did I ever wait to promote you to commander?"

"Ogden, are you telling me that you waited to promote me, tell me it isn't so." Bell teased Ogden

Trydent tried to refocus, "Thanks Kieper for all your hospitality, but it is time we were moving again."

"We have a long ways to go tonight and I doubt that we have seen the last of the enemy, please be careful Kieper there is evil moving this way." Shately added.

"How much support will you need? You can have fifty armed men, just say the word."

Kieper's offer was tempting but the answer came from all of the original four simultaneously. "No, I don't think that will work."

"Fuuuk!" Ogden, Jasmine, Trydent and Shately echoed like a bunch of stoned hippies from an era long forgotten, then nervously met each others eyes not truly understanding what had just happened.

Taylor was the one that broke up one of those awkward moments of silence. "Ok how many Laz Rifles? How much chow? Please tell me we have more than just Marine rations, let's all say hydrameals shall we."

Taylor's clear mockery brought a lighter mood to all involved. Nevertheless all involved needed to stay alert, personal support of each other was important but getting to the biodome was paramount.

"Look who is feeling better," Ogden laughed.

Taylor's strained curtsey reminded himself that that he felt like he had just lost a fifteen round prize fight. Battered and bruised Taylor would refuse to be coddled or allow himself to slow the group down.

The rain continued to fall increasing beyond the misting of when they first arrived at Sandstone Bluff. Wiping rain out of his eye, Trydent's statement was more of a fact than a suggestion. "We still have a ways to travel tonight and if experience has taught me anything, we still may encounter opposition."

Trydent took a final swig from the flask and grasped Kieper's forearm. "Fight the good fight old man."

"Fight the good fight." Kieper replied.

The crowd had started to dissipate. Although the draw of the legendary Trydent was huge, the rain pushed people back into their homes- theaters, stores, office buildings and other abandon buildings reclaimed and renovated. Over the many decades a strong community had developed, a community that the City had given up on. Not unlike the relative that everyone talks about under their breath at family reunions. But the bottom line was, it was community based on morality and family.

2.

Ogden addressed his men, "Bell I want you on point, and corporal you will take up the rear." He turned to Shately and waited for confirmation, she nodded her approval.

"Eyes alert soldier!" He reminded the young corporal.

"Yes Sir."

Leather spoke up because he was never someone to keep quiet if he thought he could add to the conversation. "Anderson was it? I will join you on point; I have a good idea of how to take us to the biodome."

"Let's go." Trydent looked across at everyone and caught a silent confirmation with nods.

Leather and Anderson started moving through the rain that had steadily increased over the last half an hour.

They were no more than twenty meters away from the fire pit when they heard a scream. An older man stood in front of the crowd with wild staring eyes. "Beware, evil is upon us. Everyone must flee, flee, fleeeee!" he turned and ran back into the night his screams trailing off into the distance.

Ogden caught some movement out of the corner of his eye; he turned to see a beast about one and a half meters tall make a charge toward the community fire. It roared as it slammed into the remaining citizens of Sandstone bluff.

Kieper met the attacker with sword in hand and quickly dispatched the blue demon with two quick strokes. As quickly as the first beast fell, a horde of twenty-five more broke out of the shadows and moved to the assault. Every one scattered, running for their lives. Those who could fight raised arms in defense of their world, those who could not ran away or perished.

The troupe got separated within the confusion of the attack; unable to fight together they separated into the rain and darkness of the Rez.

3.

Feeding the billions was a challenge, especially when farm land in reality did not exist. The family farm fought for its existence but took its last gasping breath in the latter part of the twenty-first century. High tech feed lots and grain consortiums plowed the family farm into the dust.

The demise of the beef industry started in an area called England with the first problem of Bovine Spongiform Encephalopathy. It was the result of feeding cattle, cattle parts. Now I ask you, doesn't that seem wrong to you? It hit quickly and hard, causing the mass slaughter of the majority of cattle.

It settled down for a couple of decades but resurfaced across the word in the last area to be engulfed by the ever expanding City. The panic rippled throughout the world and with the closure of the antiquated political borders to any shipping of beef products, Mad Cow significantly devastated the Alberta beef industry.

The mass production of beef ended in the mid twenty second century. Of course beef is still available but you have to mortgage your children to sit down and enjoy milk fed veal at the Ghetto. (Alanon's finest restaurant.)

As urban legend explains, approximately twenty million people died from France to Alaska because of the Avian flu. This was not the first reported transference of disease from animal to human, but really, a bullet was dodged. It could have been much much worse.

It hit again in the Asian world and was even nicknamed the Hong Kong flu. Canada was devastated in the early twenty first century and the chicken ranch, as it was called tongue in cheek, was becoming an economic nightmare to run.

The scare spread across the world and the chicken dance fell the way of disco.

Humans tried genetically enhanced feed, humans tried to clone sheep, pigs, cattle and eventually in desperation even man.

Even once wild animals suffered from strains of disease, chronic wasting disease decimated the wild deer and elk population of North America.

Society turned to the fish population but of course misuse/poor management of the world's environment interfered with the general feeding of the growing populace. The mercury levels in the fish population climbed with the industrialization of the planet. Salmon farming was an attempt to save the species but instead it created a whole different set of problems.

The steady over fishing of the planet's waterways wasn't enough of a wake up call for the ever growing infestation of humans on this planet.

The GDP was a myth that continued to let the corporate world rape and pillage the environment. The cost of the Exxon Valdez oil tanker spill had a huge impact on the environment but the spill generated significant funds and stimulated the economy as much as a small war. Yet the tears of Mother Earth flowed free.

The attempt to farm the Oceans of Jupiter's moon Europa had a modicum of success, but in twenty six million years the moon Europa would tell a tale of life that would surpass the denizens of earth. Evolution comes...evolution goes.

Some day the human species will be extinct, but don't lose too much sleep because the entire astro projection of all the galaxies, suns and life will eventually burnout. No fanfare, no applause, just good bye.

The Hunt

I.

Ogden fried the first three demons he was able to set the cross hairs of his Laz Rifle's sites on. The surge came hard and Ogden's power cell lost power, he looked around for Bell to get a new cell but could not get to him. The path between the two men was inundated with blue beasts.

"Hey give me your sword!" Ogden got the attention of a young spotter who was standing in a daze unable to wrap his mind around what was happening. The tip of his blade was resting on the ground as he stared at the carnage around him.

At first he did not respond but eventually he was able to shake of the horror induced trance and make eye contact with Ogden. He realized that it was in everyone's best interest to give his weapon to the stranger and it was in his personal best interest to turn and run and try and save his skin.

Taking the blade from the youth, barely old enough to have made it much beyond puberty, Ogden went on the attack. The blade was old and unbalanced but its edge was sharp and he let the unfettered blade taste demon blood as the steel flashed through the rain.

Rushing head long into the brunt of the attack, Ogden battled like a prince, swinging the blade proud, facing evil with eyes open and alert.

Rain poured as he pushed into the attack, removing each demon as it approached, each strike precise, each stroke deadly....

Shately and Trydent slipped into an alley and moved cautiously between the two buildings, back to back they cut down any enemy that showed its ugly little face, laser blast after laser blast. Shately's rifle burned down past it's power cells and she had to switch to a different tactic. Luckily she still carried her trusted blade, not as efficient as a laser but Shately wielded it with a practiced skill that sliced through limb and flesh.

Trydent battled through the weather with an old rusty piece of iron tubing, he had picked up off the street of the alley. He broke skulls, bruised faces and caused trauma beyond what a common autopsy could differentiate.

Together, more demons fell, wave after wave of attacks came to Sandstone Bluff and the two denizens of the Rez fought to defend the community that had opened their arms and embraced their troupe, even after realizing that hell pursued them with a vengeance and killed discriminately.

Trydent stepped past an old brick doorway, eyes scanning, darting back and forth to catch movement. As soon as his eyes passed the structure the beasts rushed the pair.

"Attack" Trydent yelled to Shately and spun the length of pipe upward into the assailant's lower jaw.

The blow shattered teeth and bone, sending its tarnished soul back to hell, back to the cycle of putrid hate. As the beast fell to the ground a second scrambled over its still twitching carcass to try and get at Trydent and Shately.

Shately's blade came down hard and cleaved its way deep into the area between the neck and shoulder on most animals but these where not animals of earth. The lumps that contained eyes and mouths could hardly be described as heads and there were no discernable necks to speak of. The second blow pierced the beast's mouth and even in its death throws it tried to bite back at the blade.

2.

Trydent hit the last demon in the lower leg causing it to howl, he then kicked the blue bastard square in the chest. It fell backward and Shately quickly dispatched the disoriented attacker with three precise slices across the throat. The battle had pushed them deeper into the alley.

"Here come some more." Shately advised as a half a dozen demons moved to intercept the pair.

"Let's move!" Trydent jerked his head down the alley to indicate the direction he thought they should go.

"Already on the way." Shately replied, as the demons moved quickly in pursuit....

Jasmine dropped to one knee and cut down the invading demons as quickly as her cross hairs marked the target. Bodies were littered across the clearing, blood pooled with the rain water making crimson puddles. Her Laz Rifle lost the last of its charge and she spun it around and continued into the fray, bludgeoning skulls with the butt of her rifle.

A demon leapt at her from a first story building, landing square on her back. The sheer force and weight of the creature knocked Jasmine off her feet. The two combatants rolled and Jasmine struggled to dislodge the enemy. After a few fleeting seconds of failure she rolled into the community fire trying to burn the beast.

The beast screamed in pain as it hit the coals, this was enough to loosen its grasp and give her the opportunity to break free from its clutches. A small gash across the cheek, but for the most part, Jasmine was not that worse for wear.

"Get the fuck off me!" She emphasized 'me' with a kick to the creatures face, and then she slammed the heel of her rifle into the demons skull.

Shaking water from her hair and out of her eyes she looked across the rain soaked clearing; she couldn't see any of her companions except Maxwell and Anderson who were making a stand trying to protect the fleeing residents of Sandstone Bluff as they scrambled for the safety of their homes.

To her left she caught the glimpse of the young girl that assisted Ogden's soldiers; she was pinned down with two demons cornering her between a of couple buildings. She had a sword that was a little too large for her and was trying hard to fend off the attack of the beasts. For a young girl not even into puberty, Jewel fought the beasts; she refused to go down with out a fight.

Jasmine ran towards the young girl who, although she fought valiantly, was being pulled down to the ground. Picking up the girl the demons headed into the Rez. Jasmine pursued, picking up the girls weapon she hurried to the girl's aid and after the fleeing demons...

3.

Ogden battled in the rain, swinging the blade that glistened with moisture, both water and blood, before realizing his movement forward had taken him a significant distance from the community fire and more importantly farther away from his companions.

Twenty demons had fallen by Ogden's hand; the blade was not crafted by the elite on Alanon station but in a forge located on the edge of Sandstone Bluff. Recycled metal that had been foraged from dilapidated buildings and even the occasional automobile was found.

Ogden continued to hunt, he moved with stealth and cunning, picking off straggling demons. It was never a question in his mind to run away, that is not how he thought, there was always a way to win the battle.

Standing silently behind a spruce tree, Ogden waited for his next enemy. He had never before seen creatures like those who attacked the bluff, but after the last couple of days nothing surprised him anymore. Ogden was hit with a moment of realization, small shadows scurried around him, he now was being the hunted, and his enemy had momentarily changed.

A crouching female slowly slipped through the long grass, a grey with mottled long hair. She had first noticed Ogden just after the crash into the Rez. The hunt had been interrupted several times this evening but she was a relentless feline and continued to track her prey.

Ogden's focus changed from dispatching stray demons to saving his ass. The steady movement through the shadows told him that he was quickly becoming surrounded.

A short haired marmalade shimmied out on a branch on

the spruce, its tail twitching in anticipation of the kill, tonight he would feed like a king of beasts.

Ogden decided to face his new foe head on. "Here Kitty, Kitty, Kitty." The Oberhause heir called the pride to a challenge. "Here Kitty, Kitty, Kitty." Ogden went on the offensive.

Feinting a rush at the grey he allowed the marmalade to see its opening and leap, Ogden spun and with a quick slice caught the cat in mid flight and it hit the ground in two separate quivering pieces.

Tails twitched and mewling and growling grew like a chorus from Andrew Lloyd Weber. Agitation and hunger drove the stealth out of the hunt. Another cat leaped, Ogden did not see this one coming in time, the rain of the night hampering his vision. Lightening flashed to give him the true scope of his chances, he quickly recognized he was more than surrounded, hundreds of cats moved to take their chance at making him their supper.

"AAW FUUCK," The feline landed square onto Ogden's solar plexus, springing eight feet from a long ago empty window, driven by hunger. Ogden straightened tall as each claw sank into his flesh, four paws, each one digging in, each claw was three centimeters of gripping furry.

Reaching behind him with both hands, "Here, Kitty, Kitty, Kitty!" Ogden grasped the feline with a vice like grip and crushed its neck. It violently squirmed but Sir Otto discarded the fur ball before it was done its final death throws.

Before the cat hit the ground kitty times two came for his head. The first one missed but was able to leave three light gashes above Ogden's eye brow, a light trickle of blood started to ooze from his second wound, his back was steadily bleeding, his shirt already soaked. The second of the two was caught with angered deliberation, it died quickly and Ogden raised it above his head sending notice to the feline hunters that pain was coming and it came with vengeance.

Rain dripped off him, diluted with blood, he screamed and shook his last kill. "Here Kitty, Kitty, Kitty, who's the next to die you furry fuckers."

The pride slipped back into the shadows but the hunt wasn't over. The beasts purred with anticipation the sweet smell of blood was fresh in the air and the taste of man was highly prized.

Ogden slowly rotated back out of the clearing, moving away from the spruce that served as a launching point. He watched the shadows, skipping between both peripherals, trying to track where the next attack would come from.

The next cat to leap was a four year old Siamese/Manx cross. Ogden caught him with a full blade swing that would make the immortal Babe Ruth proud.

Going for its first and last attempt at the hunt, the eight month old Calico made a mediocre attempt, but lost its nerve half way into its execution of a lunge for Ogden's throat. After it fell short Ogden kicked the animal with enough force to kill it before it smacked lifeless against the ancient brick wall.

Not a second longer than Ogden's kick reached its full apex, a black Persian, tangled with dirty hair, sank its fangs into the back of Ogden's calf. Barely escaping a strong stomp from its bipedal food source as it retreated for another attack. Blood was tasted by the old hunter and he was a sly and cunning male of eight years, he would taste blood again.

Not many lived past the age of five in this pride, but if you looked past the missing ear and the scar that traced down its left flank, the Persian continued to hunt true.

An orange Tabby clamped on to Ogden's shoulder, claws and teeth deep into his deltoid and triceps muscles, as Otto spun the next predator landed on top of the Tabby frantically clawing fur and shirt in chorus.

Ogden slammed his shoulder into the crumbling concrete of an abandoned office building dislodging both cats. The felines continued to fight each other, both lost in the heat of the battle.

The black Persian again attacked, it had long ago learned how to count to four and knew that it was best to wait at least four seconds before making its next quick pass. This cat had tasted blood many times and today it would feast again.

The smell of blood excited the pride and a steady attack from a leaping cluster of claws continued, no genetic memory of the household pet lingered with these blood lusting felines.

Alpha cat crouched low and watched the attack; the flick of its tail was in tune with the steady purr. Tonight, these cats did not kill but they would feast none the less.

Ogden finally had enough sense to flee, to turn and cut a path out of the clearing, swinging his blade with life saving determinacy.

More Kitties died and a few got the privilege of snacking on Sir Ogden Timothy Oberhause the 5th, the open space that once stressed business let the light of the moon shine through the clouds and guide Otto toward what had been a small man made lake, yesterday it was dry and would be tonight except for the rain.

Ogden stumbled forward, scrambling toward his destiny and beyond his perception of imagination. The shadows moved and meowed eager for the kill and to taste flesh again, many incensed by the smell of the blood already drawn.

Ogden pushed out of the clearing stumbling over the rubble of a forgotten business; he sensed water was his only chance of surviving the onslaught of claws and fur. He had to get his blood soaked body to the safety of water, his head pounded with each heartbeat that echoed in his mind.

The pride sensed their prey was escaping and made a last passionate charge to try and catch the fleeing victim. Seventy-five, a hundred, a hundred and fifty, the swarm of beasts surged across the expanse, leaping with the agility that only a cat could possess. Like a giant blanket the cats swarmed, gaining ground quickly on Ogden.

Ogden lightheaded due to loss of blood tripped over some concrete rubble, falling he hit his head. If he was disoriented before his world now swam around him. Instinct needed to take over or he would be finished in minutes. Ogden tried to crawl on his hands and knees, the cats continued to close the distance, 15 meters and coming fast.

Forgetting his blade, Ogden scrambled for his life disregarding any pain he felt. Then suddenly a sense of lucidity came over him and he looked at his cowardice with disdain and at that point he decided to go down swinging instead of a cowering death, begging on his knees.

Ogden turned and crawled back toward the sword that he had previously abandoned. His pursuers closed and the end drew near.

As Ogden's hand clamped on the hilt of his broad sword the first cat reached him, just in time to be sliced in half. The light of the moon forced its way through the rain clouds stretching his shadow across the night.

Ogden on his knees was ready to face death, his arrogance rising and his ire inflamed. Ogden's last act of defiance was postponed; the cats started to scatter as if scared by Ogden's meager attempt at pride.

But the cats were not running from him, they recognized a new danger, one that would stop them from making this kill tonight...

4.

Taylor was using the second power cell for his Laz Rifle, he found he had to shut one eye to prevent from seeing double. He was already a little concerned with the numbers of blue bastards, with out seeing twice as many.

He had stayed close to Anderson and Maxwell, recognizing their training and Maxwell also carried the extra power cells. He stayed vigilant and fired sparingly, knowing his aim wasn't true but good enough to fry demons when they got close.

"How are the power cells holding out Corporal?"

"Only five left sir, but it looks like the beasts are thinning out. Am I out of line sir but what the fuck are these things?"

Shaking his head Colonel Anderson had no answers. "Your guess is as good as mine, but all I really know is that they're here to kill with a vengeance and my orders are to support Commander Oberhause."

Leather asked the obvious question. "Speaking of Oberhause, has anyone seen what happened to Shately, Jasmine, Ogden and what's-his-name? If we are supposed to be supporting them we fucked up, don't you think?"

"I saw Ogden heading west on a killing spree, he almost seems to be enjoying himself." Taylor said with a pained grin. "Jasmine was headed in a similar direction, but she was quite a ways behind Ogden. Last I saw of her, she was helping that kid you got to bring you here. As far as Shately and Trydent, I got nothing."

"The goal is still Biodome 313." Anderson yelled to be heard over the rain. "Everyone will work to get there, so that is what we will do." Then he added. "Can you make it Taylor or are you better off in the care of this community?"

"You're not leaving me behind to be treated by the local witch doctor, besides I out rank you." Taylor made is position plain, anyone else got any thing to say?"

"Well, as long as I'm clear on what is happening, you can count me in. Oh by the way, what the fuck is happening?" Leather sarcastically tossed his two cents into the conversation.

"Everything secured here sir; Sandstone Bluff will have to take care of itself." The Corporal stated.

The four headed into the rain and deeper into the Rez. Biodome 313 was west, and in the west the storm was clearing.....

5.

Deeper into the Rez, Trydent and Shately pushed, not at a full run but a steady pace was needed to keep ahead of the pursuing demons.

"You realize that we're going the wrong way." Trydent advised

"Yes, right now we're heading south, we need to head that a way." She pointed to the west with her thumb. Are they still on our ass?" Shately looked back over her shoulder and answered her own question. "They're still coming."

"Lets try and get ahead and then cut through a building." Trydent yelled and pointed at the same time, visibly happy that an old church could be seen just up ahead. It appeared to be an old cathedral and the two rushed to scramble up the stone stairs and hastily into the building, that long ago ceased to hear the praise and songs of the lord.

Trydent hoped that the quick change of direction would throw their pursuers off their trail and maybe he would get a chance to catch his breath.

"Two churches in one week, somebody might think that I have found religion." Shately joked and somewhere on the other side of the world Drol chuckled to himself.

The pews had rotted away centuries ago after chemical warfare had left the area uninhabitable. The pair pushed through the building, over rubble and under archways. It was a pity that they did not have the opportunity to admire the workmanship that went into the construction of the beautiful stone work.

Dropping down at the back of the cathedral they approached an area that would give them the opportunity to rest out of the rain and be concealed.

Peeking around a pile of marble, what looked as if it could have been a statue, Shately could no longer see any sign of pursuit.

"Looks good so far, let's hope that these things only hunt by sight and not by the sense of smell," Shately spoke between breaths.

"Ok we take a short break, head out the back way and hope that we get to the biodome before the others give up on us." Trydent spoke to Shately but didn't expect her to reply.

"That last time I saw anyone, it was Otto and he almost looked like he was enjoying himself, he wielded that Laz rifle like he learned how in the cradle. He was heading due west toward the biodome."

Shately agreed with Trydent, "He will probably be waiting for us sipping on brandy, wondering why the rest of us took so damned long."

After a couple of minutes Shately took another look.

"Still looks clear." A statement as well as a question. "Unless they are waiting for us out side."

"Exploding buildings, an astrocab ride, we crashed a sentient space craft and survived, now six little blue bastards have us cornered in a church, so close to our goal." Trydent was not about to give up just yet.

"Are you ready?" Shately's eyes said more than her words."

"Ya, let's do this." Trydent agreed with a nod.

Picking up their weapons they move to the rear of the structure preparing to exit. One wall had long ago given way to the steady persistence of Mother Nature, it opened up to a vast cemetery. It was over- grown and almost forgotten but, headstones remained in organized rows. Human traffic had long ago recognized the use of the cemeteries as a safety net against hunting cats.

The storm was abating and it had reduced to a light sprinkle.

"Looks clear."

Shately's reply was simple enough. "Then let's get going."

The pair headed west among the graves leaving their demon hunters behind. But now they were seen by a different predator, these ones ancestors purred when it got its belly scratched...

6.

Jasmine ran hard to try and catch up to the struggling Jewel, as she approached one of the demons turned and attacked, the attack was designed to slow her down and let its counterpart escape with the young girl.

Jasmine stayed determined and knew her way around a weapon. All of her martial arts training came into play as she moved to engage her adversary.

A feint to the throat, then a pirouette to bring the girl's blade around and catch the beast across the back of the skull, the swing was full and nearly cleaved the head in half.

She hardly slowed leaving the minor minion of hell twitching, already demoted in the ranks of the netherworld.

Jasmine may have been raised with a silver spoon in her mouth but at this point she was a feral animal bent on killing anything that opposed her. She was still ten meters behind the Sandstone Bluff youth, and Jewel was struggling for her life, doing what she could to make it difficult for the beast to carry her off.

Twisting and punching with every fiber of her being, Jewel struggled to break the iron grip of the stupid blue bastard. As the creature passed close to a low hanging poplar, Jewel wriggled an arm free and was able to grab an overhanging branch. The branch bent under the pressure and swayed against the momentum of the two adversaries. The limb held and the demon's thrust pushed it forward until its feet ran in mid air like Wile E. Coyote. Eventually the spring in the bough snapped them both backwards.

At first Jasmine became confused as she didn't understand what was happening. She didn't slow down as the limb flung the pair, ass over teakettle, back toward her.

The beast was basically designed as a retrieval unit and was not capable of thinking on its feet. Success was based on sheer numbers of the pack; other types of demons were the brains of the operation. This one was running on its version of adrenalin and it had a single minded devotion to fetch and fetch was exactly what it was trying to do.

This animal lacked ego or personal ambition, its destiny was to repeat its existence over and over again until its controlling power either moved its soul up the ladder of evil or conversely down it would become tortured soul lost in the caverns of hell until it earned a chance to move up again.

Jewel and the demon were rolling as Jasmine caught up to them, Jewel was able to roll free but the beast grabbed the girl by the shirt, which extended its arms above the beast's chest exposing its chest.

Jasmine plunged Jewel's blade deep into the breast of the beast with both hands on the hilt. Out of breath she knelt with the blade holding her up as she tried to catch her breath.

"Are you ok?" Jasmine asked between breaths. "Did it hurt you at all?"

"I'm just a peach," Jewel sarcastically walked toward her rescuer, and then she delivered a kick to the head of the already deceased demon. Letting the frustration of the moment and emotions get to her she wound up and kicked the beast again.

"Did I say I was good, what in hell's name is this thing, stupid blue piece of sphagnum?" Then she kicked the beast again. "Oooh." This time she connected with bone...

Doug Heads Out

What is madness? Is it something that occurs in an instance or is it a slow process that slowly and methodically creeps into your mind, beginning with crying in the crib? Was it spanking as a child that led to the ultimate push over the edge or maybe it was getting a detention at school as a teen.

In the 1970's it wasn't unheard of for a teacher to physically throw a student out of the class room. But children recognized the line in the sand and knew that testing the strength of the line could prove dangerous. In grade eight, youth often tested the limits and suffered the consequences of an over-stressed teacher.

So it is the chicken and the egg dilemma, has society always been insane or are individuals who lack the emotional capacity to love a puppy the ones that perpetuate the madness?

Grade seven, the first year of junior high, is relatively scary. So only the really "out-there" kids are bouncing off the walls trying and get attention, which they thrive for and are not getting at home. By the twenty-fourth century, twenty-nine percent of the youth population had the diagnosis of attention deficit hyperactivity disorder.

Grade nine is the leader of junior high, so that leaves the damn grade eights, who will go to the lengths of covering a Kotex pad with ketchup and stick it in their social teachers top drawer just to see him "freak out".

It took a government decree in 2310 to institute control in the classroom; this brought full time armed guards into the classroom, that in turn restored a stronger sense of discipline and structure. This created a nurturing and caring environment and allowed students the freedom to learn in an emotion enriched environment. This all slowed the madness down, but madness in the twenty-eighth century could be put under the condition of rampant.

To put it colloquially, every one is basically fucked up, it is just coming to terms with your degree of fuckedupedness that people seem to struggle with. Under the microscope of social scrutiny, fucked up is probably a polite term when you consider the sheer number of cannibalistic, sociopathic mass murderers that have preyed on society over the centuries. Once again did we create them or are they creating society in they're own image?

Now being stuck under a refrigeration system with rotting food, vomit, your urine and fecal mater can create stress even if you planned it, let alone if your entire world came crashing down on you with no warning or explanation. Doug never truly had a chance; insanity crept into his mind and slammed him with a big stick. He had lost his marbles, slipped his gourd, a couple of apples short of a glass of cider, cuckoo for coco puffs, the light was on but he was no longer home. I think I made my point, Doug was nuts.

Babbling to himself he started to organize his space under the Ultra six, alcohol by his head, waist by his feet, and food on his left. He made a mental note to head to the biodome to pick up some fresh produce as his lettuce wasn't very good. "Biodome, need to go to the biodome, need to go, need to go to the biodome." He almost sang the words. "Gotta go, 'Food as fresh as the City can produce', come shop the biodome."

Doug opened a vacupack of beer and continued to organize and reorganize his little hovel, all the time humming the biodome catch phrase. "Food as fresh as the City can produce!"

Doug had no idea what was happening in the world around him as he babbled, hummed and sang and babbled, hummed and sang. He didn't see the black ships indiscriminately firing at almost any ship that either blocked their pursuit path or may have been part of the Alanon fleet.

An astroglide was knocked out of its flight path during the battle between Alanon and the Obsidian ships. It was hit by a wounded astrocab that had been strafed by laser fire that was meant for Dragonfly. Doug did not know that the astroglide existed, he did not see it spin into the bottom of the building that he was trapped in, he did not know the occupants of the glide nor would he ever even know of their sacrifice.

When the glide slammed into the building it started a slide right below the mound of debris that trapped Doug's Ultra six. The resulting movement loosened the grip on the refrigeration unit and Doug with all his lunacy slipped down toward the street.

In Doug's world he had no idea what was happening, he did know that his neat and tidy cubical was now a mess and he was now upside down with the door closed on top of him. Dazed and confused, Doug opened the fridge and staggered to his feet. If he had all his faculties he would probably be elated but right now Doug could only focus on the biodome.

Straightening is attire and dusting himself off, Doug headed west. Not because he was told, "Go west young man." but because he felt that that was the direction to take him to the biodome. "Food as fresh as the City can produce!" he giggled into the night.

Explosions and fire were rampant around this poor retched soul, he saw none of it, he continued into the maw of destruction as the City burned...

Cemetery

Trident and Shately were also fucked up but they were able to accept it and deal with it.

Row after row of graves, some with intact headstones, some with full mausoleums but many were reduced to rubble by decade after decade of erosion. History was strewn in front of them. Granite and marble markers still stood, aligned in quaint rows with the odd mausoleum standing tall and sleek on the horizon. The manufacturer's lifetime warranty kept giving and giving.

To the East there was copse of willows that had overgrown about an acre of the graves. Nobody as yet had spotted it but the ever ready feline predator started to flick its tail in anticipation. The copse was the refuse to a small pride of cats that had moved to get out of the rain.

Today's breakfast entered their hunting ground, low guttural meows started to spread through the pride. Patience was needed tonight, for by morning they could be satiated.

Stubs of information remained strewn across the field, dates, names, quotes and titles of the dead that had long ago been forgotten, all told a story if you had the time to listen.

Humanity stopped planting their dead in the early twenty-third century as it was a blatant waste of valuable ground and they're was even a huge push to use the land, excavating and cremating the remains of the cemetery, so the corporate city could develop the property.

Society's outcry stood up to the inevitable drive of the industrial evolution of the City until the mid twenty-fourth century. Now the only graveyards were the ones in the Rez and only a few survived. (Ok a poor choice of words.)

As the world moved to reclaim the Rez, the last of the cemeteries was destined to fall and a high rise would grow up in its place.

The planting of the dead may have made sense early in the history of humanity, but how could they have fathomed the extent of the human infestation on the planet earth, a prediction that even eluded the great Nostradamus of the mid sixteenth century.

Burning was far more efficient and offered as much respect for the dead as anything. But the politics of handling the dead will never become a global consensus.

Shately and Trydent moved through the rows, both still hyper vigilant, both watching for demons. Everything appeared to be safe, as there was no sign of their pursuers.

The ground was wet and slippery from the rain that continued at a light drizzle. The worst of the storm had passed and in the west they could start to see the glow of the City through the dissipating clouds.

"Have you ever felt like no matter how hard you push forward, it feels like you're backing up?" Trydent pondered their last few days.

"Ya really, it seems like I've accomplished nothing since I got drunk with Leather..." She paused and then almost made it a question "Last week?"

"What day is it anyway, Trydent?"

He stopped to think, "Actually I'm not sure and I really don't give a flying fuck what day it is, I'm just trying to stay alive."

"Do you ever think about dying?" Shately asked the morose question.

"Sometimes, but I try not to dwell on it, I've seen so much death and I know it's inevitable, but I hope not right now, how about you?"

"I think I will drown, it is a feeling that has been chasing me in my dreams." Shately turned her face up into the rain. "I even like water." She laughed and shook the excess off her head. Shately just happened to glance back after she shook her head like an lion getting water out of its mane.

"Did you see that?" Shately queried

"Did I see what?" Trydent asked.

"Over towards those trees, I think I saw cats."

"Not fucking cats, tell me that you're kidding, Shate please tell me that you're just kidding." Trydent was getting tired of running.

Shately stood still and watched. "Sorry, we got cats. We got to move, to the west." She pointed. Trydent silently agreed as he saw the low flicking movement of cats on the prowl. "I'm right behind you!" he yelled as he tried to catch up to the already sprinting female.

Trydent had rarely had to rely on many people before; he had always been the lone wolf. Right now, at this point in his life he needed to keep up with his companion.

The pride started to move faster, fearing its meal was escaping. A cacophony of mewling could be heard through out the graves as the feline attack force moved in on Trydent and Shately.

Both were experienced in the ways of the Rez and both recognized that they were being herded to the west. Luckily a graveyard was one of the safest places to survive a cat attack.

Shately pointed to a crypt just up ahead to the right. "I think that's our only hope." She yelled.

"You go first, I'll boost you, and then you work like a damn to pull me up after you...Aw fuck" Trydent slipped and slid into a pile of rubble that had once been a modest head stone. Long ago, Hector Gorman's bones were laid to rest, devoted father, loving husband, killed defending a country that no longer existed.

With bruises and scrapes Trydent pushed hard to keep up to his fleet of foot companion, knowing that he was lost without her and she would probably die if she outran him.

Shately grabbed the foot of the crouching gargoyle and swung her right foot high. The swing was short and gravity played its roll in humanity's existence, as Shately hit her apex and remained momentarily still. As she started to fall Trydent reached her and gave her the extra momentum she needed to continue to the top.

Normally Shately expected at least a couple of glasses of wine and a rose to let a man have access to her body, like Trydent's hands groped and grabbed, he tried to grip her knee to allow her to successfully navigate to the roof of the tomb, almost making her fall over the other side.

The first cat leapt, she was the alpha extreme and she used her left front paw to leave a small slash above his brow. A drop of blood splattered onto the ground below. (AB+)

Two cats planted themselves onto the back of Trydent's calves digging into the muscle, just missing the tendon that brought down Achilles.

Shately's first grab had him by the hair and she pulled him hard, her second attempt got his jacket and she assisted his scramble to the top. Trydent shook loose one of the cats that gripped his legs, sending it hissing into the rest, hundreds arching as they circled the mausoleum....

Hell of a Deal

Ha,ha,ha,ha,ha,he,he,eh.....hemph....he,he,he....aaaghh   inhale,
haaagh exhale...hahehahe.....Aw sshhiiiiit.

John Morgan, superstar, faded in and out of existence. He
fought the mental battle out of limbo to gain corporeal form in
a very small cave.

The cave was diminutive, no more than one meter high
and about three quarters of a meter wide. At just over two
meters deep, he barely fit into the grotto. The rock was rough
and several jagged edges jutted here and there, making it next
to impossible to avoid them. The enclosure, John guessed, was
volcanic in origin.

One of the first things he noticed was the heat, it was very
hot, and it was a dry uncomfortable heat that had him sweating
within seconds.

His feet were at the mouth of the enclosure and it took
John a concentrated effort to get turned around so he could
better assess the situation. The confusion and brain fog was
slowly dissipating, John new he was dead and he knew he was in
hell. The one thing John was, was a pragmatist and he learned
quickly to adapt to whatever situation he was in. That is what
made him one of the greatest players in the game of hockey.

Looking out the craggy mouth, he found himself peering
into a chasm that appeared kilometers deep, he wasn't prepared
for the awesome scope and the beauty that spread-out before
him.

He quickly realized that he was on a cliff wall that was
honey combed with thousands of similar openings; some had
heads poking out with wild staring eyes, furtively trying to grasp

the reality of their situation. But for each one reality wasn't concrete or defined, it was horror with a sprinkle of extreme anxiety and a touch of pain to complete the recipe for despair.

Across the chasm was a similar cliff face that was dotted with more caves and more horrified faces. Throughout the network of caves, there were a few residents that were trying to climb down and quite a ways down it looked as if two people were fighting to take proprietorship of one of the lower grottos.

From above John heard a scream, looking up he narrowly averted being clipped by a falling body of a female attempting to climb down from her cell. She could have jumped for all John knew; her frustration level may have overcome her sensibility level. It would take her eighteen attempts before she would finally make it to the bottom unfettered.

John saw the body hit, bounce and lay in a lump at the bottom of the cliff and before his eyes he saw the girl dematerialize and disappear.

The battle that was going one below continued but finally one of the combatants was chucked to the base of the cavern to suffer similar a fate to the female he had watched plummet to her end. Only this time he saw the losing combatant rematerialize in an opening across from him.

This got John to thinking; so if you fell, you ended back were you started. This was valuable information that he stored away for later use.

To gain any ground in hell takes a very strong will, not a misplaced whim to try and end the insanity. It is difficult to wrap your mind around the concept but before you can have success in hell you have to let go of your preconceived ideas of the fundamental principles of life and try and understand the deranged laws of the netherworld.

The last thing that goes through one's mind, before hitting the ground, during a suicide attempt is "Aw shit!" Those who survive, a significant number anyways, find all kinds of reasons to live on the way down after the choice is no longer their option.

John, never being somebody to watch the world go by, started to climb out of the cave. It was about one and a half meters down to the next cave mouth and a rough estimate of six hundred and sixty six caves to transverse before reaching the bottom.

The first one was difficult until he started to get the hang of it. Not every cave had an occupant and the ones that did became quickly defensive huddling in the rear swearing and yelling at the hockey star. It took John a long time before he realized what the commotion was all about, after his fifteenth maneuver down he came a cross a fairly feisty individual that started to kick him as he tried to traverse past.

"Take it easy, you're going to knock me down you dumb butthead." John tried to reason with the occupant.

"You're not going to take this cave, I have worked really hard to move down along the wall," replied the frantic young man. "I am not letting you take my spot."

"I am just passing by. I have no intention of taking your cave, so just relax a little bit. Why would I want to take your spot?" John asked the question hoping to try and get answers to this bizarre situation.

"Don't you get it? One cave per victim, if you take this one I go up again, it's taken me...." The man paused searching for the answer. "...God, too long to remember. I have been at this for eons."

"This place pits everyone against each other, survival of the most aggressive." He continued. "It's rather insidious don't you think?"

"Yes, I see how that would keep everyone mistrusting each other and prevent any chance of cooperation. You have to litterly climb over people to get down. Thanks for the information, good luck." John was sincere with his recognition; this was a very valuable piece of information.

John continued to climb down, passing the lost and dissolute souls, each fallen from grace and now tortured into submission. After what seemed like an eternity John found an empty cell amongst the honeycombs of suffering and was able to rest. Looking down John estimated that he was about a third of the way down. Most of the retched excuses for humanity huddled in the back never getting beyond the fear and terror that is hell.

Below and to the left, he could see a very large beast approaching, a lot larger than the demon that had killed John after the hockey game. This monster was much bigger and lacked the pink luster of the assassin.

Looking up toward the many openings of the molten rock wall the demon starts to laugh, "Is there any among you brave enough to face the pain that I will unleash onto your worthless existence."

There was no response from the terrorized denizens of the grottos.

"I thought not, if any of you worms feel the need for hurt, climb down and face me."

Giving the beast some time to put distance between them, John started down again. As he progressed he did notice that the further down the cliff the bigger the caves, thus giving incentive to climb down and appropriate better accommodations.

Again he was attacked by one of the cave dwellers, this one almost succeeded in knocking him to the rock floor below. John had to physically over power his attacker, trying to reason didn't seem to work and eventually chucked the man to his fate. The poor fool really had no chance of defeating John, after all John was a professional athlete and in peak physical condition. Being dead was not a factor.

At his rate it would take a concerted effort to make it to the ground and once there then what? It took great will from John to stop his mind from swimming into desolation.

John waited and rested in the now empty cave fighting the despair that continued to attempt to overwhelm him. The trip to the floor of the cavern was relatively uneventful and John had no more conflicts with the residents of the individual caves, most huddled in the back unable to face what ever demons haunted their minds.

Hell was not all emotional pain, the demons the patrolled the catacombs knew how to inflict physical pain, but enjoyed the emotional games played with the fallen souls. It took a truly demented demon to patrol the vastness of hell and John would learn this first hand, but for now he would keep a low profile.

John was able to find a cave along the bottom that wasn't occupied, this was much larger than the one he had materialized in and he was able to curl up into a corner and try and rest, he wept like a child not truly knowing why. He continued to feel sensations such as hunger and thirst, the heat was almost unbearable and although he had no source of water he continually wiped sweat from his brow.

Time slipped away and so did reality, John tried to keep a grasp on his senses but found himself losing his ability to hold on to his sanity as he huddled in a corner, for now a haven from the screams and anguish.

Out of his reach of certainty, he thought he could hear someone talking to him and again started to gain his senses back.

Standing at the mouth of his cave a man stood before him and addressed his situation. "Your new here aren't you?" the man asked.

Still a little confused John replied. "Yes, I believe it has only been a of couple weeks, but honestly I really have no idea."

"That's the effect of this place, it all eventually flows together and you lose track of time and truth. If you're already at ground level and it's only been a couple of weeks, it makes you an exceptional person. It takes centuries and sometimes never to climb down from the honeycombs." The stranger explained.

"So, this is hell, isn't it?" John asked the visitor. Not waiting for a reply he added, "How long have you been here?"

"Now that is a question worthy of an answer. I was alive around the time of the First World War, How long ago was that? I have no idea, I do know that I have been wandering the labyrinths for more lifetimes than I care to imagine." He looked pained as he tried to remember his past.

"What happens around here? Is it always like this or does stuff happen?" John questioned the stranger looking for answers to explain the sense of despair that continued to try and devastate him.

"Not much excitement, except the head demon. His name is Belphegor and he is one of the essential demons of the devil himself. You can wander through the caverns as long as you don't cause too much trouble and are willing to take a little punishment."

"What do you mean by a little punishment?" John pushed.

"Belphegor believes he is funny and he takes pleasure in causing pain, he will try and mess with your mind and will try elaborate deception to set you up. He finds this hilarious and afterwards will add a bit of torture just for the fun of it."

"This place sounds charming." John's sarcasm seemed to help him cope with the insanity of his predicament.

"It can become tolerable after a time, but you will have to learn to roll with the punches and sometimes some well placed grovelling can avoid a session of torture, just try and stay under the radar. Belphegor can sense any challenge, so learn to back down." The warning was very real but John L. Morgan would end up learning some of these lessons the hard way.

"If you have been here since the First World War, I would say you have been here for over nine centuries."

The stranger laughed quietly to himself as he recognized the sheer enormity of John's estimation. But the levity was quickly lost as he turned back to the main cavern. "Belphegor is coming, take heed in what I have told you, hell doesn't have any heroes."

The stranger moved quickly to get out of the way of the approaching demon; he had learned centuries ago that sometimes it was better to run away.

John moved to the back of his cave trying to look inconspicuous, he huddled down in the corner hoping the demon would pass him by. But today luck was not on John's side, today was a day John would try and forget.

Leaning down to look inside the cave Belphegor spoke to John. "Mr. Morgan you are looking rather pensive today. What is the matter? You don't like the accommodation?"

The stranger was right Belphegor did consider himself funny and the demon laughed as if he had made the best joke in years.

John could feel the demon in his mind, probing, testing, and looking for weakness. "Get out of my head, your invasion into my mind is unprovoked." John's instincts had him challenging the demon before his rational thought over rode his need to stand up to a challenge.

"Unprovoked" The demon's laughter roared, mocking John. "You come into my home and tell me my actions are unprovoked, do not condescend to me Star." His disdainful use of calling John a star belittled his celebrity sports status back in the City.

John, not used to being pushed around, stood up out the corner of his cave and faced the demon. "Your kind can not hurt me any more, I am already dead, a gift from your brethren."

"I have not begun to hurt you yet, Star. Do you think thumper gave you a headache, what I will do to you will make your past pain look like nothing." The demon was just stating facts, bragging was just the way it appeared.

The demon's appearance showed little emotion, its black eyes were like large pools of oil. They stared with out looking from the sockets that were deep into the horned skull. The beast was dark grey with pustules that oozed puss and blood. Belphegor was a demon of ancient and evil origin.

"I will rip you apart muscle by muscle, until you're the main show in an anatomy class, hanging there with everything exposed. Believe it or not I have limited combinations of how I can torture you. Right now I am in my third cycle of possible combinations." The fiend gloated.

"I think I will start with paper cuts and work up to finishing nails tapped into your tibia and fibula. My record is nine hundred and thirty six nails per bone. Would you like me to try and break my record, Star?

The demon wasn't just boasting, John felt pain, pain like he had never felt before. His screams echoed through out the caverns of hell. Giving reminders to the other denizens of the catacombs that pride is a sin to be reckoned with and sometimes it is better to humble yourself and grovel like the stranger suggested....

Race to the Biodome
I.

Taylor started to move west, "Our goal is still Biodome 313." He continued to limp along but never hesitated to take the lead.

"Maxwell and Leather you watch the rear." Anderson gave the order with out any preconceived notion that Leather was his insubordinate.

Leather wasn't much for taking orders from strangers but he put his pride in the backseat for now and took up the watch from the back. "Watch for cats, they're as big a threat as anything right now." He advised loudly to be heard over the rain.

The area was strewn with the dead, remarkably very few of the residents of Sandstone Bluff had fallen, mostly it was the demons that laid in humps on the ground. The shaken community worked around the carcasses tending their wounded and their dead.

The four men moved on, they headed west to try and catch up to the rest of their troupe before it was too late.

Anderson caught up to Taylor, "Are you going to be able to keep up this pace?"

"I'm feeling pretty good." Taylor gulped. "Try and keep up." His wink was lost in the night and the rain but his playful attitude was returning.

The four trudged on leaving the confusion and death of Sandstone behind them. Taylor pushed him-self determined to catch his boss and he was becoming accustomed to the young Miss Jasmine. As they headed west into the mist the night continued. Nothing seemed to get in their way, no cats, no demons of any sort, and no assholes with the idea of taking anything of value from unsuspecting travelers.

The Rez was a harsh place to live unless you belonged to a community, or you had the ability to kick proverbial ass; you tended not to live very long. There were old people that existed in the Rez but none that lived on their own.

Both Leather and Maxwell were good soldiers, although they were from very different worlds they both believed in doing the right things for the right reasons. Given the right circumstances they could fight their way out of a corner.

Maxwell, was a young man from a space station that produced space ships with cutting edge technology, capable of reaching the farthest edge of our solar system had hardly even been to the City. Leather, was a man of similar age, who rose through the ranks in a world that technology had all but abandoned.

War ravaged the land and left it almost uninhabitable for centuries, an apocalyptic horror that dominated corporate greed. Neither man truly understood their part in the story but both believed in somebody and were willing to follow them into hell.

"Hey, do you serve on a starship?" Leather liked small talk it helped him relax.

Maxwell was a little uncomfortable with Leather but yelled back, "It's a star base not a ship. But yes I get to go on missions on a ship. It is called the Dragonfly."

"Cool, do you get to fly it?" Leather pressed.

"I'm...part of the flight crew." Maxwell's pause was showing his obvious inability to chit chat during a mission. "But no I am not a pilot."

"Hey now that's really cool, I have been in an astrocab a couple of times when I was sent to deliver special packages or go on a meeting." Leather seemed sincerely interested in what the young Corporal had to say.

Relaxing a bit Maxwell added. "The Dragonfly is an atmosphere class battle cruiser." Almost confidently he continued. "I have been on fifteen missions."

"Corporal, can the chatter." Anderson gave the order.
"Yes Sir."

"Come on, lighten up man." Leather went to the Corporal's defense. "I like to talk it helps me keep calm."

"I want the Corporal focused."

"Don't fret boss man; I will make sure our asses are covered." Not getting a response from the Colonel, he pushed a little farther. "Trust me, this is my world."

Anderson ignored Leather and repeated his earlier order. "Corporal Maxwell, you will cease and desist all unnecessary communication."

"YES, Sir." The corporal saluted.

Leather looked at Maxwell with a 'are you just going to take that?' look, not understanding the military hierarchy. He turned toward the Colonel and gave a limp wrested mock salute; which put a smile on Maxwell's face.

Leather knew that he would struggle with the idea of taking orders and felt sorry for his new companion. Of course there was discipline within the communities of the City but it wasn't as demanding as the military that the Alanon station ruled with.

Both men would have to learn to accept each other's way of doing things, but for now they simultaneously thought. "I can't believe I have to work with that asshole."

2.

The rain had pretty much ceased to fall from the sky, scattered droplets occasionally hit Jasmine and Jewel but no longer was there a constant wiping of rain from their eyes.

The Rez seemed to have relaxed and calmed while the local denizens lay patiently waiting for a break in the weather. Some were hoping to get in a hunt before the dawn began to light up the abandoned streets.

Raptors started to stir, knowing that the nocturnal beasts would have a small window of opportunity to forage and hunt.

Some would ignore the usual caution and push past the sensible routine because hunger is one of the greatest driving forces for all animals. Humans no longer included, as the concept of an empty belly was made extinct centuries before.

Biodomes and food factories feed the tens of billions of people in the City. Flavored proteins, carbohydrates, fats, starches, sugars all laced with vitamins and minerals flow out of the food factories. Three corporations control eighty-eight percent of the production and twenty-six micro factories produce the remaining meager twelve percent. The food industry produce bar after bar after bar, every flavor under the sun and every combination of ingredients depending on taste and fad.

Consumption of bar proteins was phenomenal given the swarming populace of the twenty-eighth century and it was a major business within the corporate world.

Humanity has planned for every eating style; low carbohydrate, carbohydrate loading, extra protein, fat free, caffeine reduced or tripled depending on one's needs, if one wants it, and it is available in any combination your neurotic mind can fathom. Pick a plan any plan. Fast packed nutrition charged with vitamins and minerals.

Of course anyone with reasonable credit could purchase fresh produce and the balcony gardens thrived on the three hundred and fiftieth floor. The high apartments were in the clouds and the mist gave a similar affect to the tropical rain forests of a world gone by, allowing for production of fresh food. A fresh turnip or Brussels sprouts sold for premium credits but there was a barter system developed at some of the local markets.

Jewel had never tasted anything as exotic as brussel-sprouts, carrots and turnips were staples within the Rez and a meal that wasn't pasta had to be potatoes. Mashed, boiled and of course fried, what ever your preference.

Pay for a fresh strawberry at any restaurant in the City and the waiter smiles as his tip goes up significantly.

Biodomes were credit factories, not just for the fresh produce but also for the tourism factor. Citizens planned vacations around the vast gardens that began with prairies and vegetables and ended in pine hugging trails along mountain sides. A series of trails crisscrossed throughout the domes ranging from green circles to black diamonds as difficulty increased with elevation and there were controlled camping experiences for the people with the credits.

Jasmine's first experience in the Biodomes was with her grade six camp, she let a young boy neck with her under a trailer and even allowed him to touch her breast. Ok, actually they were just nubbins, boobettes, as they were very responsive to the touch but barely at the training bra stage. He ended up following her around for the entire camping experience and later in life lost his head in an astrocab accident not more than five hours ago.

Jasmine stayed close to the young girl, after almost loosing Jewel to those blue assholes earlier, she didn't want to take any chances.

"So what is the name of your ship?" Jewel started to question Jasmine.

"I don't have a spaceship. I actually fly an astroglide, a single seater Vette." Jasmine told the young girl with obvious pride.

"You own a Vette?" Jewel's facial expression said everything. "Can we go look at it or even go for a spin?"

Those simple words hit Jasmine; she had forgotten that her Vette was still parked outside the graduation facility; hopefully it hadn't been tagged and towed yet. The police were still probably investigating the attack and the media were having a feeding frenzy with the last few days' events. Death toll had probably passed the six hundred thousand mark at least.

Not really that significant when you put it in perspective, hardly one percent of the entire City's total population. But it was just starting and before it was over fifty times that number would be dead.

"I tell you what, if you can help me get to the biodome, I promise to take you for a ride in my Vette." Jasmine dangled a carrot in front of the girl hoping to motivate her.

"That's not that far away, where's your glide moored anyway?" Jewel was anything but bashful. She was determined to get a ride.

"Not anywhere even close." Then Jasmine reflected to herself 'I hope she is alright.' Not loud enough for Jewel to hear.

"What?"

"Nothing she assured the young girl"

"You know if you're good and really sneaky, carrots are easy to garden raid, but don't get caught or you could become a *Ward Of The System*." She emphasized the last bit with a practiced ease as it was the standard threat told to all youth of the Rez.

All kids raised in the Rez were taught how to avoid "social services", because very few learn how to adapt to the social expectations of the City. Very few residents of the Rez would be able to adapt to the speed and rigors that go with living in the City. Even after extensive behavior modification training most youth that are apprehended for their own good fail miserably, not fitting in to the energy bar eating machine that is the advanced human existence.

"I snagged a cabbage once." Jewel bragged. "Not something that is easy to eat and it sure doesn't sit well with the fart machine. Phew, what a stink." She waved her hand behind her butt and laughed thinking fart humor was the greatest.

Jewel drifted off with the memory and suddenly added, "And if I took it home and my mother found out she would have had a fit." She put her hands on her hips and used a sarcastic high pitched voice to imitate her mother. "How many times have I told you to stay away from the Biodomes, Julie?"

"My mother calls me by my given name, I think she is the only one even Pops calls me Jewel. I guess it's OK but I like Jewel it makes me sound precious."

To Jasmine it was like Jewel never shut up, question after question and frequently not bothering to hear any answers, just endless prattle. Jasmine thought to herself; 'was I ever this yappy?' She tried changing the subject. "I tell you what, you get me to the Biodome and next week, if this is all over, I will take you for a ride in my Vette."

This seemed to refocus Jewel. "OK, follow me." As she headed west the rain slowed to a light drizzle.

This went on for nearly an hour until she fell silent; which put Jasmine on alert. "What is it Julie?" using her given name to set the importance of the question.

"Cats!" Jewel hissed.

"How close?"

"Just over there." She pointed. "Not too bad but we should run for a block or two and try and lose them." Jewel seemed to stand prouder as she felt important being relied on by an adult, an adult that flew a Corvette.

"Let's boogie." Jasmine started a fairly fast pace.

Jewel ran hard but made sure that Jasmine could keep up the pace, after a couple of blocks she started to slow down. "I think we should cut through a building now that we have left them behind. Cats will follow the smell and surround the building thinking they have us trapped. This one has a second story connector to that building and we can cross and sneak out undetected."

Jewel had no idea that the connector was once called a breezeway and joined two sections of a mall, for that matter she didn't even know what a mall was. Inside the shell of the old building it took a little time to find the way to the second story, finally an old escalator still extended upwards. It was a four foot jump to the next floor.

"Be careful Jewel the floor where you're going to land might not be safe." Jasmine cautioned the impetuous lass.

"Be careful the floor might not be safe." Jewel mocked back, her tone similar to the one when she imitated her mother.

"Jewel!" Jasmine tried to stress the importance of caution and hoped she could quell the rising attitude.

Jewel rolled her eyes and easily made the leap. "Throw me my blade." Jewel tried to get her weapon back.

"Move aside." Jasmine made the jump and Jewel yelled 'Baah' as she landed trying to be funny.

The two continued along the second floor that could have been ladies' wear in another time and looked for the causeway.

Most of the flooring in the walkway had long ago rotted away, lost to the elements. A couple metal girders still ran across to the other building. Jewel started across without hesitating.

"Be careful, please." Jasmine mothered.

Jewel's face said it all when she stopped and looked at her, very plainly her entire body said 'I am not a little kid and you're not my mother!'

She traversed the girder quickly, Jasmine started to realize that this was the world the young woman grew up in and was more in her element than she herself was.

Jasmine made it across but lacked the ease that her companion had used. She made a mental note to try and relax and let Jewel guide her in her own way.

"Over here." Julie gestured with her arm. What was once an emergency exit was now a gaping whole in the side of the building, but the iron stairs leading to the ground were still intact. Rusted and filthy but would probably hold their weight.

Looking out into the dawn, Jasmine could see a clearing to the north and she quickly recognized danger. One of the giant pink demons that accosted her at her grad was standing with its back to their position.

"Get down Jewel." She grabbed the girl by the shoulders and pulled her down out of view. "Shit will this ever end?" she asked no one in particular.

"What!" Jewel tried to shake free of the grip, but was not even close to breaking the vise-like grip of the frightened Jasmine.

"Jewel, Please! More demons." She rasped in her ear with obvious urgency. Jewel immediately stopped resisting and the two crouched low in an embrace that lingered for emotional strength.

Slowly Jasmine crept her way along to the edge of the opening; she peered carefully around the concrete hole and toward the clearing. Yes, she was right; it was a demon similar to the one at the grad party and the ones stalking her group.

As her eyes adjusted she realized the demon was not alone. A human stood before it with blade in hand. The two were squared and prepared for battle. The human began to waver and dropped to one knee, after a couple of seconds he was again able to stand and stepped toward the demon as if a challenge was being made.

A sudden realization hit Jasmine like a baseball bat, it was Ogden and he was hurt! Without thinking she stepped out from behind her cover and stood in full view of the clearing.

"OGDEN!" She screamed as loud as she could. She saw the tall man glance in the direction of her second story lookout, and then he moved at the demon with a swinging blade, he went into battle with the force of the name Oberhause...

3.

Trydent and Shately still continued to breathe with a labored effort as their feline foe circled and surrounded the mausoleum, many trying to leap up but could not get any grip on the weather worn marble.

"Come and get me you sonsofabitches!" Trydent yelled as he held one of the dead cats that had clawed a hold of the back of his leg. He shook the dead animal taunting his brethren that were accumulating around the grave.

"Your leg is bleeding." Shately mentioned, a little worried for her companion.

Trydent hardly heard her as he persisted to yell and swear at the cats. He glanced over at her, seeing that she was looking at him with concern. "What?"

"Your leg is bleeding."

Trydent dropped the cat into the mewling throng and took a look at the back of his leg; it was torn up fairly well with six or seven gashes. "That's just great, now I have to worry about infection."

He wiped the blood away from his leg with his hand, it wasn't bad but he hit the nail on the head with his fear of infection.

"Well, this is a pickle." Shately looked down to view the pride. The clouds were clearing and dawn was swiftly approaching. "I guess we might as well sit down for a bit." Shately suggested.

"I wish I had one of those fancy-dancy rifles of Drol's." Trydent pretended to shoot cats along the graves, making firing noises as he went.

Exhausted the two sat on the roof of the mausoleum. The roof wasn't flat but was slightly rounded, there wasn't any concern that they would slip off the edge. This was one of their more insignificant dangers to concern them.

"So is this night ever going to end?" Shately asked while shaking her head.

End, what a concept, a phrase that bewildered him as he still wasn't sure when it all started. He could barely remember the night he met Drol. That moment caused his life to multiply by experience to the fourth power. The things that had just happened were of no consequence, sleep and a regular meal seemed like a lifetime ago.

"Sit down." With an uncharacteristic sigh. "Ya, I guess we might as well sit down for a bit." Finally figuring out what Jasmine had earlier said.

"What do you think, about an hour and a half until sunrise?" Shately's question brought Trydent back to the living.

Back to back they waited for the early dawn attack of the Owls, raptors of the night that learned to hunt at dusk. Mostly because its feline prey was usually wrapped up in the hunt and didn't finish until sunrise, a feeding frenzy of hierarchal standards.

The pride's alpha ate first but often when a big prize was brought down a new alpha was born. The weak, meek, and sick ate last if there was any left. So when the raptors started to fly, rarely was the alpha anywhere close to the kill. Even as cats were being taken, hunger drove their feline sisters to continue to feed.

Ask any four star restaurant and they will tell you they relied on hunger as the number one driving force in all species to keep the credits rolling in.

"So I've spent some time with you over the last couple of days but don't really know Shately the person, so tell me your story." Trydent asked.

"My story?" Shately was almost surprised at the question. "I'm a Rez brat just like you, my parents were refugees from the corporate insanity but Sandstone Bluff took them in without asking a lot of questions.

"You know I have been to Sandstone on several occasions for various reasons, do you remember me passing through?"

Shately pushed against Trydent her back pressed up against his. He had to brace his feet to keep from sliding forward. "Careful now, you don't want to knock me off and turn me into cat food."

Ignoring his comment she continued, responding to his inquiry. "I was around; once I brought you a basket of fruit when Kieper asked me and you didn't give me a second glance."

Completely bluffing Trydent lied, "I saw you but it is not polite to ogle the leader of the community's serving wench."

"You're so full of shit Trydent."

"We are all full of shit," he reminded her. "There is no other way of existing, there is too much to cope with."

"So what's it all about, this whole existence thing?" Shately went a little serious. "I mean really, when the day is done why do we keep plugging away at the insanity?"

Stretching his leg trying to lose some of the stiffness from the cat wounds and giving him a chance to think about his answer, Trydent stalled. Then he sighed. "Don't ask me any tough questions, I'm just the dumb fuck that let a cat get a hold and rip up my leg." Pausing again before continuing. "I really have no explanations. Since Drol caught me at the top of the stairs I have been running on instinct."

"Only since then?" Shately's push relaxed somewhat, "I started running on instinct when my father was brought in on a stretcher and the remains of my mother were never found.

There is always somebody or something preying on the weak and the innocent."

Almost on cue an owl swooped down low and grabbed its kitty prey giving Shately and Trydent a chance to become circumspect and think on the last few hours of their lives and wonder where the next few days would take them.

4.

The three soldiers moved through the Rez unhindered, keeping a pace that Taylor could maintain.

"Any signs of the others?" Anderson called to Leather, who was several meters away covering the rear. Leather kept to the shadows keeping hidden.

"Nothing, no signs of anything, not even an odd stray." Leather ran to catch up to the waiting Colonel. "This is really a quiet area of the Rez" he added. "We are less than an hour's steady walk from the Biodome and there is usually a lot more activity this close to the edge of the City."

Anderson listened to his Rez raised companion hoping to hear something he could use.

"What do you think, continue to the Biodome and if everyone isn't there do trace backs into the Rez and look for our people?"

Colonel Anderson was surprised at Leather's plan and literally did a double take. He wasn't expecting for the weird looking guy from Sandstone Bluff to have any sense of discipline.

It was obvious enough to offend Leather. "Listen, I am not just a pretty face." He hesitated, and then let his smart-alecky attitude surface again. "I'm also hung like a horse."

His smile said more than his words and very unexpectedly Bell started to laugh. "Of course you're not stupid, you're just undisciplined. I'm sorry it won't be a problem again."

"Now you're just being condescending." Leather got his shackles up and stood a little straighter with out realizing it he was trying to intimidate Anderson.

"No, no please, I am sorry. No disrespect intended. I just didn't know your capabilities." Bell stuck out his hand giving Leather a chance to shake it.

"Welcome to the Rez Colonel Anderson, remember what they say about assumptions." Leather hesitated looking for something witty to say. He then smiled "they're not always accurate." He laughed as if this was the funniest thing he could have said; thinking the lack of the joke was somehow funnier than something actually amusing. (Leather was twisted.)

"Don't assume again." Leather caught Bell's eyes as an equal, and then he tilted his head as if to say 'I will take over if you fuck up once...I mean just once.' He then grabbed the other mans hand in a handshake to say all was good.

"Let's move." Bell turned and headed west shaking the excess water from his hair and went to find his childhood friend.

The four continued down the rubble strewn street under the almost dissipated rain. Taking turns Anderson, Maxwell and Leatherdove rotated from rear to second to lead, circling Taylor as he wasn't quite one hundred percent, his injuries catching up to him.

"How you doing?" Bell spoke in an encouraging tone, as he passed by Taylor.

"Trying not to slow us down too much." Taylor honestly answered picking up his pace as he spoke. It was evident that Taylor was hurting but at this time it had to be endured or Taylor would have to be left behind.

Forty-five minutes and fifteen uneventful blocks later the glow of the biodome took over the sky. Biodomes could be seen from space during the dark period of the planet's rotation. The four pushed on and as they approached the final few blocks the sky had cleared and the City shone with attitude. The early morning light danced off the droplets of the rare rainfall and fires that were burning throughout the City cast an additional light. It could be considered beautiful if one overlooked the cost of the luminosity and the death that came with it.

People started to appear, not just from the Rez but civilians from the City looking for a safe haven away from the growing war. Of course there were also several City dwellers that liked to venture into the Rez for a few blocks just for thrills and kicks.

Each man concealed his weapon; there was no reason to scare the crowd anymore than was already occurring, but all stayed diligent, watching closely as the crowd grew. Even at this hour the Biodomes bustled with tourism but the look on the faces was one of worry and concern, there were no tourists today.

"Corporal, you stay in the street and make your self visible, Taylor and I are going into the Dome to see if we can find the others. You allow any of our troops to find you. Set up a line of claymores just in case some unfriendlies decide to crash the party."

"Yes Sir." Maxwell accepted the command.

"I will stay in the streets and down a block. For the most part I will stay hidden and give you fair warning if these party crashers of yours show up. Hopefully I will find any stragglers pulling up the rear." Leather told the group his plan.

"Works for me," Anderson agreed."

"Be careful," Taylor spoke to everyone, he was appreciative that not one of them had complained that he was slowing them down and they all showed support.

Taylor and Bell turned and pushed through the crowd heading into Biodome 313. The mass of people was growing and it was difficult to get through as everyone else was determined to get off of the City's streets.

Leather slipped back into the early dawn's shadows and used the darkness as cover to blend into the morning. It was better if the enemy didn't see him both for surprise and to give fair warning of attack to the team. He really didn't care that much about the gathering multitudes, when the time came he would cut down his enemy and if that caused a panic he would use it to his advantage. So what if a few indifferent bodies got in the way...

5.

A steady flow of raptors started to sweep low grabbing cats on the fringe of the pride, Each feline on the first sweep went to the chicks that were waiting impatiently, squawking with hunger.

Every child in the Rez was taught how to draw a hungry pride of pussies into a cemetery and wait for dawn. A social gathering on top of the safest mausoleums was akin to a picnic in the mid-twentieth century.

Trydent and Shately waited for the dawn as taught within the family of the Rez. But it was Shately who stirred first, this was not the first cemetery she had slept in. She took a second to shake the evening's moisture, water continued to stretch her comfort zone and she was starting to struggle with the reality of her dreams.

"What ya thinking?" Trydent asked.

"You're awake?" Shately was surprised to hear his voice.

"Ya, I didn't really sleep." Trydent stretched. "Never really enjoyed nights in the cemetery."

"I don't know, there were some warm summer nights when the entire community sang songs and made an evening of waiting for the raptors." Shately's fondness for her childhood memories shone through her description.

Cats started to scatter as shadows started to stretch across the headstones grabbing graves with every angle the sun offered. Long fingers searched the marble looking for answers and remembering family. There were a lot of fathers, husbands, grandfathers etched for eternity but long forgotten. The life cycle continues Born, Eat, Breed, and Die.

Seventy-five percent of the felines had realized it was time to flee after ten minutes since the first raptor struck. The remaining twenty-five either knew how to grab a bite of flesh and still get to the shadows before being taloned or were so incensed with hunger they refused to escape. But as it is with the cycle of life, the raptors fed and the felines fled and eventually it was time for the two to move on again.

Shately stood up on the marble burial vault stretching her cold and wet body.

"Give me a hand up." Trydent asked. "My legs are really starting to stiffen up pretty bad."

With a little feigned effort to try and get a little sympathy and Shately's assistance Trydent got to an upright stance. "Ok, now I have to get down."

"I could give you a push." Shately teased, starting to feel very much at ease with her Rez counter part.

After a couple of deep knee bends and calf stretches to loosen up, he jumped back down to earth. He landed with a wince but had been much worse off in his life. Shately landed lightly beside him and they headed west one more time.

"Do you think they waited for us?" Trydent thought out loud. "Of course they did, you the little golden girl with the destiny."

Shately scowled, "I just hope everyone is still alive." Not liking the idea of having to be relied on. She had started to become quite fond of these people in the short time she had come to know them.

Trydent headed out of the cemetery pushing hard in a misguided masculine attempt to prove to Shately he was fine. (Trydent always had to prove himself; a boy growing up in the Rez learns testosterone.)

Together they would make it to the biodome; through hell or high water their destiny was already written. For now they needed to catch up to their comrades and it was always more difficult to gain access to the biodome during shift exchange.

Trydent, although he tried, could not hide his limp. He winced with every step and with movement his leg had started to bleed once again.

Shately extended her arm and pointed to the horizon, as they came around a corner that opened up their view of the sky line. Where the Rez and the City met lights danced as the City was ablaze and the glow was enhanced by the occasional blast of light.

"Looks like the world is falling apart." Trydent shook his head in disbelief. The whole fiasco was spinning out of control. Fueled by mistrust and greed.

"If I did not know what was really going on, all this carnage that has the City burning is almost beautiful. The colors are dancing against the sky." Shately had to gulp back her emotion and wouldn't look at Trydent in fear that he would view her as weak for showing tears.

"I didn't realize you were such a sentimental poet."

Shately ignored him for a few minutes choosing to stay quiet and get back the control that she found slipping away.

"I hope this is all worth it." Trydent finally broke the silence, recognizing Shately needed a chance to save face. "Because for the life of me, I don't know why anyone needs anything from me."

They walked toward the glow in the sky, keeping a quick pace that would take them to the biodome. The next twenty blocks were covered with a needed haste under a veil of silence. Both had grown up in the Rez but didn't feel at all in their element, it was the war that was dragging them into its maw that was causing their distress.

Keeping an eye on the shadows Shately stayed vigilant, half expecting a demon of sorts to leap out on the attack. She stepped around each doorway cautiously, nodding to Trydent and giving him the lead. It was a steady practice that kids were taught early when they grew up in the Rez.

As they approached the perimeter around the biodome, public traffic started to increase steadily. Even as war ravaged around them people continued to flock to the biodomes. Looking for some place to feel safe.

Humanity is an animal, a creature of habit that needs to have expected and repetitive outcomes other wise Chaos tends to reign supreme. This morning Chaos, in all its glory, played havoc on the world with a grin of evil satisfaction.

A couple of blocks from the biodome they came across a fallen building that lay strewn over the main road going in. It wasn't completely uncommon to have to detour around rubble when traversing the Rez. Shately stepped around the corner as Trydent covered the rear from attack. When she recognized human movement she halted and signaled Trydent to stop. She slowly walked into a scene she would have never expected.

A group of about nine teenagers stood around a fire swaying in semi unison, enjoying the moment through chemical enhancement.

Realizing the grim truth of the situation she became incensed. "What the fuck do you stupid lame ass pieces of bat guano think is going on? Can't you see that the City is coming down around you?"

The nine turned to take a look at the new person on the scene, apparently a screaming lunatic to entertain them; this was all part of the experience for them. It is not that they could begin to understand her lecture, but they did seem to comprehend her urgency. None of these youth cared about this woman or whatever theory she was pedaling, they were having an 'end of the world' bash and she could join them or she could fuck off, no real preference.

Shately couldn't accept the kids 'It's not our problem" attitude. These weren't kids of the Rez; they were youth of privilege who were raised with all the perks and luxuries that go with living in the City.

"Don't you get what's going on here?" Shately continued to push trying to get them to understand the severity of their situation. "There is a war going on here and you fools find a need to stand around a fire and get wasted."

She stridently moved toward the group but before she could reach them she felt hands on her shoulders and there she was firmly pulled away from them. "Shately, let it go! It means nothing." Trydent spun her around to try and make eye contact.

She made a feeble attempt to resist but was overwhelmed. "Why, why, why?" she sobbed into Trydent's chest letting him rock her gently in a hugging embrace.

"Come on, we have survived demon attacks, explosions, laser fire, cat hunts and now you're going to let some stupid kids push you over the edge?" He tried to calm and reinforce.

"Then who are we saving this stupid world for, them?" Shately took her face away from Trydent's face and looked up. "Why should we fight for a future that gives these idiots a chance to breed?"

"You know it is bigger than these few fools." Trydent said. "There are a lot of things worth fighting for."

"Name a few." She challenged as she openly wiped tears from her cheeks and eyes.

Showing a gentler side, that he typically kept hidden, he used his index finger to wipe a tear out of Shately's eye. "I believe you know there is still good in this world because I can see it in your blood shot eyes and I know when you look at me you can still see it in mine."

The world slowed down for the pair as they looked into each other's eyes and it was all of a sudden simpler. Shately was able to find something deep within herself and smiled a pouty little girl grin, slightly embarrassed at almost losing faith in Trydent.

The moment ended abruptly as one of the teens, a female who could barely stand yelled out. "Get a room, why don't you." Slurring her words.

This broke the mood rather drastically and the two felt instantly uncomfortable. Shaking it off Trydent moved to head out again. "You gonna be ok?"

"I will be in just a second." Shately replied then she turned and walked toward the young girl who killed the mood.

"Hiyasysster!" her words slurred she greeted Shately with arms wide expecting a hug. Or she might have thought that she could fly and was trying to take off. Who really knows what goes on in a mind on drugs.

Without warning or explanation Shately threw a punch that caught the unsuspecting drunken imp square on the jaw. The poor wretch crumpled instantly, the blow was a knock out.

"Wow did you see that, man?" came from one of the other youth.

Turning back to Trydent with a devilishly satisfied grin she quipped. "I'm better now, let's go."

Taken aback Trydent was caught off guard by her actions, he made a mental note not to offer his new friend a hug when she was pissed off.

They walked away, refocused on the task at hand of getting to Biodome 313 before the others left without them...

6.

Bell pushed through the crowd that was looking for refuge within the biodome, trying to escape the chaos that was overtaking the City. It wasn't a mob yet but the tension was thick and it wouldn't take much to push the crowd over the edge.

Taylor stayed closed to his compatriot, and let the larger man make way through the mass of people. He too was on edge and was expecting the worst. It didn't help that his head was pounding and he ached all over. But he continued to think, he was determined to help Ogden on this mission even if he could not fully understand it. He looked out and assessed his surroundings; the crowd for now was staying off the gardens and crowded along the paths. There was a steady drone of concerned conversation that gossiped through the throng. These were the healthy; the wounded started to congregate outside the hospitals hoping for a chance to get help.

Riots had broken out at more than one of the Rejuvs within the City. They started when the critically wounded were put into the Rejuvs to try and save their lives and other people were dying around them. Security that was trained as controllers not negotiators tried to suppress the terror but were quickly subdued after their crowd control energy prods ran out of power. The death toll climbed exponentially.

The wave of terror rippled toward the biodome as several blue skinned attack squads bore down on the population, killing and inciting panic. Nothing could prepare the people of earth for the carnage that was unleashed on to the planet.

Bell read the crowd as he looked for the other members of the quickly shaped team. After a thorough yet deliberate search through the crowd, Bell turned to Taylor. "Listen, I have to head back out and discuss strategy with Corporal Maxwell, I need you to find the path of least resistance. Make sure that if we need to hide in the hills for a while we get there first."

"Got ya Bell, I'll get a supply of vegetables, we may need a nutrient supply for a couple of days."

Taylor shook Bell's hand. "When you're coming give me a sign to let me know, so I can let you know were I am."

"I will try and keep it as low key as possible but I don't think we will be that lucky. You will know when we are coming by the commotion that has been following us for the last day. Expect all hell to break loose."

After another hard scan through the crowd to look for any of Ogden's friends Colonel Anderson headed back through the swarm, he came to the conclusion that he would probably need the claymores he had Maxwell set up. A defensive perimeter would give them an edge to survive a possible stand off.

He had to work at not getting annoyed with the egocentric mass. Frequently he moved people out of his way, because he was at the point where some of his decisions, including slapping idiots who couldn't grasp the concept that they were in his way, would not be beneficial to his purpose. Bell cursed his myopic plan and swore steadily as he bounced into the lost and desolate souls of humanity, trying to find refuge were ever they could.

The churches filled up fast and soon the congregation spilled out into the street, the faithful huddled and preyed in and around the cathedrals.

There was a steady flow of refugees pouring into the dome and going against the flow proved to be difficult, but Bell's size and uniform gave him some latitude of control over the crowd. Finally after a solid battle with the throng, Bell made it outside and it didn't take him very long to find his corporal; as he was following orders to a tee.

Maxwell was making himself visible, giving everyone the opportunity to find him.

"Corporal!" Bell yelled.

Maxwell turned back towards his commanding officer's voice and caught sight of him moving toward him.

"No sign of anybody inside yet. It is going to prove difficult to find anyone in this craziness. If it becomes a fire fight you make sure that everyone gets in then blow the claymores."

"Yes Sir, I have ten mines set up, a ten meter perimeter around the entrance to the biodome, Sir."

"Well done, keep alert. Any sign of our friend Leather?" The military man could not help but smirk a little when he mentioned Leather's name.

Maxwell started to say he hadn't seen anyone as he saw three of the team walking toward them, he pointed and yelled above the din. "Well it looks like Leather found Shately and Trydent."...

Asmodeus

Several hundred centuries and numerous incantations later
Asmodeus again returned to the realm of man to spill his putrid
hate onto those in his way.

Serapaet was a Greek slave, born into the servitude of a
minor official, who was an aid to a fringe politician. Sera wasn't
pretty, she had a look about her that was exotic, almost oriental.
Nor was she very capable so she was given menial tasks and
would often make mistakes unable to complete anything that
included forethought.

Serapaet was the offspring of a slave who drank way too
much, she used alcohol as a numbing agent. She tried to mask
the feelings that came from being a whore, a begging in the
streets, would do anything for a piece of bread, bought and paid
for whore.

Her mother's coping mechanisms were Sera's downfall as
she was born with Fetal Alcohol Abuse. Not that anyone knew
what that was or ever considered that spirits offered to them by
the Gods themselves could negatively affect an unborn child.
Sera was just considered simple and even as a slave had very
little worth.

On this pleasant fall morning Serapaet was given the task
of going to the market within the city to get a basket of olives.
The market was a couple of miles from the compound were
Sera lived so she set out early to try and avoid the crowds. These
were her instructions and she was capable of following basic
instructions as long it was pick up or delivery. The start of the
trip was uneventful and she made good time.

Today Serapaet was feeling good, the sun was shining she had a drachma to buy her breakfast and the market was always full of wonderment and excitement. But today if she knew she was going to become the center of the excitement she would have gladly taken the three lashes for not following through with expectations. For now she was clueless to the fate that trotted toward her, an incident destined to become entwined in her life just ten blocks ahead. Life is funny sometimes (that's peculiar not haha) when it winds up and kicks you when you least expect it.

Sera was humming an old bedtime rhyme she had learnt as a child. Eight blocks away, Sera came across the first vendor selling Potatoes by the gross, thousands of bushels of spuds for half a block long, a staple in any society.

Basic greetings were passed as Sera traversed the market way, many familiar faces but she did not really know anybody outside her master's compound. As each block passed, stalls of produce became more and more available, anything and everything was available with the right currency and a slick tongue could haggle out a fairly good deal. Serapaet was not supposed to try and negotiate. Her job was to pick up olives and return the deal was already made.

The specific olive stand was a full twenty-five blocks away, her master had a standing contract with an olive merchant, who was her master's niece's husband's uncle. But family is family and that is priority in the common market.

Five blocks away, the smell of bread wafted through the air, the bakeries and meal kiosks were becoming abundant. There was always a myriad of delectable edibles scattered throughout the market. Some with tables to sit and discuss the world according to the opinion of the times, some just to eat and go.

Lamb skewers, cheeses, fruit, flat breads, being sent to the market always made Sera happy. She passed many temptations on her way to get the olives.

"How about a bite Miss?" one of the vendors offered her cheese and fruit.

"Sorry, don't have two drachma to rub together." She lied. She was looking forward to a plate of honey ham and goose eggs on flat bread, served from a vendor just one block farther.

The eggs made Sera almost croon while she hungrily devoured them but she saved the honey ham until the end savoring the sweet smoked flavor. Today was a wondrous day!

Three blocks away, Serapaet passed an olive stand the vendor recognized her and did what he could to convince her to purchase his olives as they were of course the finest olives in all of Greece. She explained that she did not make those decisions, apologized and continued on. As she walked away the olive merchant tossed her an olive, trying to brag that if she explained to her master how delicious they were, he would undoubtedly reward her for showing shopping savvy. The olive was beautifully ripe and she put the flavor on file to compare to the couple she planned to inevitably sneak from her master's supply on the return trip.

She was one block away from a destiny that was as cruel as anything nature had in store for the young girl. As if the cosmic jesters had a deranged sense of humor, Sera stopped at a flower stand to enjoy the subtle fragrance of some of the local cuttings. She liked flowers they made her feel pretty. But as fate would have it something was about to go horribly wrong.

Bending low to smell the sweet scent of the petalled wonder of nature, Sera was caught off guard by a common honey bee that at that moment had also been attracted by the flowers. Fight or flight those were the bee's choices and unfortunately for Sera the insect went for the former rather than the latter.

Completely startled and somewhat panicked Sera ran into the street waving her hands at her hair trying to shoo the bee that seemed intent on stinging her. The drastic movement pushed her into the traffic of the market and ultimately pushed her into the path of her destiny.

A local regiment of mounted soldiers happened to be riding by as Serapaet burst screaming into the street. The lead horse was ridden by a the Sergeant of the regiment, a heartless jerk who believed the world owed him better and would take whatever from whomever whenever the situation gave him the opportunity.

The poor girl startled the Sergeant's mount and it reared throwing its rider. He wasn't physically hurt but this man was an emotional cripple and he did not handle being the brunt of any joke and his men started laughing, none completely out loud and openly as they recognized his violent disposition.

Sera's panic vaulted past the bee attack and she dropped to her knees and started to scream and cry. Shaking off the dust and dirt from his bruised ego the Sergeant now needed to try and save face in front of the now growing crowd, "Somebody shut that little bitch up, why is she crying anyway I'm the one who was thrown from the horse?"

A young soldier grabbed Sera by the hair and screamed into her face, "Shut the fuck up if you know what's good for you."

This caught her attention enough to reduce her wailing, to sobs of uncontrolled gulps that she could not suppress even though she understood the danger she now faced.

An old woman who long ago stopped worrying about bullies such as the like of the Sergeant cackled laughter at the embarrassed regiment leader. "Did the big man fall on his ass?" She harassed.

"Keep that sharp tongue in your mouth old woman if want to keep it." The Sergeant warned. He was correct because by law insulting a government official was punishable by tongue removal.

"Tough guy, hassling an old woman. Don't you have any other ways to prove you're a man?" she challenged back.

For now the Sergeant moved his attention back to Sera his anger at her fueled by the old woman's insolence. "Bring the girl to me." He commanded his young soldier.

"So what is all the commotion about slave?" he started his interrogation. "What could possibly get inside that worthless head of yours to have you attack a Sergeant at arms in a public market place?"

Through broken sobs Serapaet tried to explain how she was admiring the flowers when a bee stung her and...

The Sergeant was able to pick up bits and pieces of her explanation but didn't look for any reason to console her; he looked for an opening to make himself look better.

"Bees? What do you want to know about bees?" He twisted her words to suit his petty purposes. Grinning to the crowd that had grown to a mass he played his audience. "How about we teach her something about the birds and the bees, something that will teach her to pay attention to what's important."

He was getting himself worked up, he continued to talk to the crowd and his soldiers. "How about we teach her about the bees and the..." he paused for dramatic effect. "...and the snake." Grabbing his crotch to emphasize his lewd interpretation of the snake, he leered to his men.

"Please, sir" Sera pleaded with the Sergeant. But he wasn't listening to her. He was getting his respect back (His deluded misinterpretation of respect anyway.) and right now the crowd was starting to come around, hoping to see a show.

"You two," He pointed at a couple of his men. "Grab a hold of her and bend her over the retaining wall." The order was given.

Serapaet had begun to calm down but she now recognized that the real danger had just started to raise its ugly head. She started to struggle and try and break free. "Help, help me please!" Her pleading fell on deaf ears, some too scared to assist and others as demented as the Sergeant enjoying the free show.

The soldiers had difficulty holding the terrified young girl as she was close to hysterics. "I said hold her still, you couple of dung eaters." One of the soldiers, afraid of being put on report with a need to try and get out of this nightmare held Sera by the throat, almost crushing her windpipe.

"Ok, maybe not THAT still." Looking across at the rest of his men for approval he added "I want her to squirm a little bit." His lecherous grin brought an uneasy round of laughter from some of the more sensible soldiers, others roared at the joke and this just urged their Sergeant on.

The leader of the patrol felt no guilt, a person needs a conscience to feel guilt and besides it was his inalienable right by birth to enact whatever punishment he felt was warranted to this slave. The rape wasn't overly brutal in a physical sense of the word, emotionally, it was like all rape, the psychological equivalent to pounding the psyche to a pulp.

The sperm had set and thus awakened Asmodeus, the demon of lust, the first minion of Beelzebub, right hand to the lord Satan blah, blah, blah....we all know who he works for.

If humanity didn't begin to play their cards better, they would find evil walking the earth in numbers so great it would be impossible to oppose it. An evil that would lead a pilgrimage of pain and exploitation. The Apocalypse was predicted and was heading to an apex of epidemic proportions.

The market was a commotion, nothing was said to challenge the Sergeant's rape, but whispers of the righteous slowly passed the word. A balance continued to be fought for humanity's soul. The evil needed to be kept at bay, always gnawing, gnawing, gnawing.

Serapaet never recovered from the morning's ordeal and she returned to the compound without completing the task she was sent to do. She didn't even feel the lashes she received for her failure and she wasn't counselled, supported or even cared about.

Unfortunately for her unborn child Sera's mother's coping methods became her own and she drowned her pain in many cups of mead and wine. Disruption of the fetal development was distinct and permanent. Seven and a half months after the rape in the market, Tapius was born to neglect and squalor and his soul was filled with hate and corruption at conception.

Serapaet could not love this abomination, she resented its very existence and Tapius grew up cold and heartless and eventually would take out all his pent up anger and hatred toward his mother on hundreds of girls. The cycle of pain continued...

Back to the City

I.

Jasmine yelled to Jewel "We need to go NOW!" and started to quickly move down the metal staircase that escaped along the outside of the mall.

She moved very quickly disregarding safety as she rushed down the rusted metal with the agility she found deep inside her, hidden where we keet instinct and automation. She kept an eye on Jewel but didn't wait for her, for now the focus was on getting to Ogden and she had to have faith that Jewel could keep up. The need to get to Ogden and support him against the demon was vital and too much was at stake to squander precious moments explaining to the young girl the importance of what was happening. Shately had to believe that Jewel would recognize the urgency and keep up.

It took an excruciatingly long three minutes to get to the street below; the pair hit the ground on the run moving toward Ogden. Jasmine's worries that Jewel could keep up were promptly abated, the young Rez kid was easily keeping pace.

It was only three blocks to the clearing were Jasmine saw the two squared off to do battle, what was a short distance seemed like a lifetime to Jasmine. She ran, her heart raced, the adrenalin soared. Jasmine's mind was not keeping up and she swirled with ramblings and doubt.

They passed an old three story brick walk up and out of the shadows and darkness an orange cloak appeared, fluttering out of nowhere. The breeze was mild but the silken finery flowed out into the street blocking Jasmine's path, it was hypnotic and translucent in the morning sun.

"It is about time Drol...Ogden is...There is a demon...You have to help...Ogden is in danger!" Jasmine panted her concerns with a stress that was already past panic.

"Calm girl." Drol placed his hand on Jasmine's forehead and all her worries and fears appeared to slip away and a trance like condition came over our heroine and she started to sway and teeter.

Drol caught her as she fainted away and laid her softly to the ground. "Sleep awhile my princess." He whispered into her ear.

Drol turned his attention away from the sleeping woman to see Jewel grinning at him with love in her eyes. "Drol!" she giggled and ran up to give the little man a huge hug.

"Julie, the jewel of the Rez." Drol fondly returned the embrace.

Stepping back Jewel put her hands on her hips in mock scorn. "You haven't visited me in months, and you promised me an adventure. I have been stuck in Sandstone with nothing to do."

"Now now young lady you know my work takes me to far away places and my time is at a premium." Drol shot back.

Jewel relaxed her assault and gave him another hug. "I know but I get sooo bored sometimes."

"There is nothing on this planet that can completely occupy your attention all the time, and as far as an adventure what would you call the last seven hours, a picnic?"

Almost surprised Jewel looked hard at her old friend. "It's starting?"

"Yes it is starting, so I remind you to start to exercise extreme caution. You always have to keep going, no matter who you have to leave behind, remember always keep going."

"I remember what you have taught me, I'm not just a kid."

"You're a kid but an extraordinary one, who sometimes needs to be reminded to focus on what is important." Drol slipped a little lecturing in. "I'm sorry but I do worry, nothing has changed."

"Maybe not for you but I'm twelve, the world is changing by the hour, Hell I was attacked by blue monsters."

Drol scowled at Jewel. "Language, young ladies don't need to cuss."

Rolling her eyes Jewel directed her attention at the now stirring Jasmine. "Hey, she is coming around. You have to teach me how to do that one of these days."

Drol Ignored her.

"Ogden, run please run." Jasmine mumbled the words struggling with consciousness. She was not coherent but there was still urgency heard in her words.

They turned their attention to Jasmine. "Hey Jazzy, it's time to wake up, wakey wakey."

Jasmine was not alert enough to respond to Jewel. Getting a little more forceful she grabbed Jasmine by the shoulders she started to gently shake her. "Jasmine it's time to go." This seemed to help center the woman who had earlier rescued her from the blue beasts.

"Ogden's in trouble, we have to go NOW!" She tried to sit up unsuccessfully.

"Slow down you just took a big emotional blow, now on the count of three...one...two...three and up." With assistance Jasmine was able to get to a sitting position.

"Drol!" her sense of urgency wasn't at all hidden.

"Yes Jasmine." Drol tried not to be overly condescending.

"It's Ogden, he needs our help." No longer boiling over, Jasmine was beginning to relax.

"Ogden is doing what he needs to do; there is nothing you can do for him right now." Drol tried to assure Jasmine. But she was not ready to give up on her friend.

"But it was one of those pink bastards." She pushed

"Yes, I know all about that, it will be all fine, you still will need to get to the biodome, and the rest will be waiting for you. You can't wait for Mr. Oberhause; he has a destiny to fulfill of his own."

Jasmine's faculties were returning to her and she was able to stand with only minimal assistance from Jewel. She was determined to save Ogden and refused to let it go, Ogden could be killed. "Please Drol, please...."

Drol moved past sensitive and caring. "Jasmine!" he spoke forcibly, "you need to concentrate on what you need to do and that as we agreed is to get to Biodome 313 and right now you're quickly running out of time."

"But it's Ogden..." Her voice trailed of into a whimper. "...it's Ogden."

Drol figuratively whipped the last hours grime from Jasmine, the evil filth of demon sweat cleansed from her existence, with the removal of excess evil and a fresh shot of pious purity, Jasmine felt rejuvenated. "Ogden will secure you passage through the remainder of the Rez to the biodome, the providence he is destined for now heads in a different direction than you need to go. His sacrifice lights the way for your success."

Jewel stepped up to give her support. "It is only about an hour's hard hike to the Biodome from here."

And without any explanation or warning Drol was gone, his cape fluttering and then he joined the wind, like the breeze against her cheek his thoughts gently whispered through Jasmine's psyche. "You have been a friend from the beginning!"

"I'm just not sure I can get used to that, he will be my quick trip to insanity if he continues to pop in and out all the time." Jasmine gave her head a shake trying to loosen some sense of normalcy in her mind.

Nothing seemed to work so she turned to Jewel and gestured with her hand to lead. Following the young girl she muttered to herself about not being given enough information and tired of always being left in the dark.

"Hey do you think I can have my sword back?" Jewel asked figuring this might be an opportune time to gain some power back.

"Would you know what to do with it?" Jasmine was surprised at her request. "How about I keep it for awhile just in case we run into any more trouble."

"But it is mine, you remember that."

"Sure kid, just don't go hurting yourself or anything." She hollowly promised Julie, and then mumbled to herself. "When is any of this going to start to make sense?"

But it would be a long time before Ms Phillips would be able to make any sense out of Ogden's death. He was only in hell, not that far away, when as always you put it into perspective, only a couple of missed heart beats away.

The two got back on track Jasmine was barely capable of anything more than one foot in front of the other...repeat.

"Are you going to be OK?" Jewel was honestly concerned about her welfare.

"Fuck if I know..." one step ahead of the last....repeat... "Hey Jewel, we need to try and help Ogden." Jasmine was still groggy and confused.

"If we get a chance, you know I am there for you, I got your back." Jewel tried to console her.

"I don't doubt it for an instant; did you know that I graduated second in my class of about two hundred?" Jasmine's concentration continued to waver. She tried to focus on her connection to Drol knowing it would lead and support her. Well it would lead her somewhere, somewhere better than where she was right now.

Dawn was grabbing it's cycle amongst the shadows and reflections, light hit the blade and flashed into a corner that had not seen anything but shadow for decades giving new life to the Rez. The power of the blade pulsed quietly and unknown.

Earlier yesterday she had promised her mother that she would stay close to Sandstone, Jewel was already in trouble for yesterday's transgressions and she felt a pang of loss when she realized that she probably would never get that lecture.

Jewel had been to the City's edge several times but hadn't gone much past the Biodome to the west, she could almost hear her mother's voice explaining that it was a dangerous world and kids disappear every day. As many times she stormed away from her mother yelling, "Why does everyone have to treat me like I'm some kind of kid!"

Now Jewel stood just outside of the City, wishing to hear her mother, wishing she had the opportunity to say goodbye. Staring, knowing, looking at the evil that lay ahead she knew she had to be strong just as Drol had taught her over the years. She dug down deep into her psyche and offered what she could to Jasmine, putting her left arm under Jasmine's right shoulder and worked to catch the occasional missed step.

She knew it would be only a little while before Jasmine would gain back her composure and fight forward again, she believed in her.

It was easy to catch a flow of the tragic lineups. The poor wretched fools continued to line up because that was what society trained them to do. Everyone hoped that they had chosen the fast line and even more critical the line that would lead them to safety.

"Get the fuck out of my way!" Jasmine was on edge, she brushed the crowd out of the way, trying not to be overly intrusive but frequently getting a little rough. Committing the cardinal sin of line jumping normally could easily cause a fight, but this morning this crowd was a couple of notches below riot mode and could be easily incited to mob mentality. It quickly got to the point of a mass of undisciplined bodies pushing forward; Jasmine now had to make eye contact to make it clear that she was getting to the biodome with a scowl that was sixth degree black belt. More often than not the crowd took the flight option rather than the fight response.

Jewel, finally becoming overwhelmed with the sheer hectic insanity of the situation, grabbed Jasmine by the shoulders and yelled over the noise, "OK, remembering that I'm just a kid and you have a lifetime of coping skills, you need to soldier up and get me through this. I don't think I can do this alone."

That seemed to be enough to grab Jasmine back to the land of the kick ass attitude, with eye contact from Julie came recognition and shame at her inability to take control back. She needed to get back and live in the now, because now was now and she would have to be at her best to get through this crowd and make it to the biodome. The rest of the journey had to be made with attitude and there would be no "excuse me sir" or "pardon me mam." Jasmine would have to do what it took to move through the throng. Even if it meant that a few friendlies got hurt along the way.

The crowd was thick and completely enveloped the pair, "get me through this!" Jewel pleaded with Jasmine. "Now, please, I need to get out of this NOW!" claustrophobia had overtaken the young girl who was used to the relatively low population of the Rez.

Holding onto Jasmine's shoulders she started to push her through the people, it didn't take long for Jasmine to catch up to speed and start removing the obstacles out of their way; leaving a pile of bodies in their wake. Jasmine had stopped asking and started knocking the heads together of any fools that wasted more than five seconds of their time. Jasmine's mind was screaming at the crowd but she had a silent continence that spoke volumes and most people willingly got out of her way, but she held true and maybe she slapped a few people out of frustration but the stupid morons wouldn't get out of the way.

It didn't take Jasmine long to get her ESTROGEN flowing and she could feel the burn, helping her marshal arts training take over.

The florescent signage of the biodome pulsed ahead of them while the city burned behind them the dawn was ablaze and nowhere did a fiddle play. The steady stream of refugees was actually just beginning, society lined up, hoping this was the line to personal salvation and survival.

Jasmine, with Jewel in tow, knocked and bluffed her way to the biodome with a, get busy living or fuck off and die dictum, that had them cutting through the multitudes. She ignored hysterics and hoped for forgiveness as she assaulted her way to the local fresh vegetable factory.

The battle had just started when Jasmine had got past her loss of confidence, and there were still a lot of innocent bystanders between her and their goal.

"Jewel!" Jasmine almost screamed "Stay close, real close. Don't be afraid to cry out if we get separated. If you need my help yell loud and do it fast."

"Not a problem." The usually chatty young girl kept her response brief and to the point, hoping that she didn't need to yell for help.

The explosions to their right were unexpected and it knocked Jewel off her feet as the crowd was sent flying, scattering bones and flesh like shrapnel. Intending to disrupt the enemy's progress, Anderson did not know Jasmine and Jewel would be caught by the impact of the perimeter mines. The first wave of the blue demons was taken out as they attacked from the edge of the Rez.

They came from the west, rounding the edge of the great half sphere using it for initial coverage. Their attack cut down the average Joe public as they instinctively tried to get to the Biodome. Each life a metaphor for acceptable loss and fodder for the cause.

Jewel stumbled from the blast, she struggled to regain her footing and get above the flailing bodies, arms and legs entwined and fueled by panic. She couldn't even yell as she had the wind knocked out of her. Finally after some struggle she was able to roll the body of an elderly man who obviously wasn't successful at any diet as he could be the poster boy for obesity, off herself. She stood looking for Jasmine and finally got her breath back and called out for her new friend. But she wasn't able to get Jasmine's attention as she had been briefly knocked unconscious from the blast.

Jewel did catch the attention of someone though, a demon, large pink and packing a Laz rifle. "That was easier than I thought!" The demon laughed! "I thought it would be a bigger fight to kill your friend Jasmine. Please tell me, is she close by?"

"I'm not going to tell you anything."

The giant beast started to move toward the young girl, knocking stragglers out of his way. One of the biggest flaws of this level of Demon was overconfidence; they really thought that no human would have the ability to defeat them.

The beast was impatient for the kill and raised his Laz rifle up only seven meters away from his prey, and just as he was about to pull the trigger a wild eyed stranger stumbled in front of Jewel.

The Laser fire caught him square in the back and he grabbed Jewel by the shoulders to try and gain it's balance.

Jewel held his gaze and realized that he had just saved her life, he had no remorse only satisfaction, the kind that comes when you feel that you have accomplished something important.

"Thank you." Jewel mumbled, not knowing what to say.

"I did it! I made it to the biodome." Doug died with a smile on his face and Drol joined him in the satisfaction of a plan coming together.

"Get out of the way, you fool I need another shot." The demon's frustration surfaced as annoyance.

Jewel tried to lay Doug to the ground, lacking the strength to do it gently he fell with a thud. No longer needed, Doug took a deserved rest.

"Now that's more like it, just hold still you little brat, this will only take a second." The demon did not get the opportunity to aim his weapon as Jasmine positioned herself unnoticed behind the ugly beast and swung Jewel's sword severing his head from his shoulders. "Jasmine two, Pink bastards nothing." She panted with satisfaction.

Catching him from behind and unsuspecting, the demon was sent back to hell.

Jasmine looked over at Jewel, "Hey kid you all right?"

Jewel started to giggle. "You should see the look on your face, and you're asking me if I am alright."

"Come on." She held out her hand and took the girl's. They turned and headed through the bodies toward the biodome.

"Hey it's Jasmine and the Kid," she heard Col. Anderson yell, but was not able to feel past the surreal pleasure of saving the child from the beast.

2.

Leather waited in the shadows, watching the world unfold before him, more like becoming unglued. The crowd had steadily spilled into the Rez as it was becoming difficult to gain easy access into the Biodome. Groups were motivated in several ways, looking for support, trying to console each other through the insanity and following the line ups they had been conditioned to do since their youth.

Some kids were having a party around a fire, trying to enjoy what was turning out to be a bad day. Each one trying to enjoy the artificial stimulation of their cerebral cortex, dopamine and serotonin levels synthetically enhanced. Basically they were fried, fucked, frelled and just a little unfocused, but the party was on...Dude.

His heart leapt as he saw Shately emerge into the clearing, but it did not take that long for the feeling of elation to fade and a pang of loss skip across his heart. He watched Trydent approach her and true affection was exhibited as he consoled her. It would have been a moving moment if not for his feelings for his old friend. The whole scene was knocked back to reality when Shately walked away from Trydent and approached one of the partiers and in true Shately form decked the drug muddled teen.

Leather gulped in a quick breath and sighed, he knew a long time ago that she was never his but he had always hoped in the back of his mind that someday they would be stuck with each other. He couldn't help the smile that gripped his continence, when the stupid girl chose unconsciousness over shutting her mouth. The solid left hook was never seen coming and it would be a while before she would gain consciousness. But it didn't really matter as the group would all be dead in a matter hours after being over run by Hell's soldiers.

Ultimately he hoped for her happiness, but if he interfered he might have to explain to his grand children how he was partly responsible for the end of humanity. Now, he had culpable deniability. He had to give his head a shake as he realized the rationalization of bullshit he tried to get away with even to himself.

He let them approach with out any sign of his position almost breaking down with the pressure of jumping out from the shadows and yelling "BOO". Worst case scenario, she reacts without thinking and slugs him in the nose pushing shards of bone into his brain. Best case, she laughs it off and hugs her old friend. Normally Leather was a bit of a gambler but this morning he decided to lean towards caution and let his presence be known.

He would greet both his allies with warmth hoping to increase his chances for success, believing in their cause. He let the pair have their moment and then stepped out of the shadows letting his presence be known.

Trydent was the first to spot Leather; in the darkest part of his mind he cussed his luck, wishing the demons would have eliminated the competition for him. He shook it off recognizing that Leather had potential and could be a valuable ally, even if he had ridiculous hair. Trydent had grown to respect Shately and if he could be part of her life even in a small capacity he would be proud for the opportunity.

"Leather!" Shately was happy to see another ally, "It is so good to see somebody else who survived the night. You wouldn't believe the last six hours."

"If they were anything like my evening, you should be congratulated on your success at surviving," he replied. "You always had a way of spicing up the ho-hum life."

"How about the others?" Trydent asked, trying not to appear jealous. "Are you the only one to make it this far?"

"No, three of the military bunch are already in the Biodome, Anderson, Maxwell and the little effeminate guy, I forget his name."

"No Jasmine or Ogden?" Shately was disappointed.

"Sorry, that is all so far." He gestured towards the west motioning them to hurry. "It is just up ahead, maybe the others came in a different way."

It wasn't long before they came across Corporal Maxwell and Colonel Anderson. Who apprised them of the situation stressing the claymores and what would be considered a safe distance away.

"Taylor is inside securing an escape route and getting supplies. Still no sign of Ogden and Jasmine. I never did see what happened to Ogden but Jasmine went after the kid. You know the one, the lippy girl who showed us how to get to Sandstone."

Anderson started to give orders; he naturally took over when Ogden wasn't around. "Corporal you stay here and cover the front, let the claymores fly if there is any sign of the enemy." He stressed "any" pushing the meaning.

"Shately, Can you give Taylor a hand? He is gathering food as we speak."

"Works for me." She replied, not giving thought to where the directions were coming from. "He could probably use some assistance after the beating he took when we landed."

Trydent didn't wait for Anderson's directions. "Leather why don't you join me inside and we can scan the area for Ogden or Jasmine, maybe they slipped in without being seen."

Everyone had something to do and a purpose to fulfill, it just wasn't obvious to them what that purpose might be, as Drol had not revealed everything just yet.

Corporal Maxwell took his post without question and waited for the inevitable attack. It didn't take long for the first wave of demons to rampage through the crowd that had been amassing outside the Biodome. Many could not get out of the way as the entrance to the gardens was clogged with desperate citizens just looking for some kind of salvation. Families tried to stay together but were pulled apart by the mob that was panicked by the attack.

Maxwell knew his role and that was the role of soldier. Soldiers followed orders even though they knew innocent lives could be lost. But there was much more at stake and he blew the charges to stop the onslaught of blue evil that poured into the crowd.

He had no idea that the squad that followed was close behind, nor had he actually seen any of the pink Captains of Hell's army. They were dispatched as assassins and each had targets given according to the dark lord himself. In the confusion nobody had briefed the corporal that these pink monsters even existed, for that matter, even his commanding officer, Ogden's best friend, wasn't told the entire truth. Not as a deliberate move to keep him in the dark, only an oversight that resulted in a lack of flow of information due to time and circumstance. But destiny is by no means a lottery and this was a destiny that explained the purpose of why humanity was in the hands of the Angels yet evil was pursuing.

Heaven heaved at the gates, wanting to exact righteous justice onto the evil that spread across the planet, but the city taught one lesson, natural selection doesn't allow for take-out and off sales is a foreign language, so the pearly gates remained closed for this was a battle to be fought by humanity's soldiers.

Maxwell relied on the chain of command to make decisions for him, so when bodies started to fly he remained stoic and held his position. We all remember the victors vs. the vanquished history lesson and at this point victory was the only option

There was still hope for Ogden and his team and even as the dust settled after the perimeter mines exploded that hope began to reveal itself. The view cleared and he quickly realized that Jasmine was only a few meters away and could use some assistance. Jasmine stood behind a rather large pink beast and she swung her blade with all her worth cleaving it through its neck. Dropping to one knee Maxwell took aim at the skull of the beast but he did not need to fire as Jasmine's blow dispatched her enemy.

"Security breach controlled Sir." The words were spoken as thoughts out loud, not really directed at anybody.

He allowed Jasmine some time to gather herself and refocus. "Over here." The young soldier called. He got no response from her, both were caught in their own spinning reality (or lack there of).

The crowd did not know where to turn and flee, there was no place to run, uncertainty exploded in front of them but certain death pursued them with a vengeance.

Humans with dark souls drove the good of heart with fear to perform cowardly acts to try and save themselves. Innocents were trampled by the fleeing heading in all directions not knowing where they were going, not knowing which way they had come.

Maxwell moved, he moved as fast as he could over the strewn bodies, the wounded reaching out groping, and pleading for assistance. Yelling as he pushed through the throng he again tried to gain Jasmine's attention. She didn't hear him. Her focus was on her young companion Jewel and making sure she was safe.

Maxwell was still a soldier and wasn't relying on blind emotion to make his decisions. With a clenched jaw he approached the two females. He tempered his desire to scream at them to follow him with his training to make sure their travel to the Biodome was secure.

Grabbing Jasmine by the shoulders, Maxwell mistakenly misjudged her sense of self preservation. She spun around hard with her blade ready to cleave her possible assailant's skull open.

Narrowly missing the biggest headache of his life he was able to avoid Jasmine's blow.

"Jasmine! It's me! Corporal Maxwell." He yelled. She regained enough of her faculties to recognize the Corporal as a friend.

"Corporal I am sorry, forgive me I am a bit edgy right now." She apologized.

"Hey, we made it." Obviously surprised at her proximity to the Biodome, only two hundred meters from her destination.

"Mr. Oberhause?"

This caught Jasmines attention and she looked him hard in the eyes. "Ogden, I believe is dead." She paused as the truth of her words hit home and she was able to accept his death for the first time. "We need to move on... Without Ogden...into the biodome...it is important to keep going."

"Mr. Oberhause is dead?" not believing it was possible, the man everyone on Alanon Station thought would cheat death on the river card every time.

Jasmine turned back to her prepubescent companion. "Come on." Placing her arm around Jewel's shoulders she guided the young girl through the bodies and blood that littered the once active docking space lot. Endless traffic long ago finding no place to park, crashed when fuel loss became a factor.

"Behold, he cometh with clouds; and every eye shall see him, and they will also pierce him: and all kindreds of earth shall wail because of him." (Revelations 1:7) Leaving Revelations behind them and humanity to try and gain back some respect, the three moved toward the Biodome.

"Anything else I should know, Ms Phillips?" Reverting to military speak. Helping Jasmine and Jewel to the entrance Maxwell sought answers.

Jewel bewildered finally spoke. "He seemed happy to die for me..."after some heavy thought she added "Damn you Drol you never warned me about any of this shit."

Poorsoulswithcreditsinhandhopingthatexcommunication could be bought off and calm was only a pay-cycle away from salvation. The Question was how many fools lost their chance at eternity by betting on the wrong horse. Death rides a pale horse.

With some effort the three entered the crowded biodome, leaving the carnage behind them. People stared blankly at them recognizing the need to give them a wide birth. Trydent caught sight of them and moved quickly to intercept. "Jasmine, you made it." More a statement of fact than anything else.

Shately was close to Trydent and rushed to give Jasmine a hug. "Holy shit woman who stole your lunch credits?" she tried to tease to lighten the obviously dark mood. "You're looking a bit rough around the edges don't you think?"

Jasmine had no choice, she started to giggle due to sheer exhaustion. "You think I look bad, were is the mirror, you do understand terminal bad hair day?"

"Yes, we all have had a bad day," Trydent refused to take a back seat in any conversation. "Now give me a hug and explain your last few hours."

"My last few hours?" Shaking her head. "Now that is a question that will need more time."

Taylor interrupted the reunion. "Grab a pack, grab a pack, grab a pack" he gave orders to pick up the food supplies he had gathered. Starting with Maxwell, then Anderson and finally Trydent who was the only one that spoke.

"Which way we going Taylor?" He asked accepting that the attaché had a plan in place.

"Just up toward that big pine." Taylor pointed toward the edge of a boreal forest that rose up after the rows of vegetables. "I have Alpha camp set up just inside that clearing.

Trydent turned to Anderson for interpretation. "Alpha camp is basic ribbons around a clearing to give an area to be cleared for a basic bivouac after some of the ground brush is cleared."

"Lead the way." Trydent offered to Taylor. Anderson accepted Trydent as his superior officer only because he believed in Ogden's dedication to the man.

Trydent asked the next question unsuspecting of the response. "So we are just waiting for Ogden?" Silence said more than the troop could vocalize. Jasmine's look told him the truth before she spoke.

"I am pretty sure Sir Ogden Timothy Oberhause the 5th is dead. One of the pink bastards got him." She sighed before continuing. "I never actually saw him fall, but I watched him attack the demon and he was wounded before the battle.

"Wow, I thought he would out live us all." Shately spoke quietly to Taylor.

"Drol told me that we need to continue on and this includes getting Jewel to Praith." She gave her young friend a hug as she mentioned her name.

"Actually, Drol said that this Oberhause guy is continuing to fight the battle some place else and Jazzy needed to meet you guys at the Biodome and then all of you need to continue to Praith." The hug was given an extra shake and then Jasmine ruffled her hair in acceptance of Jewel's perspective and explanation of prior events.

"Again with this Praith, we have been hearing that name all along, since back in Drol's apartment." Shately expressed her frustration. "What do you think; we continue into the Dome and hope a magical city just appears out of thin air?"

"Ya, I guess that just about covers it." Trydent didn't mean to be mocking but his tone had a sarcastic edge to it.

"I presume this means we move on." It was a statement that didn't need explanation Jasmine's words were understood by everyone.

Not really opposing but shaking his head in opposition Trydent intended to speak words of doubt but he found himself saying , "We keep moving...let's hope thing can't get any worse."

Without any thing else to say Shately looked at her friends knowing they had all lost their minds, "We keep moving." She stepped up and held Jasmine and Jewel, a hug of pure love and trust.

Trydent grabbed the group and inflicted his version of dedicated affection, clumsy as it was, he was learning. Honestly at this point in Trydent's life he really needed to hold somebody and was thankful just to be held back, the basic serotonin response where safety sometimes overrules wisdom.

Weak at the knees Trydent enjoyed the basic of hierarchy of needs.

Shately caught Trydent by the elbow.

Jasmine felt lost and on the verge of panic.

Geoff fed Elvis.

Doug was accepted into the Pearly gates.

Ogden faced his destiny.

To Hell with John

John again regained corporeal form, no time actually passed during his regression to one of Hell's lost souls, then again a million years of pain seared though his existence. Surreal confusion tap-danced on John's mindscape, and then abruptly he returned to reality in a sudden explosion. This time he was lying on the ground in the larger cave on the lower level of the catacombs where he had first found himself.

"So you can make progress in Hell." John's thought process was muddled but there was still enough synaptic firing to elicit that simple comprehension. "You can make progress in Hell."

Flashes of pain inflicted by Belphegor pulsed though his mind. "AAAAAAGGGHHHHHH!" He realized he was screaming and had to make a conscious effort to stop, but even after he was able to control his wailing the echoes of the screams reverberated through out the catacombs.

Hell wasn't exactly vacation property in the Hamptons. Pain and suffering were just the normal existence and Belphegor ran a tight shift.

People on Earth start their lives against impossible odds and when finally they can't make the grade or they were never taught any better, poof the pearly gates reject you and you end up in Hell. Life is messy and after people are given the option of personal gain verses moral precept, (remember that something as simple as gluttony is one of the seven deadly sins.) too many poor choices gets you an invitation to Belphegor's realm.

OK maybe Belphegor didn't run that tight a shift, yes he did know his job well when he actually applied himself, but he was the Demon of sloth so he had a reputation to uphold.

He was basically lazy but when you were dealing with eternity you had some time to spare. Belphegor made up for it by being exceptionally evil and exhibiting a very warped sense of humor and ironically he was kind of funny.

John started to shake, he knew he should stop but wasn't able to, the walls of the cave closed in on him in a claustrophobic incontinence of the mind. Pushing hard with his hands and feet he slammed himself up against the cave wall. He wasn't ready for the pain yet so when his hands sliced open on an edge of volcanic obsidian he couldn't focus beyond Belphegor's poor bed side manner and the nine hundred and thirty two finishing nails that had pierced the tibia of the MVP of the NHL championship, giving shin splints a whole new meaning. At this point he couldn't relax enough even to catch his breath.

John finally grasped who he was and that was more than Belphegor could give out, he knew he had to find a way to move on. (Because you can make progress in Hell)

After time passed (how much is confusing) he was able to sit on the floor with only a minimal amount of holding himself and rocking back and forth. John tried to focus on a positive memory, he recalled a simpler time as a child when he played hockey for fun with his friends and he got his first kiss from a girl after the game. John was completely caught off guard when a young girl scurried into his cave apparently looking for a place to hide. At least that is what she tried to tell John.

"GET THE FUCK AWAY FROM ME!" he screamed at the fool who was frantically looking for a place to conceal herself behind something.

When it's all over and you're finally dead, do people feel good as they pass or are they terrified? There is the urban myth of walking toward the light that has been so convincing, people in their final moments consistently see a tunnel of light because they have been conditioned to do so, after centuries of anecdotal confessions after surviving a near death experience. When you die half the time you're thinking "awe shit" as tragedy strikes your family. But humanity copes the best way it can, holding on to what ever optimism it can.

In John's world coping was everything from videoreality, "Please stay Glued," to the latest synthetic endorphins to over stimulate the entire psyche but numbing the masses was considered pragmatic.

Getting low she ducked behind a stalagmite, "Sorry buddy, but I think Belphafuckinggor is on me, so if he comes in and rips you from limb to limb and I use that opportunity to slip out undetected I apologize in advance for being a bitch. For now I am looking to save my ass, we may have a chance to get better acquainted some other nightmare from now, but today how about you take one for the team."

Her apology meant nothing; John had no idea what the little chick in a toga was trying to tell him. It wasn't the fact that she was speaking in Greek, her native language. At this precise moment in his existence John would be lucky to comprehend a second grade reading class. John was raw emotion. His eyes looked to understand but his brain was quickly losing its capacity to contain the screaming. Fear is in the mind not the eye, and had a way of gnawing deep into the psyche.

Controlled by his emotions John did not see the shadow as it was cast against the back of the cave, flickering from the flames that were fueled by tortured souls. He barely noticed Belphegor lean in to check on his latest project.

John gripped at the wall expecting excruciating pain, hands ripped raw from the black glass but John did not feel any physical pain nor did he hear the demon roar with laughter at making him lose incontinence.

This was not the moment, recognizing that adding pain to John's terror wasn't a priority for this morning Belphegor continued his rounds looking for a bigger challenge. Hoping to find a soul that hadn't been tortured in a while, maybe an angel or something. Belphegor did not recognize how special John Morgan was.

John continued to grip the wall and stare with wild eyes, looking nowhere, seeing nothing, wishing he was dead...oh ya, he was.

"Hey Master, we ok, sorry about the earlier letting you take one for the team thing and me hiding. You don't understand just yet but you will. No hard feelings, right?" The girl spoke to him as she slipped from her hiding place.

Both survived Belphegor's rounds, he was looking for someone else to torture. "It's ok, gladiator, it will be bearable." She was no longer hiding as the threat had moved on for now. The caretaker of souls was fairly predictable, and would not be back for a couple of cycles.

Trying to console John the girl moved closer but he wasn't very consolable right then. "Get away from me!" John hissed through his teeth. "Just get the hell away from me." It trailed off into a whimper.

The young girl did not give up that easily; she had been around the catacombs of hell for a very long time and recognized a rookie easily. Rarely did she meet one with such strength of terror this low in the catacombs.

"Hey Gladiator." She spoke with tenderness. "Hush hush, everything can be tolerated with time, but you will need to learn to concentrate. Trust me sir, you need to concentrate on my voice."

There was a soothing tone in her voice, a soft steady cadence that helped to ease the terror that gripped him. John's staring focused on the hope that was intonated with controlled deliberence.

"What is your name Gladiator? You're in charge, try a deep breath, you are in charge, never forget this." She continued to try and comfort him.

John began to relax, and slowly moved off the cave wall, his hands bleeding from the obsidian shards that jutted from the walls. Bleeding was an understatement; his palms were shredded from trying to back up the cavern wall.

"Deep breaths, gain back what you once had, relax and don't let the bastard win." Her monotone mantra continued to sooth John down into his muscles and he finally did start to relax, letting go of the emotional nails driven into his shins.

The young girl had learned how to cope with evil; she had been introduced to the concept on within the streets of Greece centuries before but she had learned her lessons of how evil can be dealt with amongst the endless caves and tunnels that went nowhere and often ended in pain.

"Now focus, sir." She paused briefly to let her words sink in. "LET GO, let go NOW!" She slapped him with the hypnotic suggestion to sleep and he did not have the will to resist.

John L. Morgan drifted off, the MVP lost his form and continued to battle, a battle of will to survive with a modicum amount of sanity. This time he went on his own without Belphegor's help, he worked on healing himself...

Fallen Friend

High above the great grey circled, silently watching the world unfold below him.

Ogden watched the cats scatter; his sword glistened in the moonlight, mostly covered in feline blood, the steel that dripped with corpuscles flashed the moon rays into the dawn.

"Ya, screw you and the litters you will eventually spawn." Ogden did not understand why the cats gave up on their attack but for now didn't care. "Stupid cats."

Using the butt of the hilt he pushed himself off his knees. Feeling drained due to loss of blood and fighting the stinging pain, Ogden still had enough adrenaline flowing through his system to push his right hand up above his head brandishing his kitty covered blade in admonishment.

Metabolic rate running on pure endorphins, he taunted his attackers. "Fuck you, you soul sucking stupid Bitch." He screamed at the alpha feline.

Ogden needed to take a deep breath and it was labored, painfully gripping his back muscles in a bloody spasm. He understood that this would have to be a short victory and should probably turn and run but the moment was precious as he stood proud above the flicking tails that retreated into the shadows, hissing and arching right out of an October thirty first calendar.

A cold tickle hit Ogden at the nape of the neck where the hair just starts and shivered down his spine. He knew it was important to turn around; the precognizant fingers tapping him on the shoulder like an uncle messing with his nephew's gullibility were not just for fun. Turning around he looked back to see another pink multi jointed killing machine smiling behind him, looking like the cat that just ate the canary.

The Beast laughed at Ogden with more insult than mirth. "Stupid mortal, get back to your knees and grovel, you will learn your place before this day is through."

"Bow to the likes of you?" Ogden openly challenged him, "Not today."

"Start to beg, what kind of pathetic deal will you try and negotiate?" The beast's attempt at ridicule and intimidation were lost on Ogden.

Ogden was still hyped by the attack from the cats and he dropped to one knee feigning collapse. He stuffed the blade of his sword into the ground to support himself and to catch the sum of his transgressions. Ogden had been blessed away from the devil's clutches and he reached back to grab an inner strength, a strength of soul that pulsed through his senses. Holding his hand out as if to stabilize himself Ogden coughed up a mouthful of blood that spattered on to the feet of the demon.

The raptor continued to circle dropping down to get a better approach.

Ogden enjoyed the disrespect that sprayed across the pink metatarsals of the Demon. The Beast roared with displeasure and stopped his progress forward. The Beast kicked Ogden with the blood covered foot catching him square in the mandible, sending him sprawling backwards. Disoriented, Ogden tried to work quickly to right himself and regain his weapon. Ogden controlled his breathing and raised up to accept the demon's challenge. Squaring off on his knees he tried to remain upright and proud.

"OGDEN!" His name echoed through out the Rez. The cry sounded like Jasmine, but right now he had to concentrate on the beast in front of him.

Thinking to himself, he knew he needed to get closer to the demon to destroy it and send it back to hell. He recognized that he needed patience and that it would probably cost him his life, but in his condition Ogden realized that his life was already forfeit.

Forcing himself back to his feet he stared the demon in the eyes. "What do you think you're smile at? Asshole. Did your mother give you that dye job or what?" The taunts gave Ogden a chance to try and refocus. "Had any dates with Flamingos lately?"

Ogden dropped back down to one knee and snapped his sword six inches from the top of the blade, hoping to give the demon a false sense of control. A feint calling on an aggressive response, Ogden waited for the attack.

"Human, have you learned nothing, nothing at all? You are already dead, I have a boiling caldron of oil waiting for you to spend a couple of lifetimes of existence in." Shaking his tooth filled smile that would challenge the Grinch the beast continued to mock his prey.

"I have already killed one that looked just like you," Ogden challenged.

Standing again with an exaggerated wobble he added, "I am hoping there were a few hundred more of you're filth in the ships we destroyed."

"You will have to kill thousands like me if you intend to win this war, Mortal."

"Win this war?" Ogden was taken back; "What bloody war are you talking about Pinky?"

The rain had stopped and the air was still very fresh after the shower, it was refreshing to Ogden to inhale the moist air. It almost smelt green as the dehydrated planet sucked up the rain, a rare treat.

Down dropped the winged warrior, swooping in for the attack.

"So, are you going to kill me or what? Boiling oil you say, I am sure it is going to sting at first but I always liked a hot soak with a good book." Ogden laughed surprising himself at how ready for death he really was.

He accepted his sacrifice to humanity, with humility but his sanity tore at his conscience which fought to find an inner peace within all the confusion. Ogden was not used to losing and would fight until there was no longer any fight left.

Ogden Timothy Oberhause grabbed the remaining shard of his blade from the ground, disregarding the cutting of his palm to really get a good grip. Ogden slipped the blade behind his back into the waistband. Exposing his palms he allowed the demon to see the blood.

"You know it takes the human animal several minutes to completely bleed out with even a cut along the carotid artery. With your wounds I give you ten maybe fifteen minutes tops."

"You are going to let me bleed to death? I believe your deal with the devil warrants a far more savage death, are you a pussy demon all pink and pretty. My job is to die, that is ok, but give me some respect." Ogden goaded the beast.

"Come at me hard and give me a chance to defend myself or is pink just a limp excuse for red."

The Demon shook itself like a confident lion and prepared to rip out Ogden's throat. The Demon grabbed him by the Adams apple looking for a secure kill, cutting off all breath to his lungs. Frantically trying to catch his breath Ogden reached out to scratch at the demon's face. Not having any effect on the beast, it breathed into Ogden's face an intrusive acidic stench that sprayed across the Oberhause heir stinging his eyes.

Still gloating the stupid pink bastard didn't think as Ogden continued to use his right hand to make a ineffective attack, his only response was to grab the wrist to control the flailing. All of a sudden Ogden's left hand was the only limb free in the battle and he still had the six inches of broken blade stuffed into his pants. He looked deep into the demon's cold dark eyes and reached behind with his left hand grabbing the shard.

"Who are you fooling?" The demon chuckled at Ogden's struggles. The attempted of subterfuge was missed by the minion of Hell.

"I can snap your skull with my bare hands you puny piece of slug slime." The word slime barely left the demon's lips when he was hit by the diving raptor. A great white owl swooped across the demons face, talons piercing its eyes, digging into the orbital flesh.

Caught completely off guard the demon screamed, third trimester fetuses squirmed in their mother's womb at the sound.

The distraction was all he needed, he thrust upward with all his might forcing the shard under the Demon's jaw and up into its skull, dissecting its brain cross laterally. The beast went into spasms releasing Ogden who fell across the rain drenched clearing. Ogden had no chance of standing, he was not even capable of rolling over. Both lay shaking, one was is its final death throws and the other would soon follow. Both destinies were connected to Hell.

Laying on his side Ogden continued to breathe through labored attempts that resembled more gasps than inhalation. He opened his eyes, half surprised to still be alive and half wishing he was finally dead. It took a couple of seconds but he finally focused on the small man in front of him, his cape fluttering in its orange glory. "Drol?" he spoke the name still unbelieving, not able to understand what was happening, not comprehending his fate.

He was quickly engulfed into Drol's wraps and folds that had no real form or feature, more like colored wind against his cheek, gently caressing his last moments on the planet called City, once known as Earth.

"Sleep my young friend, continue on your journey." Drol encouraged Ogden to accept his fate.

"Sleep?" Ogden was confused. "I have to get to the Biodome, remember, Shately, Trydent, Jasmine...I heard Jasmine yell my name."

"I is ok, you have done enough." Drol cradled his head.

"Just relax and remember..." Placing his palms on his forehead. "Remember to trust John."

Then Sir Timothy Oberhause the fifth passed on. No Angels heralded him, no parades were held, Otto died. No fanfare, no applause, just inexplicably dead.

And Heading To Hell!

Made in the USA